I0740030

Gone Pecan
By Cherie Claire

Cover Design and Interior Format
© THE KILLION GROUP INC.

GONE *Pecan*

CHERIE

AWARD-WINNING AUTHOR

CLAIRE

Gone Pecan (gȯn pē-kan)
A South Louisiana expression meaning to split, to leave.

Dedication

Wayne Dyer once said that everything that happens to us has a blessing built into it. I have lived in California on several occasions and worked for some fabulous publications, but certain circumstances at a couple of them — many unpleasant and unfair — led me back to Louisiana where I belonged. Now, I see the blessings in those hard times and I thank those who put me on that track, regardless of whether I liked it at the time or it was the fair thing to do.

Chapter One

ALL IT TOOK WAS THE taste of pecans.

The thought of gooey sweet insides made from sugar and cane molasses, the flaky crust that includes dollops of lard, and giant Southern pecans arranged in a spiral pattern — if Dewey didn't get a slice of her grandmother's pecan pie soon she was going to lose her mind.

These sensory bombs were happening way too much lately, pummeling her with memories of her Louisiana roots. Dewey would be watering her purple and gold daylilies in her Santa Monica yard and hear the LSU Band start up *Hold Them Tigers*. Merging on to the 405 Freeway and she'd suddenly smell crawfish boiling. But the worse so far was standing in line for her daily Starbucks skinny latte with an espresso shot when Mamaw's pecan pie topped with Blue Bell vanilla ice cream invaded her senses, a yearning so intense she almost unraveled on the spot.

"I am definitely heading off a pier."

No one turned at her spoken admission; it was L.A. where people talked to the heavens, with or without Bluetooth. In fact, the man in front of her was carrying on a lengthy discourse of a screenplay involving zombies, fairies with psychic powers and Zac Efron to some entity inside his earpiece.

Dewey rolled her eyes. After a decade living in the City of

the Angels and working at *That's Entertainment*, the Hollywood lifestyle had lost its luster. Almost on cue, she spotted this week's aspiring actress.

"Caroline." The tall blond in high heels and skinny jeans waved from across the room.

Dewey waved back and hoped that would do the trick, but the woman sauntered over, grinning a brilliant smile and giving Dewey invisible pecks on both cheeks.

"I thought that was you. Or is it Dewey?"

"Dewey to my friends. It's a nickname my mom gave me, has to do with a Cajun musician she admired."

The aspiring actress's eyes glazed over so Dewey turned the attention to her with a sigh. "I'm sorry, but I don't remember your name."

"Natasha Kelly," she said with an overabundance of enthusiasm. "We met when I came into the office to deliver my demo for *And Then The Rains Came*. It's a small independent feature that a group of really innovative creatives shot entirely in their living room. A brilliant piece of filmmaking..."

Now it was Dewey's turn to tune her out. No doubt Natasha would be repeating this tale several more times that day and could probably use the practice, so Dewey let her ramble on while her thoughts returned to that decadent pecan pie.

When Natasha finally took a breath, Dewey piped in, "I'm actually one of the editors. I know I was in Peter Dunston's office when you gave your pitch last week but I was probably there to bring him coffee."

Not true, it was production business with the magazine's publisher, but definitely nothing to do with determining if Natasha's movie got reviewed. Natasha's countenance fell. "Oh," was all she said, turning quickly and retreating back to her table.

"Nice to meet you too," Dewey said to the actress's wake.

It never ceased to amaze Dewey how fast people could change courses in L.A. once they deemed a person unnecessary. Her Southern family would have been appalled at the rude behavior, but Dewey was used to it.

Besides, today Dewey could relate. She had her own speech to rehearse. After years of serving as one of several production editors for the premiere Hollywood trade publication, she was going to insist on the managerial position she had been performing for weeks, ever since Marianne Faust had jumped ship to People magazine. Her boss, Bill Ferguson, called it a trial period. Dewey saw doing two jobs for the price of one as corporate abuse.

Today, she would confront Bill and demand an answer. Six weeks she had served as manager of production and was doing it damn well, thank you very much. Dewey felt confident and excited.

"Make that two shots of espresso," she told the clerk.

There it was again. In a rush, her taste buds craved a shrimp po-boy, jumbo Gulf shrimp lightly seasoned, battered, and fried, served on crispy French bread. Dressed.

"I really am going crazy."

The clerk smiled meekly and handed Dewey her change. "Have a nice day," she said with a weak smile.

Dewey headed to her office across the street, downing her coffee in an effort to shake the piercing homesickness that appeared at any time. No matter what the outcome of her promotion, she would leave work at a decent hour, visit the grocery store on the way home and do what she should have done weeks ago.

"What I need is a big bowl of gumbo," she said to no one. "Dark roux, rice, sprinkle of filé. Then I'll be fine."

The problem was, she wasn't fine, and began to doubt she ever would be. What excitement she had felt arriving in Hollywood to work at the premiere entertainment magazine had long evaporated into the drudge of magazine production. She missed her early years writing, particularly on the food pages of the Los Angeles Times where she worked the test kitchen and developed recipes. She had loved that job but editing at *That's Entertainment* offered a lot more money and prestige, a move her father insisted would pay off in the end. Trouble was, the only passion Dewey found in work these days were the hours spent in her own kitchen, experimenting with Cajun and Creole dishes for her *Louisiana Simple* food blog, anything that reminded her of home. She was getting quite good at it, in fact, offering trademark Louisiana dishes into simple and non-time consuming recipes. Her blog was actually becoming quite the rage and the next time she saw Mamaw she was going to get that secret ingredient she put in her pecan pralines.

There it was again. The taste of the creamy, sugar substance infused with pecans and a hint of something extra invaded her senses. For not the first time, she wondered if Mamaw had put a *gris gris* on her, a Cajun spell to get her back to Louisiana. She was always threatening to find a way.

Dewey grabbed the New York pages on her desk and headed for the morning budget meeting. Time to make demands, she assured herself, carrying her confidence around her like a shield, marching into the massive conference room head held high.

Her bravado plummeted when she spotted Ronald Fabrizio sitting to the right of Peter Dunston, the two discussing like old friends some film they had seen over the weekend.

"What's Ron doing here?" she asked Bill.

"We decided to have Ron try out for the managerial position as well," Bill replied. "Thought he should be included in on the meetings from now on."

"Oh." Frigid cold water thrown on her face couldn't have startled her more.

Bill looked up, appeared to realize that he had dropped a bomb without thinking and regrouped. "Peter and I just talked about it this morning, Dewey, didn't get a chance to tell you first."

"No, you didn't." Dewey could feel the coffee burning a hole just north of her navel. She tried not to appear as shocked as she felt, but watching Ron laugh at some joke Peter was relaying felt like being thrown into a nest of gators.

"Don't worry about it," Bill said. "We'll explain it after the meeting."

Peter must have noticed Dewey's arrival and subsequent surprise at finding Ron in the room for he cleared his throat and called the meeting to order. "As you all know we have a position open in the production department."

Ron grinned broadly, looking around the table at everyone but Dewey. What a brown-noser, Dewey thought.

"And Caroline has been doing a fabulous job," Peter injected, sending Dewey a half-hearted nod.

All eyes turned to Dewey and she braved a smile, trying to appear as if nothing was out of place. Think like that actress, she instructed herself. Pretend I'm on top of the world.

"We're going to continue the trial period two more weeks and let both Dewey and Ron show us their stuff," Peter concluded.

"What?" She hadn't meant to say it out loud, but the shock was too much. Was he for real?

Peter was too important for delicate employment issues — *Hollywood Magazine* once called him the most powerful man in town — so he deferred to Bill to establish the details and began discussing front page stories for the New York edition. Dewey was sorry she had asked for those two shots of espresso for they seemed to be ripping open the lining of her insides.

Ron, on the other hand, sent her a snarky grin before launching into his opinions of the day's best stories.

How dare him? Dewey thought. What did he know about print production? He joined the staff as a web editor. Granted, he had won awards for his innovative online packages, but he knew nothing about print journalism.

"I'm almost positive Paramount is going to make a move for Leonard Spade for *The Time Bomb* in the next week," Ron said, grinning like a cat that ate the canary and only he knew where the body was buried.

"Spade's still in rehab," Dewey retorted. "He's not doing projects right now."

Ron refused to look her way, answering to Peter instead. "He left rehab this weekend."

"And you know this how?" Dewey asked.

Peter tapped his pencil on the desk. "Ron and I played golf with Spade's agent this weekend. He's out. If Mark can get the story let's make that the top feature in New York. They're film-ing there at the end of the month."

"I'll get Mark right on it," Ron said.

They played golf together? She was so screwed. This day had turned from hope and promise into the depths of hell. She had to come up with a plan to dazzle them over the next two weeks. And fast.

"Caroline." The front desk receptionist stuck her head into the room, adding, "Excuse me, everyone."

"Yes?" Dewey wondered what on earth could be important enough to interrupt the morning budget meeting.

"Your grandmother's on the phone. She said it's urgent."

Peter exhaled and Dewey knew he wasn't pleased. One didn't walk out of meetings with the most important man in Holly-wood. Hell suddenly loomed that much deeper. "I'll only be a minute," she told everyone, avoiding Peter's gaze.

When Dewey reached her desk, she briefly closed her eyes to steady her breath. It wasn't unusual for Mamaw to call during work hours, but rare for her to call her out of meetings.

"What's wrong?"

There was a long pause on the other end, too long. So not like her talkative grandmother who figuratively traveled through town, around to the neighboring parish with a quick stop at the beauty parlor before getting to the point.

"I've checked into Our Lady of Perpetual Help."

Dewey had heard this threat before, many times. She rubbed her brow and exhaled. "Mamaw, I'm in the middle of the morn-ing meeting."

Mamaw said nothing and the hole in her stomach intensified.

"I will come home as soon as I can, I promise. I told you before I'm trying out for this new job and it now looks like it will be two weeks longer. As soon as I find out about the pro-motion I will head home."

"You're not listening."

For a moment Dewey imagined Bernice Guidry, hailing from a family of *traiteurs*, or Cajun faith healers, knew about the sensory bombs happening to her daily. Mamaw knew everything. "Ma'am, I am listening."

"I done told you I would do this," her grandmother announced. "And it's done."

Mamaw was tired of living alone in her "big house" in Lafayette, Louisiana, and she had stated this on several occasions, the last being Easter. Michael and Sandy lived next door and Mamaw's house was less than twelve hundred square feet, but those were mere technicalities.

"Wait, did you say you checked in?"

"That's exactly what I said."

"To Our Lady of Perpetual Help assisted living?"

"*Mais*, you hard of hearing?"

"How?"

Her grandmother huffed on the other end. "You and Michael always thinking you're the center of my universe. I got friends."

Of course, the Holy Trinity. Claudine Thibodeaux, Jeanette Dugas and Bernice Guidry had been tight friends since elementary school. And Jeanette's grandson had a truck. She had heard about all this at Easter as well.

"This is crazy," Dewey said.

"What's crazy is you and Michael not talking for fourteen years."

Dewey rubbed her forehead. "Please don't bring up Michael right now."

"Of course not. You never want to talk about it."

"Not a good day, Mamaw."

"So when is? What's crazy is my family living in limbo and acting like it's all perfectly okay. You want a good day, you come home."

Dewey leaned in close and whispered the details of the promotion, adding how she had arrived that morning full of hope and found disappointment starring at her from across the conference table. She implored that it was only two more weeks and she needed to be there to fight for her job. After her long explanation, there was nothing but silence.

"I said, you coming home?"

How does one answer an obstinate grandmother, Dewey thought, at a loss for words. In those moments of indecision, Mamaw huffed once more and demanded her ultimatum.

"You're got to be kidding," Dewey said at its conclusion.

More silence. Dewey's chest tightened realizing her grandmother wasn't joking.

"Come home," were the last words Mamaw uttered before hanging up.

Still holding the receiver in her hand, Dewey thought of how other people's grandparents slip into senility and say crazy things. Mamaw had perfect control of her senses. And yet, while gazing at the photos staring back at her from the walls of her cubicle, snapshots depicting happier times in her youth, she wondered if Mamaw had a point. There she was, at twelve, she and Mamaw visiting Peuvre Pop's grave on All Saints Day, polishing her grandfather's tomb after a night of trick-or-treating, then setting out candles and having a picnic on top of the cold, white marble. The air had been exceptionally clear with a slight but biting wind blowing in from the north, the first cold day of the season. Dewey could smell the cedar trees in the cemetery, feel the excitement of a late fall chill arriving in sub-tropical Louisiana, not the buzz of a Hollywood newsroom where the smell of Starbucks was the only sensation.

There were photos of the Cajun Embassy, friends she had made at Columbia journalism school when she had created a gumbo during Carnival. It had been her balm to the pain of not being home for Mardi Gras, but when Elizabeth Guidry and Maggie Mallory had smelled the delectable creation, they had followed the scent, the gumbo soothing their homesickness as well. Funny, Dewey thought, how life repeats itself.

Almost lost behind endless memos and jokes lining the cubicle wall was the photo taken at Tyler's christening. She and Michael had argued, then retreated to separate areas of the VFW Hall where the reception took place. Somehow, someone had managed to sweet-talk them into a photo with Tyler. After all, he was their godson.

Dewey argued to no one but herself that having that photo on her desk was because of Tyler. But who was she kidding? A day never went by without her starring into those dark Cajun eyes of the man who was once been her best friend.

Dewey heard the board room door open and looked up to see staff members filing out of the morning meeting, Peter, Ron and Bill laughing over some guy thing, she was sure. Peter even stopped and placed a friendly hand on Ron's shoulder, a rare gesture for a man who routinely screamed at editors and made people change jobs to "shake things up."

She was definitely screwed.

When Bill sauntered back to her area, she asked if she could have a word. He immediately assumed it had something to do with the promotion and crawfished back into his office. "Need to get on that HBO preview," he muttered.

With all the bravado and egos in Hollywood, the city was a pit of wimps.

Dewey followed him and plopped in the Charles Eames chair across from his mammoth desk, feeling as uncomfortable as the fiberglass and plywood construction. "Bill, my grandmother's not well and she's been moved to a nursing home." That was true, wasn't it? "I need to fly home right away."

Thankfully, Bill knew that Mamaw had practically raised Dewey so she didn't have to explain. "Take all the time you need," he said a little too eagerly, which sent a deep chill up her spine. Out of sight, out of mind.

"I still want to be considered for the job."

"Of course." Again, too much teeth.

"I put in six weeks, Bill. That has to count against two future weeks of Ron's."

"Take as much time as you need," Bill repeated. "Family is important and these things can take time. Don't worry about a thing."

It was all too easy, too nice. Ron had said the right things when playing golf with the boss and a decision had been made.

It's a boys' town, Dewey had been told by a female executive producer upon arrival to Hollywood. Some things never change and probably never will.

So that was that, she thought, trying to appear brave and not cry. Bill must have sensed her defeat for he quickly added, "Nothing is decided yet, which is why we said two weeks. Go home and take care of business and then come back when everything is settled. Okay?"

Dewey nodded, managing to add one last thought. "I did a good job these past few weeks. I deserve it."

It wasn't the speech she had perfected all weekend, and it definitely hadn't been delivered with the confidence of the aspiring actress in the coffee shop. But it was the best she could do.

Bill nodded. "Yes, you did. Call us when it's time to come back."

She thanked him for his concern, then kicked herself for doing so. Southerners were like that, bred to be nice and gracious in the worst of situations, which was probably the reason why she wasn't getting the damn promotion; she lacked the back-stabbing gene that made one successful in Hollywood. Yearning for the sanctuary of her car where she could let loose a long, hysterical cry, Dewey grabbed her purse and left the office, smiling vaguely at the well wishes of the few people she called friends.

Suddenly, all the pain of the past six weeks — hell, all the hard work and loneliness of the last few years — came raging through her like water bursting from a ruptured dam. It all came back to one decision she had made fourteen years before, one she had made to impress two people. One of those people was about to be really disappointed in her. Again.

And in the process of climbing the corporate ladder, she had disappointed the one person who meant more to her than life itself.

Within a few hours Dewey had bought a ticket, took a cab to LAX and was on her way to New Orleans. She took a deep breath as the plane descended upon the Louisiana wetlands, touching down in what some people call the Big Easy.

To Dewey, it was anything but.

Chapter Two

MICHAEL RACED UP THE RAIN-SLICKED stairs, hoping he hadn't missed her plane. He entered the Louis Armstrong airport, glancing at his watch and realizing he was at least twenty minutes late. To make matters worse, the New Orleans airport appeared deserted, the usual hordes of tourists strangely absent.

"Damn."

He glanced at his watch again. As soon as Dewey had called from Dallas, letting Sandy know her flight and arrival time, Michael had hit the Interstate. Ten minutes later the skies had opened up and hadn't finished pummeling him during the entire two-hour trip. As he gazed at the flight monitor searching for her plane, thunder rolled, rattling the overhead windows of the terminal.

"Everything's delayed," a uniformed man said to his right. "The airports west of us closed down for a while."

"Thanks." Michael skimmed the flights until his gaze landed on Dallas. Great. The plane had been delayed but was at the gate now.

Michael ran for the American Airlines wing, pausing at security and waiting with a handful of people. He checked his watch again. Three people in LSU T-shirts and shorts bounded into the arms of what looked like waiting family. A toddler ran toward a woman carrying two armloads of presents. Three airline attendants passed security, trailing their baggage behind them. Had he missed her?

Michael was about to rush over to baggage claim when he spotted a lone Dewey heading down the aisle. If he hadn't been there specifically to retrieve her, he surely would have missed her. Unlike her usual attire of trendy clothes — at least on the few occasions he had seen her — she wore an oversized sweatshirt, jeans and the same Converse shoes from high school. A ratty old backpack was thrown over her shoulder, causing her sweatshirt to list starboard. Her light brown hair, an aspect of Dewey he had always adored, was now blonde and cut into one of those hip California hairstyles where pieces poked out at various angles. Mused from the flight, her hair seemed to rebel against the ridiculous constraints of style, forcing its strands back to its normal state and making her appear ten years younger, almost as if she had stepped out of her senior year and time had never passed between them.

But, it was the dark circles above her cheeks and the bloodshot eyes that made Michael's heart constrict the most. He knew whatever argument he had had with Mamaw, Dewey must have had it worse. Because despite Michael's stubbornness to bridge the gap between them, despite his reluctance to talk about what happened, it was Dewey who had actually gone pecan. It was that last thought, that painful memory still fresh after all those years, that made Michael resist pulling her into his arms.

"Dewey."

She nearly collided into him before hearing her name spoken, her head bent in deep thought. When she looked up, the pain in her eyes made him reconsider that last thought about a hug. After all, they had been best friends once.

He opted to remove her backpack, slinging it effortlessly over his shoulder. Sandy would have laughed, had she been there. "The things you do to express emotions," she would have said with a shake of her head.

"Do you have baggage to pick up?" Michael asked.

Dewey blinked. "What are you doing here?"

"You needed a ride to Lafayette."

"I have a rental. I told Sandy that."

Michael adjusted the backpack and started walking toward the baggage claim. "Do you have baggage or what?"

Dewey, who almost reached the same height as Michael but who could never maintain his long strides, rushed to keep up. "Michael, you didn't have to pick me up."

"Yeah, well, here I am."

Dewey halted suddenly, her eyes brimming with tears. Michael was bent on getting her suitcases and hauling her back home that it took him a few seconds to realize she wasn't by his side. When he looked back and witnessed her heartbreak, he almost did give her a hug.

"She's fine. Nothing has happened."

She pulled her tangled hair behind her ears, the tears precariously close to brimming over.

"She's fine," Michael repeated, stepping closer. "I saw Mamaw today. Trust me, it's nothing to worry about."

Dewey stared at him with a haunting, somewhat accusatory gaze, making Michael feel twice as guilty for sending their grandmother into an assisted living facility. He let the backpack drop and stepped close enough to breathe a fruity scent he could have sworn Dewey wore in high school. Memories came flooding so fast it almost choked him, like too much water gulped on a sweltering day. Michael forced them aside. He wasn't going there now.

"Look, Dewey, the reason Mamaw is in the home is because we had a fight this morning. She got mad because I wouldn't agree with her, threatened to stop talking to me and, well, she did."

Dewey's gaze grew even more suspicious. "When was this?"

"Today."

"When?"

"You want to know the time?" God, was she for real?

"What did you argue about?"

Michael exhaled and offered up a sly smile he often gave his students when they presented him with excuses. "You mean *who* did we argue about?"

Dewey shook her head, her eyes never leaving Michael's. When she spoke, her voice rose with each word, as if incredulous to be speaking such an atrocious statement.

"She's not going to talk to us until we get married?"

That was basically it. Mamaw had complained about their years-long estrangement, nothing new there, then started making demands. By the end of the conversation, she presented her ridiculous ultimatum — the two of them had to get married or she would never to speak to them again.

"I take it you got the same conversation I did."

Dewey's eyes grew larger. "Yeah, this morning. I can't believe she's doing this to us. It's insane!"

Welcome to his world. "*Mais*, so is dressing up like royalty for Carnival, but it seems to be quite popular here."

"Michael, she can't be serious!"

Michael picked up the backpack and took Dewey's elbow, leading her toward the LSU menagerie at the baggage claim while snatching the ticket from her fingers. "Why don't you go cancel your rental car and I'll pick up the luggage."

She paused, turning enough to meet his eyes, her gaze begging for hope. He almost laughed at the absurdity of it all, but then they were standing together on Louisiana soil. Maybe the old lady wasn't as crazy as they thought.

"She got you home, didn't she?"

Before Dewey could protest, Michael turned her around and pushed her gently toward the rental car desks. Then he headed off to find two pieces of luggage with smiley face badges.

Oh, for a drop of sanity in her bloodline, Dewey thought as she handed her online reservation printout to the woman behind the Enterprise counter. Maybe that was why she had put up with Hollywood all this time. It was insanity that made sense, something she could wrap her logical mind around.

That only brought back the hurt and frustration of the morning, making the knife reappear and her stomach rumble.

"Damn," she muttered. First Mamaw, then work, now Michael. She would have a full-blown ulcer by morning, she knew it.

"Excuse me?" the Enterprise woman asked.

"Is everything clear? Can I go now?"

The woman handed back the form, along with a card. "All clear. And if you need a car while you're in Acadiana, we have an office on Johnston Street in Lafayette."

Dewey hadn't thought about that. How was she going to get around? She didn't want to bother Sandy with all she had to do and she really didn't want to rely on Michael. What was he doing here anyway?

"Thanks." Dewey pocketed the card, called her mother and left a message on her answer machine that Mamaw was fine, could she please call back and offer some help, then headed in Michael's direction. To his credit, he had retrieved her luggage.

"How did you know which ones were mine?"

Michael slung the backpack over his shoulder and picked up the bag as Dewey realized he remembered her smiley face obsession. Still, it had been fourteen years.

"We're on the second level," was all he said as he led them out of the airport and into the muggy night air that was typical Louisiana. The humidity hit her like a wall.

"Wow. Forgot how this feels."

"How what feels?" Michael asked from ahead.

"It's October and it's hot."

Michael paused briefly, sending her that sly smile he had performed earlier. She used to see it regularly in high school, when he needed to get out of an assignment or was caught skipping school, something he did on a regular basis. And it usually worked. "This isn't hot."

Technically, for Louisiana standards, it wasn't hot. But it sure as hell was hotter than the cool night balminess of Los Angeles in fall. Her sweatshirt absorbed the humidity like a towel as they trudged up the stairs in the outdoor parking garage.

"You've been away too long," Michael continued. "You think seventy-eight is a heat wave."

For some reason that comment smarted, made her feel like an outsider. "I'm not a tourist, Michael. I know what real Louisiana heat is."

He paused at a pick-up truck and dug into his pocket for keys. That sly twinkle re-emerged. "And yet you date other men."

He meant it as a joke, like he meant all his good-natured ribbing. Cajuns were notorious for cracking jokes and teasing each other; it was an expected ritual. And on any other occasion, she would have laughed. But he was referring to *their* heat and that, plus the damn mugginess invading her lungs, stole the breath right out of her.

Michael quickly sobered, no doubt realizing his error and finding himself in water he did not want to swim. They had never spoken of her leaving or the three weeks of wild sex leading up to that infamous event. Nor, had they mentioned their lapse of good judgment at Tyler's christening a few years before when, after an hour of arguments and cold shoulders, they ran into each other at the familiar bayou shed and went at it again.

It had been hot all right. So were Dewey's cheeks at the moment.

Michael frowned, unlocked her door and deposited the luggage behind the seats. Dewey pulled her hair behind her ears nervously, wondering how they were going to communicate during the two-hour drive to Lafayette.

Then she realized what was before her.

"Oh my God. You still have the pick-up?"

Michael moved to the driver's side, sending her a semi-hostile look over the hood. "I'm a high school teacher. I don't have the luxury of owning a new car."

Dewey ran a loving hand over the crimson hood. "Why would

you, anyway? She's your baby."

Michael said nothing, entering the truck that once carried them to freedom and various states of carnal bliss. "*Bonjour Clotille,*" Dewey said to the truck as she climbed in as well, remembering the feel of the vinyl seats and the musty smell of the twenty-year-old dashboard. "*Comment ca va?*"

"Like you'd be able to understand her if she spoke back."

Dewey spoke fluent French, had learned it in immersion programs at elementary school in New York and throughout her studies in college. But she never let on to Michael. She liked playing the outsider in that regard, listening in on conversations spoken in French on her behalf. Old Cajuns were particularly good at that; speaking English until they wanted to communicate something the kids couldn't understand and then switching to their southwestern Louisiana patois. Michael was no different, having been raised in a French-speaking household. Anytime he wanted to talk about Dewey, he would convert to French with Mamaw.

Only Dewey had understood every word.

Suddenly, the ache in her gut took that moment to intensify and Dewey grimaced.

"What's wrong?"

Dewey bit the inside of her mouth, hoping whatever was taking a chunk out of her stomach wasn't visible to the world. "What?"

"That's the third time you've done that since you got off the plane."

"It's nothing. Just a pain in my side."

Michael rolled down the window to pay the ticket and Dewey reached for her wallet. "I got it," he said a bit harshly, as if he didn't want to argue about it. Dewey sighed, knowing Mr. High School Teacher couldn't afford a new car, but he'd be damned to take a few dollars for a parking ticket.

"What kind of pain is it?" Michael asked as they got back on the road.

"It's nothing. I've seen a doctor and he said it was stress."

When they reached the red light leading toward the Interstate, Michael tapped his finger on the steering wheel. Then, when the light turned green, moved into the other lane and continued down Airline Highway.

"Where are we going?"

"To fix that pain."

Airline was a long stretch of commercial businesses — many seedy bars and po-boy joints — and bounded on the side by a wide-open drainage ditch. In Cajun Country, they called them coulees, something French and romantic that evoked images of bayous. In New Orleans they called them what they were — ditches full of standing water that sometimes reeked and bred mosquitoes. On a good night, wild nutria crawled along the grassy sides, munching down on the infrastructure of a below sea level metropolis. And sometimes, when no one was looking, particularly PETA and the Humane Society, the Jefferson Parish Sheriff's Department paroled the highway late at night and picked the rodents off with shotguns to keep them from further damaging the neighboring roads.

Airline was the bane of natives, an ugly, embarrassing entrance into America's Most Interesting City, and locals were all too happy to veer visitors on to the Interstate.

Dewey couldn't imagine it offering anything to calm her budding ulcer, but Michael drove down a couple of blocks, then turned into the parking lot of an all-night donut shop.

"Donuts?" she asked incredulously.

Michael shut off the engine. "Donuts and chocolate milk. Something I learned in college when I had a similar problem."

She wanted to ask what had caused his stress back then but quickly realized it was probably *her*. Or, at least she had contributed. That last thought didn't help matters any; her stomach roiled.

They entered the grungy restaurant that smelled amazingly good, a heady combination of sweet shop and bakery smells. They even managed to find a clean booth, although Dewey's side leaned grossly toward the window.

"What can I get you, dawlin'?" the woman behind the counter asked Michael in a typical New Orleans accent. Most people thought residents of the Crescent City spoke honey-smooth Southern dialects, thanks to good ole Hollywood that threw authenticity to the wind, but the truth was New Orleanians sounded more like Brooklynites, thanks to it being a port city and attracting many of the same nineteenth century immigrants as those hitting New York City. Maybe a slower Brooklyn accent with a few y'alls thrown in. No one really knew why New Orleanians spoke that way and Dewey was hard pressed to find someone in L.A. who believed her when she explained it.

"We have a special, *hawt*," the counter woman continued. "Buy three, get one free."

Dewey gazed at the shelves of donuts, round creations that held no nutritional value whatsoever, just pure sugar and carbohydrates. Who would want to eat such a thing?

And yet, the chocolate covered ones looked awfully good.

"I'll take one of those," Dewey said pointing to the sugar-laced donuts.

"And a chocolate milk and a cup of coffee," Michael added.

When the counter woman pulled out a tray of cream-filled donuts with Mardi Gras colors glazed on top to get to the ones Dewey had pointed to, Dewey suddenly felt hungry. "Uh, maybe one of those, too."

"Those are our king cakes donuts and they come filled with cream cheese, strawberry and chocolate," the woman explained. "We also have our New Orleans donuts with a praline icing on top."

"Wow." Just take a pound of fat and apply it directly to her body. Still, they looked mighty good.

Dewey debated ordering another or choosing just one or maybe her original plus the praline. Or maybe she'd just taste the double chocolate one — she wouldn't dream of eating a whole one — and chow down on the rest. But, then, it was no sense buying only one more when you got another for free if you bought three. Only four was way too extreme.

When the woman looked up impatiently, Michael stood, reaching for his wallet. "Just give us one of each."

"Michael!" Four donuts? The thought was absurd.

"Whatever you don't eat, I'll bring home."

He handed the woman a ten and she handed him a cup of coffee along with the four artery cloggers. "Cream is on the table, dawlin'," she said. "But I'm out of chocolate milk up here. Going to have to get some out of the back cool-ah."

Michael slid into the lopsided booth, placing the plate in front of Dewey. It all looked so disgusted and utterly delicious at the same time. What would her trainer back in L.A. think of her now?

She started with her first choice, feeling the rush of sugar enter her system like gas firing up a stove once the pilot light is lit.

"Well, like you said, Mamaw got me back to Louisiana. Do you think I could talk some sense into her now?"

Michael added a touch of cream to his coffee. "Not unless you want to stop by Vegas on the way home."

God, the donut was good. Dewey couldn't help herself; she took two bites then shoved the rest into her mouth and licked her lips to catch any dangling icing.

"It's insane," she mumbled.

Michael sent her a look and she read his meaning clearly. Since when did anything in Louisiana have to make sense or its residents act normal? They had parishes instead of counties, the Napoleonic Code instead of English law and drive-through daiquiris. And that was just the tip of the iceberg. If anyone added up all the unique customs, traditions, languages and culture, they'd realize that Louisiana was its own country and always had been.

Still, Dewey grappled for logic. "She can't possibly think we're going to get married."

Michael put his cup down and ran a hand over his five o'clock shadow while he sighed. He looked tired, although ruggedly handsome as always. He maintained his fine black hair longer than fashion, curling around his ears in dark waves, although it didn't reach his collar as it had in high school. They met eye to eye across the table, but he appeared taller, for some reason, or more built in the shoulders and torso. But it was those eyes that unnerved her the most — still so sensual and inviting, yet dangerous and mysterious, like a moonlit lake beckoning her for a swim only to drown her in its depths.

"Maybe she just wants us to bury the hatchet." Those dark Cajun eyes, like drops of solid ink among a sea of white, gazed at her sternly, sending a chill over her skin. "Perhaps if we make up and put the past behind us, she'll at least start talking to us again."

It all seemed so simple, but there was one small problem. Dewey starred at the third donut, wondering what was holding up the milk. "And what happened in high school…?"

"We don't need to go there."

He said it so quickly, Dewey doubted they would make it to Lafayette, let alone become friends again. She smirked, feeling the sugar hit the sore spot and register. "Yeah, you want to bury the hatchet, but I'm still to blame, is that it?"

Michael exhaled and gazed at the ceiling. "I'm not saying anything, just don't want to relive all that right now."

"Right." Dewey wiped the sides of her mouth and found what felt like half a pound of sugar. But it was nothing compared to what was eating up the lining of her stomach. "I left town and you tore up the letter. And we're supposed to pretend like nothing happened?"

Michael's gaze found her again, this time full of pain and anger. "I don't want to talk about it, Dewey. Can we please change the subject?"

"You never wanted to talk about it, Michael."

"Maybe that's because there's nothing to discuss."

"Right." A sharp pain tore through her side, burning like fourteen years of suppressed anger and hurt. "Because I've always been the one to blame."

She must have raised her voice for several people turned to look in her direction. The fact that she was close to tears kept them staring, which made the ache intensify.

"Here's your milk." The waitress placed a pint before her, something local with a dancing cow on front, but all Dewey could focus on was the accusatory look on Michael's face, the anguish so unbelievably fresh after all those years and the nasty bile rising in her chest.

She pushed the woman aside and ran for the restrooms, reaching the stall one moment before revisiting her short-lived culinary trip to heaven.

"Is she okay?" the woman asked Michael.

Shit, Michael thought. He never should have let her eat those donuts without coating her stomach first. Sugar on an empty stomach was not a good idea.

And they should have never had that conversation.

He rubbed his eyes, wishing he had gotten more sleep the night before. He had stopped blaming people a long time ago, about the same time he had given up alcohol. His father may have screwed him up as a youth, but what he did with his life now was his doing and no one else's.

Then why didn't he want to talk about high school? Why couldn't they discuss the events of that day and move on? Fourteen years and he still didn't know the real reason why she had fled the scene, leaving him in that cold jail cell. Not to mention having to face life, alone, after the death of his father.

He didn't want to relive it, that's why. He didn't want to know her inane reasons why she took that moment to hop a plane and leave town. What possible reasons could she have in leaving a best friend at his lowest point?

Michael thought of what led up to that blowout, how he had dragged her into the situation when she had insisted they "talk" first. Maybe he was afraid to learn that everything had been his fault, after all.

"Shall I go in there and see to her?" the waitress asked.

"Thanks, but I need to fix this one." He threw a dollar on the table. "If you could bag the milk, though, I'd appreciate it."

"Sure, dawlin'."

He followed the hallway alongside the kitchen and gingerly entered the women's room, finding Dewey hunched over the lone toilet inside a stall. He took out a handkerchief and wet it in the sink, then crouched down, pushing her hair back from her neck to apply the cool compress.

She sighed and leaned against the stall's side, tears streaming down her cheeks. Michael wondered if he had caused those or if they were a result of the exertion.

"What are you doing here?"

"I wanted to see how you were."

"No." Dewey straightened and took the handkerchief to use on her mouth. "I mean why are you here? I had a rental to get me to Lafayette."

As juvenile as it sounded, her words wounded him to the core.

"It's nothing personal, Michael," she continued, sitting upright.

"I'm having a day from hell and you're the last person I wanted to see."

He couldn't help but laugh. "I'll try not to take it personally."

She stood up, pushing hair back behind her ears. She looked deathly pale, so he grabbed an elbow to steady her.

"I'm sorry."

She said it with such force and contrition, Michael thought she was referring to high school.

"Sorry for what?" he asked, hoping those two small words could erase the chasm of fourteen years.

She started to speak, when the waitress knocked on the door. "You all okay in there, baby?"

They smiled at the familiar cadence of the local dialect, easing the rift between them. Lafayette may be only two hours away, but the Cajun language was as far removed from the "Y'at" accent of New Orleans as France was from England.

"We're fine, thanks," Dewey answered.

Michael took her elbow again. "Let's get out of here."

He led her along the narrow hallway into the main restaurant, then slipped an arm about her shoulders before she had time to rebel. Surprisingly, Dewey leaned into his chest, seeming to relish the opportunity to lean against him. They had been that way once, always leaning on each other when times were bad. Could they ever resume that friendship?

Michael grabbed the bag of milk and placed it in her lap after she climbed into Clotille. "Drink this when you feel up to it. You need something in your stomach."

Again, to his surprise, she didn't argue. As they made their way toward the Interstate, Dewey gulped down the milk, then starred out the window into the deep blackness of the LaBranche Wetlands as they headed west on Interstate 10.

"I miss this," she whispered, and Michael wondered if she was referring to their time together or the swampland surrounding Lake Pontchartrain.

He pulled his jacket from the back of the seat and rolled it into a semi-ball, then patted its top. Dewey looked over and got his meaning instantly, lying down on the seat, her head resting against his thigh.

They had always been like that, communicating without saying a word. Whereas Sandy claimed he lacked the ability to express his emotions verbally, Dewey could silently read him like a book.

Only one time, they had failed miserably.

She sighed and closed her eyes, falling asleep quickly. As they passed out of the lights of New Orleans and into the quiet darkness of the rural parishes and into Cajun Country, Michael ran a caressing hand through her hair. "I'm sorry, too," he whispered.

Chapter Three

SOMEWHERE IN THE DARK RECESSES of Dewey's consciousness, she heard a cell phone ringing, and as much as she wanted to ignore it, the dang sound wouldn't end. Finally, she opened her eyes, realizing she was sleeping in her old bedroom beneath neon pink and blue sheets. She reached for her purse, pulling out the tiny device that put out such a huge offensive noise.

"Hello."

"Caroline. It's dad."

Of course it was. Who else called at such an obscene hour? "Hi dad."

"Did I wake you?"

"Yes, dad." Dewey glanced at her watch, still on her wrist. She couldn't remember how she got into bed last night, then recalled Michael helping her out of the car and up the stairs. "It's six fifteen."

"Well, you had to get up to answer the phone."

It was the stupidest joke in the world, told by a New Yorker who regularly called the West Coast at a decent hour for *him*. From now on, Dewey vowed, she would turn the damn thing off before she went to sleep.

"What's up, Dad?"

"I called you at work yesterday and they said you went to Louisiana."

"Mamaw is not doing well. She checked herself into a nursing home."

"Your mom said she's fine."

This made Dewey sit up straight. "You talked to Mom?"

"I wanted to see how your promotion was coming along and you weren't at your desk or home."

"Where is she? I've been trying to reach her since yesterday."

"So, did you find out anything?"

Dewey slid her feet over the side of the bed. "There's nothing wrong with Mamaw besides being crazy as a jaybird."

"I'm talking about the promotion."

Oh, of course, Dewey thought. Her parents were never ones to think of others and her father was no fan of her grandmother, who always thought of everyone. Walter Hennessey never showed much interest in Dewey, either, for that matter, but he brightened up after learning she might be third in charge of the world's finest entertainment trade magazine. A nice title would give him something to brag about at the country club.

But there was probably no promotion and Dewey dreaded having to tell him so.

"It's too early, Dad. I told you I'd let you know as soon as I find out."

She heard him take a gulp of his coffee. "Caroline, I explained this to you last week. You have to go in there and demand it. It's been six weeks since they started this trial period and now you have to lay your cards on the table and call their game."

She really hated listening to her dad lecture her about business, careers, and the world at large. What did he know about journalism, anyway? Hell, what did he know about *her*? But, she was in no mood to argue or explain the situation. Or, more importantly, stand up to him.

"I talked to them before I left."

"And?"

"And nothing. We're going to sit down and discuss it when I

get back." That much was true.

"Shouldn't you be at work now? Why are you in Louisiana when Bernice is fine?"

Because she's my grandmother and the woman who raised me when you and Mom were too selfish to do it yourself, Dewey wanted to scream. And I pissed off the one person who cares about my happiness and not some stupid promotion!

Instead, she blew her frustrations out in a breath. "I have to go, Dad."

"You will call me when you hear?"

"Yes."

"Okay."

"Okay."

And that was that. Her father disappeared with a click.

"I love you, too," she said to the dial tone.

Dewey threw her phone into her purse, feeling the now familiar pinch in her side. "Relax," she told herself as she practiced her yoga breath. "Be the Buddha. Find your center."

Instead, the center of her temple pounded. All the meditation, Pilate's, yoga and massage couldn't stop the barrage of emotions her parents caused, everything from pain and betrayal to anger and frustration. Maybe she truly needed medication, like her doctor had suggested, to finally tune them out completely. Maybe she needed to be locked away somewhere with nothing but a pile of paperbacks as company. Yeah, she liked that idea.

She stared at the manga posters and years of Mardi Gras beads hanging off the bookshelves full of YA novels, wondering why she never redecorated her room all these years. Never was home long enough.

Suddenly, the image of Best Stop grocery came to mind, white paper in her hands, standing outside in the parking lot, leaning against Michael's pickup. It had always been like that, purchasing a slice of warm boudin sausage but never making it home before devouring every last bite.

Dewey bolted upright. Time to confront Mamaw, talk some sense into her and get back to L.A. Time to stop the homesickness bombs pummeling her at every turn.

But she would definitely swing by Best Stop that afternoon for some of its heavenly Cajun boudin.

"Hey," someone shouted out from below.

Dewey leaned down to peer outside the opened window that was providing less than adequate ventilation. Even though the hour offered a slight drop in temperature, her skin felt warm and clammy. She spotted Michael fully dressed, skillet in hand, gazing up from the next-door kitchen window. Just like old times.

"What are you doing up this early?" she asked before realizing teachers did that sort of thing.

"Get your butt down here. Breakfast is ready."

"But I have to take a shower." She ran a lazy hand over her hair to see what shape it was in, thankful it survived the vomit fest intact.

"Hurry up. You need to put something in that stomach."

She started to protest further, but he moved away from the window. Even so, she doubted she would win the argument. When did Bad Ass Arceneaux turn into an authority figure? Dewey thought.

"Hey Aunt Dewey," Tyler called out, his thin face pressed against the pane.

"Hey Boo. What ya know?"

Her godchild giggled, bouncing up and down in his chair while Sandy protested in the background.

"You coming over?"

"Yep."

"Now?"

"Yep."

"Come on!"

"Okay."

Once Tyler got something in his head, it was impossible for the hyper youth to let it go. Dewey knew he would remain at that window yelling up to her, waking up the neighborhood if not the entire city unless she headed out the door. So, she quickly showered, then pulled on shorts and a T-shirt, adding a jacket without thinking. She left her shoes behind. She couldn't wait to relish the damp St. Augustine grass between her toes and the cold, squishy gumbo mud.

Sandy met her on the back porch, wrapping her arms about Dewey and squeezing tight. "God, I missed you."

Dewey hugged her friend back, thankful there was a place in the world where someone cared enough to offer physical contact. When they pulled back, she was greeted with a rainbow.

"I like your chartreuse, magenta, scarlet — what is that hair color?"

Sandy subconsciously touched her thick strands of curls. "I know. It's a little weird."

Dewey didn't want Sandy to think she was being unkind, but curiosity got the better of her. "Did you do that on purpose?" she asked as they made their way into the house.

"She got interrupted by a phone call." Michael didn't turn from the stove, stirring something with onions and spices that smelled distinctively Cajun and one hundred percent delectable. His presence dominated the kitchen, cooking in khakis and a polo shirt with the school logo over his heart. He looked every bit as good as he did in high school, even though back then he wouldn't have been caught dead in such a preppy outfit. Still, only a hint of gray changed that familiar thick head of hair sitting on top of the best looking body Dewey had ever witnessed, even in Hollywood. Some things never changed, she thought with a sigh, including the tingle radiating from her toes to her, well, other places.

"It was my doctor," Tyler said, as he, too, threw his arms around Dewey, but this time around her legs.

She picked up the five-year-old and twirled him around, which made him laugh from the bottom of his soul. Dewey wished she could bottle that giggle and carry it with her.

"I was applying the color to my hair when his doctor called," Sandy explained. "I had been trying to get ahold of him forever so I had to answer the phone. By the time I got back to the sink, half of the color had been in for a few minutes and then when I applied the rest…"

"It's great," Dewey lied.

Michael turned at that point and sent her a puzzled expression. Dewey shrugged. Amazing, after all these years, how they could speak volumes without saying a word.

He handed her a plate of scrambled eggs, toast and Cajun home fries — thinly sliced potatoes sautéed with onions, peppers, green onions and lots of Tony Chachère spice, the magic ingredient of the Arceneaux household.

"I should have gone easy on the spice, sorry," Michael said as he placed a coffee cup in front of her.

"Hey, if I have to give up spice because of an ulcer, than bury me now."

"You have an ulcer?" Sandy asked.

"What's that?" Tyler inquired.

"It's a place in your stomach where frustrations gather." Dewey helped herself to sugar. She liked her coffee the old Cajun way – black as the devil, strong as death, sweet as love and hot as hell. She really wasn't supposed to drink it, doctor's orders, but some things they would have to pry from her gripping fingers. Especially Louisiana's own dark roast Community Coffee.

"Huh?" Tyler crawled into her lap. Dewey shifted him to one side so she could indulge in the breakfast before her. Talk of ulcers only reminded her of the day before and she was determined to move on today.

"It's nothing and I don't have one."

One bite of the eggs and potatoes made her forget about stress, job promotions, and stubborn grandmothers. She moaned, not caring if she did.

Michael sat down on the other side of the table with his own cup of coffee, sending her a raised eyebrow while a corner of his lips turned up ever so slightly. She knew what he was thinking, reliving a time when he used to make her moan on a regular basis. She almost shivered, recalling the experience.

"Shut up."

Tyler shifted and looked up at Dewey. "Uncle Michael didn't

say anything."

Dewey shoveled more of the delicious breakfast into her mouth, while Michael grinned slyly. "Yes, he did."

Sandy shook her head. "I don't get it. You understand his unspoken language? My brother drives me crazy. He hardly says a word."

Michael raised the cup to his lips, but paused before sipping. He gazed seductively over the rim at Dewey. "Some things don't need words."

Now, she did shiver. A possum ran over her grave, from one end to the other.

"Are you cold Aunt Dewey?"

Dewey pulled her jacket tight over her chest, determined not to let Michael get the best of her, although she swore she saw a smile behind that coffee cup. "A tad."

She shifted the child once more, to mop up her eggs with her toast. "How's school, Boo?"

Tyler launched into a stream of conversation that lacked all punctuation. Several times he repeated the sentences, making sure she got the message, and twice, he grabbed her chin while she ate so they could make eye contact. "Did you hear me, Aunt Dewey?"

"Hard not to, sweetheart," she answered with a kiss.

When Tyler began anew, Michael stood up from the table, then effortlessly grabbed the youth from Dewey's lap and hauled him down the hallway, still talking.

While Michael seemed amused at the child's auditory skills, Sandy groaned and let her head fall on to the table. "That kid is going to be the death of me."

"He's a sweetheart."

She gazed up from beneath a wave of multi-colored curls. "You don't have to listen to that nonstop twenty-four hours a day. And this is his better side."

"He seems to be doing good." At least he had sat in her lap. The last time Dewey had visited, Tyler spent every meal rolling underneath the table with tiny things setting him off into full-blown tantrums.

"The medicine's helping." Sandy lifted her head on an elbow, her hair still shielding half her young face. "Teachers say he's much better."

"That's encouraging."

"Yeah, well, they get the best of him. They don't have to deal with him off his meds every morning and every night. He didn't go to bed until ten last night and he's up at the crack of dawn."

Sandy started playing with the salt and pepper shakers, reminding Dewey of their teenage years. At twenty-three, Sandy hadn't been too young to have a child, but her lack of maturity didn't work in her favor when Tyler had inherited the attention deficit genes from his now long-gone dad, someone else who was good at talking too much. Or too sweetly. Sandy had fallen for his charm and impulsiveness without a second thought. He, too, had a problem sitting still. Within a month, Sandy had found herself pregnant — and alone.

"I don't know how you do it." And Dewey meant every word. She wanted children one day. She wanted them badly. But, every time she watched mothers with their kids, the idea frightened her to the core. What if she made a mistake, didn't hold their infant heads just so or accidentally hinted that Santa was a fake? What if there were special needs like Tyler's? She knew Dr. Spock had written all the instructions down, but her mother had had a copy of his book and look how wonderful she turned out.

If only someone could assure her children would grow up straight and not like her crocked upbringing.

"Michael's been wonderful. I don't know what I would have done without him."

Sandy's voice brought her back to the present, and Dewey leaned to the right to see what the boys were doing in the living room. From her angle at the table, gazing down the hallway, she made out what looked like Michael tying Tyler's shoes while Tyler tugged at a dishrag in Boudreaux's mouth. In typical fashion, Michael never said a word, didn't have to, while boy and dog growled at each other.

"He's perfect."

She meant it in regards to his relationship with his nephew, but it resounded like an echo from her youth. How many times had they traveled as friends, the three of them, only for Dewey to retreat to her room and worship Michael in silence? Sandy had suspected the attraction – and Dewey later admitted as much – but she kept Dewey's secret all those years. Still, she wasn't much better than Mamaw these days, pestering Dewey to make amends.

"Uh huh." Sandy's tone echoed high school as well.

"I meant he's the perfect one to help. Look how good they are together."

"Uh huh."

Dewey gave up. "You know what I meant."

"Yep." Sandy got up from the table, grabbing Dewey's plate in the process, ignoring her protestations to help. "I know exactly what you meant. He's been a godsend to us, taking us in when we needed a home and I needed a job. And he makes home fries every morning."

"Who makes fries?" Tyler came bounding back in the kitchen, shoes on, backpack on his shoulders. "We have fries?"

"Kiss," Sandy instructed and Tyler gave her a quick peck, before moving on to Dewey and asking, "We have fries?"

"Later," Dewey said, knowing he would exhaust the question until the right answer arrived. "I'll pick up a snack for you after school."

"McDonald's?"

"Sure."

Tyler began screaming with glee, which made Sandy wince. She quickly grabbed her son and headed out the back porch, admonishing his loudness all the way.

Dewey gazed up at Michael, realizing she was without wheels and the three of them were heading out the door. "I need a car."

"Mamaw's car is parked in the driveway around back." Michael handed her the familiar keys with the St. Christopher medal and a Paul Hébert High School medallion. "Take your time, but lock up when you leave. There's more coffee."

"We better go," Sandy said through the screen door. "It's getting late."

"Mamaw's home takes visitors starting at nine," Michael said, as he grabbed his briefcase.

Briefcase? Dewey leaned around the table to make sure she saw right.

Michael paused, as if he wanted to say something, and his hesitation made her suddenly feel awkward. They still hadn't made up or spent more than five minutes together without hostilities erupting. Not to mention the things she said to him in the bathroom the night before.

Dewey cringed, recalling the commode-hugging experience and how rude she had been. "I'm sorry."

Her words, spoken so softly she wasn't sure he heard, brought him around. "For what?"

Good question. What was she sorry for? The list was growing longer by the day, especially after wasting so much time chasing after a promotion, which, in turn, made her think she had been chasing after way too many wrong things over the years. Including her father's approval.

But Michael? She wasn't ready to go there.

"For insulting you in the bathroom last night."

He nodded, saying nothing as usual.

"It was a bad day," she amended.

"Why do I think there is something happening with you besides Mamaw."

"Work." Dewey offered up a concealing smile. "You know how that goes."

He stared at her concerned as if he truly didn't, as if teachers worked in heaven. As if.

"I have a break between third and fourth periods. Around ten thirty." He pulled the briefcase over his shoulder as Sandy honked the horn. "Stop by."

She really wanted to. She was dying to see Mr. Arceneaux — once the bane of the high school's principal Mr. Wagner — now teaching students under Wagner's tutelage. Bad Ass Arcenmeaux, the man who once talked her into making love in the school's janitor's closet right after the graduation ceremony, was mentoring Lafayette's youth.

But, she had Mamaw to work on. And that closet memory was best left in the dark. "I'll be with Mamaw at the home."

Michael grinned sadly. "You'll be done sooner than you think."

Like hell. Dewey straightened. She was going to get to the end of this mess and head back to Hollywood and nab that promotion. "I don't think so. She and I are going to have some words. I'm clearing this up today. I've got a job to get back to."

Michael smirked. "Sure you will."

She didn't know what made her defensive, the fact that Michael might be right or that he thought her a slacker granddaughter, returning home only during emergencies. His attitude prickled her skin.

"I can take care of my own grandmother, Michael."

His eyes narrowed, the old animosity returning. "You do that, Dewey."

And with those final words, he headed out the back door, the screen door slamming shut in his wake.

Heading down the hallway of Our Lady of Lourdes Nursing Home, Dewey wasn't going down without a fight. She entered the room filled with Mamaw's friends, hoping to find her rightful place among them and not continuing to be the cast-off granddaughter who was neither married nor successful in her career.

She quietly approached the group, then leaned down and gave her elderly grandmother a kiss on her cheek. Mamaw's face still owned that youthful grace juxtaposed with an old soul wisdom and exhibited the same qualities Dewey had known for years — pensive study, silent examination, unconditional love. "Hey, Mamaw. I'm here."

Mamaw, to her credit, never looked around or flinched at the contact. She kept talking with her friends as if Dewey never entered the room. The knife piercing her stomach suddenly found her heart.

"I flew in last night. I thought we could talk."

"So, what did Jonas do then?" Mamaw asked Claudine, her oldest and dearest friend sitting to her left.

Claudine wasn't as adept at ignoring Dewey. She glanced her way nervously. "Hey baby."

"Hi Claudine," Dewey answered, glad she wasn't totally invisible.

"What he do, *hein*?" Mamaw repeated.

"He did what he always does." Claudine poured Dewey a cup of coffee, signaling to her there was cream and sugar on the table. "He let that fish pull him right into the bayou."

"*Pouaille*," Jeanette said, as she shook her head of snow-white hair, always meticulously groomed, her trademark pearls at her neck. "That boy needs to develop some upper arm strength."

"That boy needs to develop some brain muscle," Mamaw said, which made all the women laugh.

Dewey couldn't remember a time when she felt out of place in Louisiana. She could remember plenty outside the state — most notably New York City and Hollywood — but here, she was home, she was with friends. Even when her mother drove her down from New York and dumped her at Mamaw's so she could pursue a film deal, Mamaw had introduced her to dozens of people who all treated her like family, hugging and kissing her as if they were blood relatives.

Now, she sat among them the outsider. The ungrateful grand-daughter. All the pain of the previous day paled in comparison.

Claudine sensed her discomfort. "Bernice, your granddaugh-ter has come all the way from Los Angeles."

"Unless she's going to do right, my granddaughter can go all the way back to Los Angeles."

"We can leave you alone, *chèr*, so you two can talk," Jeanette offered.

"Unless there's a ring on her finger, I got nothing to say."

Mamaw headed toward the window, staring out to the court-yard below. As hard as Dewey fought them back, tears poured down her cheeks. She wiped them away with a hasty hand. "I'm not getting married. This is crazy."

No one said a word. Dewey looked at each woman for support. "She wants me to marry Michael or she's not going to talk to me again."

She waited for them to agree how utterly insane the whole thing was, but neither woman spoke. Dewey ran the back of her hand over her nose, wishing for a Kleenex. "Surely, you all don't agree with her?"

Jeanette leaned forward and placed a hand on Dewey's shoulder. "You forget, dear. We remember what good friends you and Michael were."

"The best of friends," Claudine concurred. "Never seen two people alike."

"It would be a shame to throw all that away."

Okay, Dewey thought. This, she could rationalize. This, she could handle. She turned toward the back of her grandmother, standing so proudly by the window. "Michael picked me up at the airport last night, Mamaw. We've been talking. We had breakfast this morning and I'm going to see him at school later. We're working it out."

She failed to mention that his last look could have disintegrated her on the spot.

Again, Mamaw was silent.

"Mamaw, did you hear me? If we make up and be friends again, can we stop this whole charade?"

Mamaw turned around, giving Dewey hope, but she only had eyes for her friends. "How about a game of bourré?"

Claudine and Jeanette sent Dewey an apologetic look, then gathered around the room's table for their favorite card game. Within seconds, Dewey had been pushed outside the circle once again.

Both stunned and wounded, Dewey could only quietly leave

the room. The lump lodged in her throat made speaking impossible. As she made her way down the hallway toward the exit, praying there would be a box of Kleenex along the way, Jeanette ran out and touched her elbow.

"Don't be so sad, Boo. It'll all work out."

Dewey smirked through the tears. "Sure, Jeanette. I have to get married to get my grandmother to talk to me, and all her friends think this is perfectly sane. Am I still on planet earth?"

Jeanette smiled, then gave her a hug. "You're in Louisiana, baby."

That said a lot.

Jeanette pulled back to look at Dewey, then caressed her hair and wiped away her tears. "You career girls think you know so much. But, you forget, we've been there too."

Dewey had no argument with that. "I gladly admit you all know more than I do. I've always said Mamaw was the smartest woman in the world."

"Then think about what she said."

"About getting married?" This was all so surreal, like a B-movie love story made for cable. "Jeanette, Michael and I have barely spoken in fourteen years."

Jeanette gave her one of those I-know-something-you-don't smiles. "Some things don't need words, *chèr.*"

And as quick as she appeared, Jeanette was gone, disappearing into Mamaw's room for more laughter and bourré, leaving Dewey alone in the hallway with Christ looking down from the crucifix, which made her feel twice as guilty.

She gazed down at her watch, anything to escape those accusing eyes.

"Shit." Then she kicked herself for cussing in the lord's presence. "Sorry," she said without looking up.

But nine fifteen! Michael had been right. What else could go sour, Dewey thought, until hurried footsteps sounded behind her.

"I got here as fast as I could."

Dewey cringed, knowing the day could only get worse. She

turned to find her mother, dressed in skin-tight clothes and dangling earrings, eye makeup caked on like a Vegas showgirl, standing before her, breathless.

Chapter Four

"WHAT ARE YOU DOING HERE?" Leave it to her daughter to not mince words, Emma thought.

"My mother is in the old folks home and my daughter has been calling constantly on my cell hysterically begging me to come home. Am I missing something?"

Dewey rubbed her eyes with both thumbs, making Emma wonder if her daughter got as little sleep as she did. Until Emma realized she had never made it to bed. She should have slept on the Red Eye out of LAX but her mother's words, and the task before her, forced any sleep from her mind.

"Didn't you get my latest phone call?" Dewey stared at her feet, tracing a toe in the terrazzo. "Turns out Mamaw's fine. No health problems at all."

First things first, Emma thought, as she sat on the hallway bench deliberately facing away from Jesus. She was about to swallow enough guilt for a lifetime and she didn't want to start with the church. "I turned my cell phone off when the plane went up and didn't get your message until I landed forty minutes ago."

Funny, it was Dewey who appeared guilty. "She's fine, Mom. I'm sorry I got you into this."

"Into what?" Emma patted her pockets for a cigarette, then

remembered she had given them up. Months had passed without her desiring lighting up and now a drag was all she could think about.

"Why are you dressed like that?"

"Do they have a coffee shop here?" Emma glanced around but found nothing but the typical Catholic Church interior design, which made her infinitely more uncomfortable. "I could really use some caffeine."

Dewey sighed, obviously frustrated that she had come. Emma couldn't remember a time, after moving her to Louisiana, that her daughter had been glad to see her. "She's fine," Dewey repeated.

Now it was Emma's turn to sigh. "Are you never going to forgive me?"

For the first time since she startled Dewey in the hall, their eyes met. Looking into blue eyes inherited from her father, a gaze so full of pain and resentment after all the years, made Emma want to run screaming from the building. She wasn't up to this; she had explained as much to her mother.

She reached for Dewey's hand, but Dewey quickly crossed her arms about her chest.

"Look, it's me Mamaw is mad at," Emma said. "We had a fight on Wednesday and she's not going to speak to me until I resolve some problems in my life."

Dewey looked at her again and unfolded her arms. "You?"

At this, Emma smiled. "Yeah, imagine me being the cause of anyone's problems."

Dewey silently sat down on the bench beside her and Emma could feel their hip bones meeting through their clothes. Physically, they were practically twins — long and thin oval faces with large eyes, although Emma's was typically brown due to her French heritage, and hair with a mind of its own. Only thing different between them, Emma thought as she attempted to tame Dewey's obstinate haircut by pushing strands behind her ears, was her daughter had grown breasts at one time in her life. That one little gene could have made a huge difference in

Emma's early film career; she had augmentations later on in the hopes of getting roles that — not surprisingly — helped.

Something felt different today. The dark circles beneath Dewey's eyes were accounted for, thanks to Emma's stubborn mother holed up in the neighboring room, but her daughter seemed frail and way too thin. "Are you eating?"

"Of course I'm eating." Dewey ran her hands nervously up and down her thighs. "It would help if my family had a few sanity genes amidst their DNA."

"Don't count on it." Emma laughed, playfully bumping Dewey with her shoulder. "The hot sauces killed them all."

She was hoping Dewey might lighten up at the joke, but she only turned a serious look her way. "She's not talking to me, either."

Now, this was news. "What the hell did *you* do? You're the one person who's made a good life for herself."

Dewey shrugged her shoulders and rescued the hair behind her ears. "She doesn't approve of the direction my life has taken."

"Let me guess," Emma offered, "she wants you to get married and have babies."

Dewey's toes found the terrazzo pattern again, shapes that appeared like Picasso fishes or

boomerangs on acid. "Something like that."

Emma studied the floor that had captured Dewey's attention. "All the designers from the sixties must have been doing drugs to come up with that crap."

God, it felt good to see her daughter smile, but it was short-lived, turning into a hollow frown.

"Are you sure you're eating?" Emma asked, slipping her hands into her skirt pockets to keep from reaching for her daughter's face.

Dewey gave her that juvenile "bug off" stare. "I've been working a lot. The magazine's been stressful lately. It's just a little stomach problem."

Emma stretched an arm along the back of the bench. "You used to get stomach pains when you visited your dad, but you haven't seen him in months. What's going on?"

Dewey flinched, which made Emma think she had hit the right nerve. "Nothing. I'm fine."

"You've lost weight and you look pale and you're fine?"

Dewey straightened her shoulders and that haughty gaze — which most mothers witness on their teenage girls during their adolescent years — found her once again. Emma knew what was coming. Something that made it all her fault.

"I look bad?"

Forgetting that she still wore makeup from the set, Emma stood and moved toward a hall mirror, scaring herself in the process. She pulled out a tissue and started blotting the heavy mascara. "I ran for the airport as soon as we finished shooting my scene."

"What are you this time, the prostitute who stands behind the main prostitute, the one who actually speaks?"

Emma wiped away the worst, gritting her teeth against the pain assaulting her heart. Funny how family always knew just the right spot to plunge the dagger. "Thanks, dear, for pointing out the shortcomings of my career."

Dewey's shoulders fell a notch, reminding Emma that her daughter wasn't the hurtful kind. She just saved all her choice animosity for her. As her analyst explained it, Dewey felt comfortable enough with her mother to fully express herself, which was a compliment in a strange sort of way. If only Dewey would feel as comfortable in her father's presence.

"Did you get a speaking role this time?" Dewey was trying to be nice, but Emma could hear the resentment behind each word. It was her film career, after all, which made Emma drop Dewey off at her mom's. Dewey blamed Emma's career on everything else as well, including the long-overdue divorce.

If only her daughter could realize that "abandoning" her at Mamaw's, as Dewey always put it, was righting an old wrong, correcting Emma's worst error of judgment. If only Dewey would recognize that her Louisiana years had saved both their lives.

She started to tell her daughter that she had finally nabbed a starring role in a made-for-cable movie that paid more in three months than she had made in her entire career, when the door to her mother's room opened and Jeanette emerged, carrying an empty coffeepot.

"Emmeline?"

Wow, some things never change, Emma thought, taking in Jeanette's trademark pastel shorts and matching top with the pearls her late husband had brought back from Japan.

"Jesus, Miss Jeanette, you haven't changed a bit."

Jeanette's cheeks blushed, but Emma quickly discerned it wasn't from her compliment. "Please don't use that kind of talk in here, Emmeline. It may be okay in Los Angeles, but this is a Catholic establishment."

Yep, some things really do stay the same. Emma gritted her teeth. How long had she been in Lafayette before being reminded how worthless, tactless and unwanted she was? Rewind this scene and she was ten years old, being admonished for laughing in church, wearing the wrong clothes — again — and criticized for not being more of a lady. Emma wanted to run for the exit but she had a job to do. Instead, she exhaled. "Where's mom?"

"She's not talking to you."

"Miss Jeanette, where is she?"

Dewey touched her sleeve. "She really isn't talking. I've already tried."

Emma grabbed the doorknob leading into the room Jeanette emerged from and turned toward them both. "We'll just see about that."

Dewey watched her mother strut into Mamaw's room, trying to recall a time when her mother had taken charge of anything, particularly when it came to rebelling against Mamaw. She was so stunned at the image, it took her a moment before realizing she had been left in the hall. Even Jeanette stared at the door as it fell shut, empty coffeepot still clutched in her hands.

What was she waiting for, Dewey thought, relishing in the idea that her mother might make things right for once. She followed her into the room where Claudine stood watching as Emma gave Mamaw a piece of her mind.

"If you want to be mad at me, so be it," her mother was saying to the same cold shoulder Dewey had received. "But why bring Dewey into this? This is between you and me, mom. You got issues with me, fine. Just leave my daughter out of it."

"Emmeline…," Claudine said, trying to either soothe her or point out that Mamaw wasn't responding.

"She turned out fine, you know. She's up for a big promotion in Hollywood."

Dewey cringed.

"I'm the one you want to punish. Just don't punish Dewey too."

"Emmeline," Claudine repeated, her tone turning brusque.

"It's Emma!" she retorted harshly. "When will any of you ever get that through your heads?"

Claudine blanched and an awkward pause ensued. Her mother had breached polite boundaries with her elders and Dewey felt inclined to interfere. "How about we all sit down and have some coffee. I think Miss Jeanette is…"

"You don't have to talk to me in such a tone, *Emma*." Claudine folded her arms, eyes narrowed.

"I'm sorry, Miss Claudine, but why do you all insist on calling me by a name I detest."

"It's a lovely name, Emmeline." Jeanette was now in the room, looking every bit as defensive as Claudine. "Your father, God rest his soul, gave you that name."

This made her mother pause, but only briefly. "I prefer Emma, have been doing so for almost fifty years. Do you all think you could call me that now?"

The three women launched into a conversation Dewey had trouble making out. Jeanette was discussing something to do with etiquette, Claudine made comments about Emma's dress and makeup while Emma stood proudly in the middle, hands planted on her hips, fighting them all off. Although she really shouldn't have felt this way — considering the elderly women in the room had cared for Dewey when she had been placed in Mamaw's care — for the first time in Dewey's life, her mother was making her proud.

Then Mamaw spoke. At first, Dewey thought she had imagined things, but it was no mistaking the French emerging among the English bickering or the proud brown eyes demanding attention.

Everyone stopped talking and listened to Mamaw's commands, but only Emma couldn't understand. With no emotions in her voice Mamaw kindly instructed her friends to stay out of the family problems, to let her handle things her way and to return to their game. Within seconds, the two women became silent and sat back down for another round of bourré. Emma, with all her wind and fury, deflated as the Greatest Generation discussed life in a language she didn't understand, since Cajun wasn't cool when she was young and the older generation refused to pass it on.

Emma watched the group conversing, no doubt about her, trying so hard not to let her chin drop or the tears well up. Another new emotion ran through Dewey as she watched her mother become the outsider, much as Dewey had been only minutes before. Now that Dewey thought about it, how many times had she seen that exact pain shine in her mother's eyes? How many times had Dewey relished in the fact that she understood what her grandmother was saying and her mother did not, enjoyed the torment it caused her?

This time, Dewey sympathized. For the first time in her life, Dewey felt a need to come to her mother's rescue against her unreasonable grandmother. She breathed deep, amazed at where she now stood. "They're not talking about you."

Emma turned her gaze to Dewey, her eyes glistening with unshed tears. She crossed her arms about her chest. "I don't care."

Like hell. "They're discussing bourré. Miss Jeanette's talking up her hand but she's really bluffing because she hasn't a prayer with those cards."

Jeanette gasped and looked up at Dewey, spewing forth some

prime French words. Emma gazed sadly at her daughter through her repressed emotions, offering up a small smile which infused Dewey with a bit of confidence.

"Now Miss Jeanette," Dewey said in a motherly tone, "I don't know what kind of language you're used to in Lafayette, but we'd appreciate a little more respect in a Catholic establishment."

Before anyone could retort or accuse Dewey of being rude to her elders, she grabbed her mother's sleeve and pulled her out of the room. They said nothing all the way to the car. When Emma hit the seat and Dewey roared the old Toyota into action, her mother's sails lost all wind and she crumpled like a jib on a dead sea.

"Are you all right?" Dewey asked.

Emma said nothing, shook her head. How many more surprises would Dewey receive that day? She had never witnessed her mother at a loss for words.

"Home then?"

Emma nodded, closed her eyes and fell fast asleep, but not before Dewey noticed the tears lingering on her eyelashes.

Principal Patrick Wagner stood at the entrance circle of Paul Hébert High School, greeting and sending home the hoards of teenage students as he had every day since he started his career in education. Kids needed a positive role model, he vowed way back when, an adult who consistency showed them he cared. So every day, morning and afternoon, he planted himself at the school's entrance, greeting the students by name.

Nothing had changed in the thirty years he had been at the high school, yet lately he felt restless and uninspired. He couldn't put his finger on why, although Bernice Guidry had a few theories. That is, when she was speaking to him.

"Hi, Mr. Wagner."

Jennifer Latiolais smiled up at him beneath a head of untamed curls and way too much purple makeup on her eyes, juggling a

Starbucks cup along with her enormous backpack load.

"Caffeine isn't good for teenagers." Lord, he sounded like a public service announcement for a health organization. He smiled back, hoping to defuse his off-the-cuff authoritative comment to one of the few students that he never had to worry about. "You might want to get decaf once and a while."

"Okay." Jennifer waved as she trotted off to her extra-curricular activity of starring in *Oklahoma*. She strode past a couple deep in a passionate embrace, the boy's hand cradling one half of the girl's backside.

"Mr. Savoie!"

The boy would have continued regardless of the interruption, but his latest flame jumped at the sound of Patrick's voice.

"You have five minutes to catch your bus."

"Yeah, five minutes," the teenage Lothario replied, attempting to resume the kissing. The girl, on the other hand, wasn't so eager with the principal watching.

Yep, some things never changed, Patrick realized. Every year there was one tough nut with raging hormones who used his charm and good looks to entice half the female school population. Rewind a decade and it was Michael and Caroline. Rewind further and, well, he didn't want to go there. They were all caught in some endless film loop, watching the same scenes over and over again.

"You enjoying this, old man? Maybe you want an orchestra seat so you can get a better view."

If Michael hadn't grown up straight, Patrick might have thrown in the towel years ago. The boy was one shining accomplishment — one of his finest teachers — and he gave him hope. Not to mention that Patrick had been one bad seed himself and look where he now stood. Even this smart-mouthed kid might one day be a success story.

"Oh, I doubt you have anything new to show me, Mr. Savoie." Patrick placed a caring but non-intrusive hand on to the girl's shoulder. "But this young lady might want to be in the front row to see your parade of girlfriends that come through these doors every week."

"Say what?" The girl turned and sent Warren Savoie a scathing look.

"He's lying," the boy answered, retreating like a crawfish in a mud hole.

Patrick didn't answer. He didn't have to. The girl stormed off, running to catch a bus pulling away at the curb.

"Just because you don't get any, doesn't mean you have to ruin it for the rest of us." Within a heartbeat, Savoie was gone, disappearing down the corridor toward the football field.

"Glad we weren't like that."

Michael paused at Patrick's side, watching the remnants of students heading out the front door.

"Hauling you out of jail was one of the highlights of my life."

Patrick really shouldn't have said it. After all these years the two of them could discuss just about anything but the night Caroline left and the horrible incident leading up to it. That episode had been off-limits. With reason.

Michael said nothing, so Patrick braved further. "Speaking of, I heard Caroline was in town."

To his credit, Michael offered no emotion. But then, he hardly ever did. "Did she come by?"

"Here?" Patrick gave a quick look around, expecting to see her among the last of the teenagers heading home. "Did she come by the office?"

"I don't know." Michael let his briefcase drop off his shoulder. "I thought she might visit during my free hour but she never showed."

Michael was trying not to appear disappointed, Patrick noted, but then so was Patrick. In a matter of seconds Patrick's heart had leapt and fell. Funny how old wounds never heal.

"Now's the time to make amends, my friend," he said, placing a friendly hand on Michael's shoulders. "Don't you think it's time to bury the hatchet with Caroline and move on? At the very least, get Mamaw speaking to you again."

Michael winced and rubbed the bridge of his nose. "I'm really sick of that cliché. Who buried what hatchet, I'd like to know." With a smirk, he added, "Or is it the one sticking out of my back?"

"Martyrdom is not like you, Michael."

To his credit and maturity — something absent fourteen years ago when Michael blamed everything and everyone for his pain — Michael smiled and nodded. "I could say the same for you."

Patrick eyed him curiously, placing his hands on his hips in his finest principal stance. "What does that mean?"

Michael settled his briefcase back on his shoulder and slid on his sunglasses. "And to think, I get shit for being a bachelor at thirty-two."

He started toward the faculty parking lot, but Patrick refused to let him have the last word. "Not as if I didn't ask her. What's your excuse?"

Michael didn't turn around, but waved as he headed toward his car.

"Stubborn kids," Patrick muttered, although he wondered if Michael was right. If Bernice wasn't speaking to him, no doubt she wasn't speaking to her daughter either. Would Emma come back to Lafayette? Would she ever tell Dewey the truth about what happened?

Maybe Bernice was right. It was time to right old wrongs or at least lay them out on the table.

Crap, Patrick thought. He was resorting to too many overused clichés today. Then he thought how only educators admonish themselves for using clichés.

"I'm going crazy," he said to no one.

But he did something he swore he would never do. He pulled his cell phone from his breast pocket and called Emma Guidry.

Chapter Five

April, fourteen years earlier

DEWEY STARED OUT HER BEDROOM window, listening for sounds from Michael's back porch. She wished he would move to the shed and bang that damn baseball. At least he would be expressing something. He had been eerily quiet through the Mass and burial. So still and silent, she shivered every time she met his eyes.

She didn't blame Michael for being in shock. The whole town was either mourning or in shock themselves at the passing of Frank Arceneaux. Michael's father had joined Lafayette residents and tourists at Festival International downtown, a Francophone fete that annually attracted people from around the French-speaking world. Michael and Dewey had passed him on their way to the car. It was late and, as usual, Mr. Arceneaux was drunk.

Michael had insisted on driving him home, but his father resisted, calling Michael a host of names. Dewey didn't know what happened next, for Michael had pushed them off toward their car while he and his dad argued without an audience. When Michael finally made it to the car, he was furious.

"Let him kill himself then," Michael had muttered to himself.

Which was exactly what he did. It didn't happen immediately following their argument; Frank Arceneaux had visited two more bars until he had point two-five percent alcohol in his bloodstream, enough to plow his car head on into a telephone pole, killing him instantly.

The police had come hours after Dewey and Michael had made it back, Michael saying nothing on the ride home, then stomping off to the house he shared with Uncle Peter and slamming the screen door shut in his wake. Dewey had awakened to the sound of the police radio emanating from a patrol car and watched Michael from her bedroom window quietly receiving the news from Sheriff Landry. Mamaw had joined them, holding her hand over her mouth and weeping, all the while grasping for Michael's hand, his arm — anything — but Michael had moved out of reach. That said it all, Dewey thought as she watched Michael walk on to the back porch steps, his head bowed. From that moment, he had silently moved away from them all.

Dewey debated about what to do that afternoon after the funeral. Michael had accepted the well wishes of those offering condolences, nodding his head numbly. He had been a comfort to his stepsister, Sandy, although avoiding his stepmother completely since they never got along. Then, after performing the duties expected of a son, he disappeared. Took Clotille and rode away.

Not talking to Dewey through the services hurt enough, but deserting her without so much as a word to his supposedly best friend pained her to the core. But then, just looking at Michael was painful.

The truth was Dewey wanted him, had ever since last summer when the planets had shifted and a desire rose up in her as she watched him washing Clotile without his shirt, his muscles glistening in the sun and his body sculpted into tight Levis. Since that moment of sexual awakening, all Dewey could think of was wishing for Michael's hands on her body, his lips touching hers — his lips kissing everywhere. She stole a shirt of his and kept it under her pillow, breathing in his scent every night. She spied on him from her bedroom window, wore tight sweaters in his presence and found unique ways to brush up against him, although the gesture usually made him uncomfortable and testy.

Sandy was the first to suspect, cornering Dewey one day in the school's courtyard where she was smoking cigarettes with her regular group of potheads.

"You're crazy," Dewey had said, trying to push Sandy off the scent. "He's my best friend."

"Yeah, well, he's my stepbrother and even though I don't feel that way about him, I'm not blind. He's turned into a damn good-looking guy and he's sweet deep down, although he'd be the last to admit it."

Dewey hadn't thought of Michael as sweet, but she had seen him come to Sandy's rescue on occasion at school. He never admitted as much, of course, considering his resentful feelings towards her family. Sandy actually *lived* with his father. She got the best of the old man, whereas Michael received the leftovers.

"It's okay, Dewey. I'm not going to say anything to him."

A wave of relief flowed over Dewey and she felt like crying. She loved Michael so much and it felt good talking to someone about it.

"Jump his bones," Sandy had advised that day. "If he doesn't feel the same way, he'll be polite about it. You know how he is."

Dewey really didn't. That was one area she never dared enter. "I'll ruin the friendship."

Sandy reluctantly blew out one last inhalation of smoke as the bell rang, then snubbed the butt with her toe. "He loves you. Nothing will change that."

Dewey knew he did. What kind of love was the big question? He had been dating other women in high school, nothing that seemed to stick. Would she be another sexual exploit or would they actually become a couple? Lust aside, Dewey wanted more from a relationship with him, and it scared her thinking they might start down a road he would not want to finish.

If she had been a well-adjusted girl from a normal loving family she might have asked him straight out and taken her chances.

But she couldn't risk rejection again. Especially from him.

Someone turned off the lights in the Arceneaux household and the whole world turned dark and silent; even the crickets had fallen asleep. Dewey gazed down at Michael's back porch and its lone glow, watching the sliver of him visible beneath the porch light, Michael staring off into the night.

Now was the perfect time. Leaving her room in only her nightgown, she slipped down the stairs and out the back door without a sound, her feet relishing the cool texture of the backyard mud and the light dew coating the early morning grass. She softly approached him, not knowing what she would do or what to expect.

As her foot reached the bottom step, he looked up, his eyes still void of emotion. But he saw her now. She took another step, touching his forearm, then moved up one more until she stood before him.

Before she had time to think, to plot her next move, Michael grabbed her hips and pulled his face into the lace of her bosom. Dewey leaned forward, allowing his hands more room around her and buried her face into his hair. As one hand slid up the hem of her nightgown, she let her own travel down the length of his back.

Michael broke free and rose, stepping down two steps so they met eye to eye. Without so much as a breath between them, he took her face in his hands and kissed her soundly, nothing sweet and friendly but wild and sensuous. It was dangerous and thrilling, fraught with pain and emotion and need. When his hand slid up her thigh, she didn't think twice, so caught up in the passion that had finally come to fruition.

He paused and then headed down the steps, taking her hand and leading her toward the back shed at the bayou's edge. Dewey followed him into the darkness of that night, knowing she would have followed him anywhere.

Chapter Six

THEY HADN'T SAID ANYTHING THE night they slipped away to the shed. Not one word until it was over. She had offered Michael condolences, but in reality so much more. She had been his for the taking, a worm dangling on a line waiting for a bite. And he had swallowed her whole.

Damn, Dewey thought as she opened the shed door and peered inside. The walls had been sheetrocked and the back windows replaced with weather stripping in its conversion to guest room status, but the old furniture and family items remained, including the endless photos of Michael's on the wall and his old photography equipment gathering dust in a corner.

Dewey gingerly sat on the bed, now a double as opposed to the ratty twin they used so long ago. Back then, the rugged shed had felt like the Waldorf Astoria, any place to escape to and liberate their passions.

She closed her eyes, fighting off the painful memories that sucked the breath from her. Twice. They had made love twice that night. The first awkward and rushed, the second slow and exhilarating, sending Dewey into an insurmountable bliss. She vividly recalled every moment.

"I got what I wanted," she said to no one. And had ruined a friendship in the process.

Dewey ran a hand over the chenille bedspread, wondering who slept here now, hoping it wasn't Michael and another woman, sneaking out for a little privacy at night. Heaven knew he wouldn't get much of that with Sandy and Tyler in the house.

She jumped off the bed as if the thought burned her skin, then reprimanded herself for doing so. What did she care what he did with his life? According to Mamaw he had more than his share of women. More than likely had one now.

"What am I doing here?" she mumbled, pacing the small room. What did she have to go back to, either?

Dewey paused at the desk at the opposite end of the shed, gazing over the collection of photos randomly pinned on the wall, many with their edges curled skyward, a hazard of the humid environment. The shelves above held boxes of more photos, no doubt Michael's rejects and experiments from his years of photography.

Along the wall there was Mamaw in her garden, waving him off. Sandy as an awkward teenager constantly following them around. A few family dogs, long gone. Uncle Peter, before he came out of the closet and moved to New Orleans, selling Michael the house. And endless photos of Tyler.

Dewey's heart lodged in her throat. Two people were absent among them all. Michael's father, naturally. And herself.

She wrinkled up her face to fight off the emotion. She wasn't going to cry again — she was tired of crying. And what did she expect anyway?

The tragedy of it all assaulted her. Suddenly, what Mamaw had threatened made some type of insane sense. Dewey and Michael had had the best of friendships, the tightest bond. With one argument, or lack of, it had all passed away.

Gazing at the collection before her, the reflections that make up a life, Dewey realized the gaping hole she had caused him. Her life wall had one just as big.

Was it really her fault because she had left without a verbal explanation and he had refused to read her letter? Should she correct the mistakes of the past, tell him what happened and move on?

Yes, she could apologize and move forward, renew their friendship and make amends. Yet, one question remained, the one that had forced her away fourteen years ago. Did Michael truly care for her, or was all the wild lovemaking a teenage distraction offered by an adolescent boy wild with grief and pain?

She could forgive him anything, but she couldn't bear continuing a friendship where she pined for him in silence, watching his every move, trying not to be hopelessly in love. They had crossed a threshold that spring and there was no going back. She couldn't return to being nothing more than a friend, watching him date other women, love other women, marry some Cajun girl. Could she?

Dewey fell into the desk chair with a sigh. Now, what was she thinking? Of course she could make amends, be friends again. It wasn't like she was still in love with the guy.

"Shit." She rested her elbows on the desk and dropped her head into her hands. Here we go again. This was the reason why she left Louisiana in the first place.

"I'm going to get me a giant bowl of gumbo, maybe a po-boy, and get the hell out of here."

"I was thinking more of boiled shrimp."

Dewey spun around. She hadn't heard Michael approach and his presence gave her a scare. Besides, he was not the person to be sneaking up on her at that moment, especially there, at the scene of the crime.

"What are you doing here?"

Michael huffed and entered the shed. "I own this place."

He dropped on the bed and leaned back on both elbows, forcing his polo shirt to stretch across his chest. Like a lightning bolt reaching down from the heavens to strike her dead, Dewey felt a rush of electricity run down her spine. Damn, after all these years, the man could still race her pulse.

No, she commanded herself, she was not going there. It was time to move forward.

"I didn't make it to school."

"I gathered."

Was there a hint of disappointment in that statement? God, Dewey hoped as much.

Sobering, she straightened in her chair. "I was busy with Mamaw."

He said nothing, continued staring. Something about that gaze pinched a nerve, like a guitar string plucked too hard.

"I set Mamaw straight," Dewey lied, wondering the instant it came out what brought on such a juvenile reflex. Or maybe she didn't want to admit he was right, that he might know her grandmother better than she.

"Uh, huh."

He wasn't buying it, which pissed her off even more. She wanted to march across that room and slap the ambivalent look off his face, but then she wanted to cross that distance and do other things as well.

She looked away, biting the inside of her cheek in exasperation. Maybe she didn't have time for gumbo. She needed to get away from here, from all these memories, from all the still-lingering desires.

"She'll come around." He leaned forward to a sitting position, rubbing his hands on his knees, as if he sensed that Dewey longed to flee. Or maybe she wanted to believe he wished to keep her there.

Did he?

The walls of the shed appeared to press closer, cutting off her air. She remembered the night of Tyler's christening, when the two of them had fought so hard, their first argument — hell, their first talk — since Dewey had left and she had sworn to hate him forever. Then he had found her on the back porch, and apologized enough to have that photo taken with their godson.

So many times she had thought to put that photo away. It reminded her of too many things missing in her life, including the great sex she and Michael had shared in that very shed shortly after taking that photo. They hadn't meant to, just bumped into each other by the bayou's edge and one thing led to another, silently, of course. Then someone had called someone's name — she couldn't remember who — and they both pulled on their clothes and rushed off, everything back to normal.

Well, Louisiana normal.

Dewey stood abruptly when the image of them locked in carnal pleasure came to mind. "What am I doing here?"

Michael's gaze, so cold and angry, met hers. "Yeah, what are you doing here?"

"I don't know." Her lungs ached. She needed fresh air, but leaving the shed meant walking past him. She felt trapped like an alligator with a noose around its nose.

A silence ensured between them until Michael sighed and dropped his head into his hands, pulling his thick black hair through his fingers. "We're not going to get anywhere this way."

She didn't see how a truce was possible, considering their constant animosity, but she didn't move, staring at a photo of Mrs. Greene on the wall, Michael's most hated teacher in high school.

"Mrs. Greene?" The realization hit her like a sledgehammer. She couldn't believe it. Dewey was completely absent yet he had *her* on his wall? "You have a photo of Mrs. Greene on your treasured wall?"

Michael looked up, following her gaze.

"Wow, I guess I rate really low in your book," Dewey said with a smirk. "You have her and not one of me. And you want to make amends?"

Michael stood and drew closer, which would have made Dewey nervous had she not received a jolt of angry injustice rushing through her veins.

"Why are you so mad at me?" he asked between clenched teeth, stepping so close she could make out the signature red specks inside his dark, mysterious eyes. "I'm the one you left in the jail that day, remember?"

"What makes me so angry, Michael? The fact that you don't think I have a right to be angry. That nothing of importance could have been in that letter I left you, that I had no reason to leave."

He leaned so close she could smell his aftershave. "Couldn't you have left the next morning, after you bailed me out of jail? Have the guts to tell me whatever it was face to face?"

His energy spent, Michael headed back toward the other side of the shed, pausing in front of the bed, his hands on his hips as he stared out the window where Tyler played with Boudreaux. Dewey recognized the familiar frustration and actually understood his pain; she felt it every time she looked at him, heard his name spoken, or gazed at his photographs lining *her* walls back in L.A.

There was the fact that he might be right. She could have waited, even if that wasn't the point. She had been scared, and if he hadn't loved her as she had him, what would staying have proved? She had had the courage to put it all down in a letter once, wasn't that enough?

"Why didn't you read my letter?" she whispered heatedly, feeling as betrayed as the day she found out he had ripped it to shreds.

His shoulders fell as he let out a sigh. "Okay," he said, turning back to her. "I admit it. I shouldn't have torn up the letter. I was angry."

Dewey huffed. Who dragged whom into a school janitor's closet on graduation day, drunk as a skunk, and insisted they make love?

"*You* were angry?" This took Michael aback. No doubt he never considered that she had feelings that day, which made her temple pound. "Did you ever think that maybe I didn't wish to have my graduation dress torn off me in some dark, nasty closet by a lusty teenager who reeked of rot gut whiskey?"

She shouldn't have said it; she realized her error the moment the final words left her lips. Although he never would have indicated otherwise — the man was never one for expressing his emotions — Michael had been distraught that his father wasn't present at his graduation, thus drinking steadily since early that morning. He was also mad at Mr. Wagner who almost threw him out of the auditorium.

Dewey knew this, understood his anguish and guilt over his father's death. She went along with his insistence that they make love on school property — the perfect revenge to Mr. Wagner, but in reality something to focus his anger on. Not to mention that she had hoped the lovemaking would sober him up, enough to explain that she was leaving for New York that afternoon.

"If I recall," he said softly, anger and pain lurking behind his words, "you never minded my lust."

The guilt of the night of the funeral assaulted her. She had, in fact, been the one who started it all, the one who caused the rift in their friendship in the first place. It still didn't relieve her anger. She needed to get out of there, needed to get away from this horrid conversation that was going nowhere.

"You're right, Michael, I did."

She headed for the door, but Michael grabbed her arm. When she turned to object, she found herself so close her chest brushed against his, causing her anger to turn into something more primal.

He started to say something, but hesitated, gazing into her eyes with a new emotion, one devoid of anger and resentment. She could feel his warm breath on her cheek, his large hand still clutching her upper arm, but all she could focus on was the depths of his dark eyes and the lips that seem ready to kiss her.

He reached up, his fingers caressing her cheek, still appearing as if he wanted to tell her something.

"Tell me," she commanded him in her mind. "Tell me you love me."

Michael swallowed and frowned, then moved back, releasing her arm and the spell he had cast upon her. "I came out here with a proposition."

Anywhere else she never would have thought anything about that remark, but they were standing in the "love shed," as Michael once jokingly called it. He appeared to read her mind and smiled slyly. "Not that kind of proposition."

For a moment, Dewey felt disappointed. Until she regained her senses, moving back further and crossing her arms about her chest. "What?"

"I work with a teacher who's pregnant and has to get some tests done this week. She asked me to grade some papers for her in her absence, but it's creative writing, not my specialty."

This got Dewey's attention, something that didn't involve Michael, her mother or Mamaw. "Sure, I'll do it."

"I figured since you write that popular food blog."

"Yeah, I'd be happy to." Dewey frowned. "Wait, how did you know about my blog?"

Michael sent a look that said all. Of course, who else but the Cajun Telegraph? Mamaw.

"Michael," Tyler began calling, a small request that was quickly turning into a constant bellow. "Well, I was going to offer to buy you a shrimp dinner in exchange for grading the papers but if you're that easy…"

That was an understatement, Dewey thought. If only he knew he could have had her right there on that bed only a minute before. "Nope, sorry, you still need to pay up."

"How about Blue Dog Café then? I have an *envie* for some oysters and Sandy likes shrimp, plus Tyler likes the music."

As if Michael didn't. Dewey smiled, thinking back on Bad Ass Arceneaux and his dirty zydeco dancing, not to mention what oysters might do for that overactive libido. She wondered if he had given up dancing, both in and out of bed, Mr. Prim and Proper High School Teacher.

"Sure."

"Un-cle Mi-chael," a five-year-old voice screamed from the yard.

Michael started to leave, then paused and headed back toward the photo wall. He pulled a box from a shelf and placed it into Dewey's hands.

"Mrs. Greene has nothing on you," he said before leaving Dewey alone in the shed.

Dewey fell back on to the bed, the box resting in her lap. She gingerly opened the lip and found a sea of photographs, all variations of her face.

"Holy shit."

There were photos of her attending class, working in the yard, reading a book on Mamaw's back porch. There were many of her through her window, no doubt taken by Michael from his. One was her laughing at a crawfish boil. Another had her fishing by the bayou, the infamous shed in the background in its former seedy glory. A whole roll seemed to have been taken of her walking through the halls of Paul Hébert High School.

And all were shot without her knowledge.

"I can't believe this."

"What can't you believe?"

Dewey jumped for the second time that day, the photos falling haphazardly into the box. "Jesus, doesn't anyone knock anymore?"

Emma gazed around the open doorway that led to a rugged porch. "Guess I missed the doorbell."

"Never mind." Dewey hurriedly placed the lid on the box and shoved it beside her on the bed. Suddenly, she knew why people called it jumping out of your skin. There were too many surprises for one day, too many jolts of emotions.

Emma entered, gazing around. "Wow, someone fixed this place up. I remember when…"

She didn't finish and Dewey didn't prompt her. The last thing she wanted to hear was her mother having wild sex in the love shed, which, no doubt, she probably did.

"Did you get enough sleep?"

Emma stretched, appearing pleased with the world. "Yeah, I did." She gazed at Dewey, concerned. "You, however, look like you could use some."

Now that Dewey thought about it, she hadn't slept much in the past couple of days.

"How's your ulcer?" Emma sat on the bed next to her and opened the box.

"How did you know about that?"

"Who else? Before Wednesday, of course." Emma riffled her hand through the photos. "Wow, someone was really in love with you."

Realizing what her mother was doing, Dewey thought to grab the box and hide it back on its shelf. But, it was too late, her mother had seen too much.

"Those are Michael's. He's a photographer. I'm sure he was just practicing."

"Who?" She picked up one of Dewey lost in thought on the porch swing. "This one is really nice."

"Michael." Her mother didn't react, which caused Dewey's blood pressure to skip a notch higher. She really needed to get back to the Coast and her yoga classes, something to calm her nerves and conquer her emotions. "He's the guy you were scared I was going to get pregnant by in high school, the one that made you talk me into going to Columbia."

She chose one of the photos of Dewey at school, gazing at something in the background. "I talked you into going to Columbia?"

"Well, you and Dad." Sheesh, how could she forget that? They practically begged Dewey to leave Louisiana and go to a "real school" instead of LSU. Her father had been afraid she would turn out like Emma, become pregnant and have to marry some "coonass nobody." Or worse, she would choose Louisiana as her lifelong residence.

"Nobody who stays in Louisiana amounts to anything," her father had said.

Dewey rubbed her eyes. Yes, she was tired.

"This one's cute."

Dewey opened her eyes to see one of she and Michael leaning against the hood of Clotille, his arm draped across her shoulders and both of them grinning widely. They appeared so happy, like the best friends that they were. When had that one been taken? Before or after the seduction on the back porch steps?

Dewey took the photo from her mother's fingers, rubbing a thumb over Michael's handsome form. Then she silently hid it into the pocket of her shirt while her mother continued her forage through the Dewey box.

"I'm going out tonight." Emma smiled at a photo of a young Dewey with Peuvre Pop watering the lawn. "Do you mind?"

"Why should I mind?"

"I don't want to leave you here with no one, nothing to do."

"Actually, I'm helping Michael grade some papers for school. We might go get some food, too."

"Who's Michael?"

She was really annoying. The only time her mother had paid attention to her in high school was to convince her that this "Michael fella" was going to lead to her ruin. Now, she couldn't remember his name?

"He lives next door." Surely, she'd remember that.

Emma turned and looked at her. "Are you mad at something?"

Dewey couldn't help but laugh. The world had gone nuts. "No, Mom, why should I be mad?"

Emma grasped her meaning, smiling sadly while she placed the lid on the box and stood. "Well, when you figure it out, let me know, okay?"

She headed across the threshold, making Dewey suddenly anxious to see her go. Before she had time to call out, her mother paused and turned back to look at her. "I love you, you know. I may not have been a great mother, but I have always loved you."

This wasn't what Dewey expected and it stopped her cold. "I know, Mom," was the only thing she could think of to say.

"You are and always will be the brightest light in my life. Nothing I have done or ever will do comes close to having you." Then she met Dewey's eyes, a sad smile gracing her lips. "Although I doubt you believe me."

If truth be told, Dewey always had a hard time believing it, although Mamaw always insisted she put way too much blame on one parent when it belonged to the other. Gazing at her beautiful mother standing there, the sunset casting a glow about her, Dewey nodded, believing her now.

A man called Emma's name from the direction of the house, and Emma suddenly grinned like a teenager. "That's my date. I have to go."

"Date?"

Before Dewey could ask, Emma disappeared around the corner of the shed. Dewey followed, just in time to see her mother give Mr. Wagner a hug and enter his car. Within a heartbeat, the couple pulled out of the driveway and drove away.

Dewey stood there, mouth gaping, one hand still gripping the youthful photo of she and Michael, wondering how much shock a person could receive in one day and still survive.

Chapter Seven

"DAMN," SANDY MUTTERED AS SHE turned off University on to the dreaded street that was the bane of her daily commute. Johnston was backed up all the way to Our Lady of Fatima, red taillights lined up like a Christmas string of lights.

She leaned her head back and moaned out loud, which relieved some of the tension. Work had been insufferable, as usual, her boss a major headache. She needed to pick up school items for Tyler's kindergarten class and dog food for Boudreaux, which meant every minute spent in traffic was one less minute relaxing at home. It really wasn't anything to get stressed over, not to mention she was bringing home dinner, which ruled out that time-consuming duty.

Maybe she was PMSing. The dreaded date loomed on the horizon.

Or maybe it was the comment Dewey made about her hair, which really sucked if she was honest. Sandy glanced in the rearview mirror to convince herself it wasn't that bad but the horrid colors stared back. "Yeah, it's that bad," she said to no one.

Frustration reigned in her veins, as her best friend Carol would say. She needed at least twenty bucks to get a decent haircut, but the twenty in her purse was earmarked for school supplies and a dog. She needed to get laid, or at least find a man who didn't run screaming when he got a look at Tyler, and no money could solve that dilemma. Then there was Tyler, her adorable baby boy who was driving her insane. Hell, she needed a life!

Her cell phone buzzed as she managed to inch forward and make out Mel's Diner above the parade of SUVs. Sandy reached into her purse, trying to locate the loud nuisance.

And then there was Michael. Her handsome big brother who provided home and encouragement when her family offered criticism. The man she loved — had always adored — who was neglecting his life to play surrogate dad.

He needed to get married, to have a family of his own, preferably with Dewey if the two of them would ever come to their senses. But where would that leave her?

The cell phone rang the theme song of *Harry Potter* again, this time sounded closer.

It didn't matter what happened to her, Michael and Dewey needed to face their insecurities and get over this stupid grudge. While Sandy lingered in celibacy hell, the two of them could be fornicating at this very moment if only they opened up their emotional prisons and admitted their love for each other.

The jingling tune rang out again and Sandy's fingers finally grasped it amid the jungle she called a purse. "I'm almost home," Sandy lied. "I'll be there in five."

"Uh, it's not Michael," the voice answered.

"Hi, Kevin," she answered gruffly. Sandy didn't have time for small talk and her coworker always seemed eager to initiate some. Casual conversation was a luxury she failed to find in a day's time.

Kevin sensed her irritation. He was good at that, too, which made Sandy kick herself for being insensitive. Then she kicked herself for being too kind. The guy had to know she couldn't shoot the breeze whenever he felt like it. Still, her mother taught her not to be rude.

"What's up?" she tried to say pleasantly.

"Just checking on you. You seemed stressed out today."

"Yeah, well, life is like that."

"Huh?"

Sandy gritted her teeth, cringing at the nails-on-the-chalk-board sound it made. "What do you want, Kevin?"

He sighed, which gave Sandy time to kick herself once more. God, she was turning into such a bitch.

"I noticed Joe ignoring you today, especially in the morning meeting. I wanted to see if you were all right."

"Damn," Sandy muttered. The man was being thoughtful and here she was trying to blow him off like the turd who really mistreated her.

"I'm sorry, Kevin, I didn't mean to be rude earlier. I'm stuck on Johnston and my A/C isn't working and…" She moved around a slight corner and realized the traffic stretched into the horizon, at least what she could make out over the enormous pick-up in front of her. "Why does everyone have to own an SUV or a monster truck in this town? Do all parents have entire soccer teams to lug around?"

"Huh?"

She didn't mean to think it, but the guy was getting on her nerves, good intentions or not. "Thanks, Kevin." She tried to remove the edge from her voice. "I'm fine. He's an idiot and I'm fine."

A pause followed and Sandy almost inquired if he was still breathing. "I heard you crying in the bathroom, Sandy."

Yeah, that was the beginning of her horrible day, right after bumping into Joe with his arms around the new temp. She hadn't meant to lose it, she and Joe had only *flirted* for the past six months, him kissing her that once at the staff party. Sandy preferred to blame it on hormones, or watching her best friend and brother lock horns over breakfast, two people who could have it all as opposed to her no-sex-single-mom-living-in-limbo existence. "Look, Kevin, it's nothing. I'm just emotional today, it's a woman's thing."

"Well, if you need to talk."

Somehow knowing he knew about her crying jag depleted her hormonal rage. Or maybe it was the fact that Kevin Blanchard, geeky glasses, bad taste in clothes and dorky shoes, was a nice guy who cared. "Thanks. I will."

"I mean it. I'm here."

"Okay."

"Any time."

"Okay."

"We can do coffee or take in a movie or whatever…"

"I got it."

Now, he was back to getting on her last nerve. The traffic picked up so Sandy had an excuse. "Gotta run, Kevin. Johnston's moving. I need my hands."

"Okay."

She hit the end button and threw the phone toward her purse, missing the enormous bag and hitting the side door. It made a funny sound, which caused her anger to come racing back. She had only bought that fancy new phone because Joe insisted on everyone owning one. He couldn't possess her soul enough during the daylight hours, she had to be on call as well, which cost her an extra fifty dollars a month for the phone. And like the pair of scratched glasses she wore to drive, she kept breaking the thing due to her clumsiness.

Finally, after another ten minutes of verbal self-abuse, and some choice words directed toward the SUV soccer moms around her, Sandy arrived home, her decade-old Honda sputtering to a stop. Within a heartbeat, a cherub face rounded the corner, calling her name.

For a moment, all the stress of her life disappeared, everything made sense. When the tiny arms encircled her neck and hugged her close through the open car door, all stood right with the universe.

"Hey Boo," Sandy said as she hugged her boy tight, relishing the smell of his fine brown hair and the soft fold of skin beneath his chin. She absorbed it quickly and hurriedly planted kisses on him before he pulled away and ran just as fast up the back porch steps.

Love was fleeting in her household.

"Come on," Tyler yelled back at her, his attention on to something new, more than likely what was on the Disney Channel or what Boudreaux was licking.

Sandy sighed and watched the blur of her son as he stole away, then she grabbed the remnants of the afternoon function and headed for the house. She forgot to call Dewey in her haste to leave work and away from Joe's lovesick gazes every time that temp came into their department. Hopefully, Michael had done the duty and invited her over. Unless the two of them were still at each other's throats.

God, she hoped not. The last thing she needed was watching those two fight.

"Hey." Dewey held open the back screen door. "What'da you bring home?"

"Leftovers from a function. We had a big bash with the City-Parish Department of Sanitation and hardly anybody ate."

"I can imagine, if they were discussing sanitation issues." Dewey peeked inside a bag. "But Michael said something about shrimp."

"We're going out to eat," Tyler announced loudly. "Uncle Michael said so."

Sandy gritted her teeth again, forcing a headache. "I can't afford a night out."

"I'm paying." Michael entered the kitchen, gazing in the bag as Dewey had done.

"No, you're not." Sandy wasn't in for a night managing a hyper child in a restaurant and playing the role of sibling pauper.

"Then let me," Dewey inserted. "I'll be happy to treat."

"Yeah!" Tyler said, clapping and jumping up and down which made Sandy's head pound.

"It's okay, Dewey. You don't have to."

"But I want to."

"I initiated this thought, so the dinner's on me," Michael inserted.

"Yeah," Tyler exclaimed, this time louder. "Let's go to the place with all the Blue Dog pictures."

Suddenly several people were talking at once, the noise getting louder and louder. Sandy imagined four white walls and a straight jacket as a happy alternative. Finally, when Michael started lecturing her about graciously accepting gifts and Tyler responded by chanting "Blue-Dog, Blue-Dog," Sandy exploded.

"No," she shouted. "We're eating here."

The talking stopped and all gazes fell upon her. Until Tyler threw his head back, crying loudly as he headed for a tantrum. Sandy closed her eyes. Yes, electric shock therapy would be a great improvement.

To his credit, Michael recognized the meltdown coming and whisked Tyler into the living room where he began to tickle and make jokes as a distraction. It took several minutes, but soon rational thought took over and laughter was heard coming from the other room.

"He's not a brat, you know."

Dewey looked over as if Sandy had gone crazy. "I know that."

"He sounds like one, but it's the ADHD, the chemical that's missing in his brain. He doesn't have the rational power to discern things like normal people. He only sees and reacts."

Dewey stepped forward and touched Sandy's arm. "Of course, Sandy. I wasn't thinking anything else."

Embarrassed both by Tyler's behavior and her own, Sandy crossed her arms about her chest defensively. "It's okay. Everyone thinks that way. He looks like an undisciplined brat. But I'm not a bad mother."

Dewey wrapped an arm about Sandy's shoulder and squeezed, causing Sandy's dreaded tears to find their way back home. "I'm not everyone. I'm his godmother and I love him just the way he is. And Tyler Michael Arceneaux is not a brat!"

Sandy wiped the back of her hand across her nose. "He's great at school. He's on the medicine then. When he's older, we'll put him on a new drug that will last longer throughout the day, but for now it's best so he can go to sleep at night…"

She felt Dewey pull her close. "Shhh. You're among friends."

It felt good to lean on someone, especially a girlfriend. Outside of Carol, who Sandy only saw during her lunch hour and occasionally at the mall on weekends when she could manage a moment away from home, she had no friends. They had all pretty much disappeared soon after the pregnancy test turned blue.

"I'm having a bad day," she whispered.

Dewey laughed, but didn't release her hug. "Now, that's the first thing you've said today that makes sense."

Sandy straightened, blowing her nose on a nearby paper napkin. "What happened with Mamaw?"

Dewey exhaled deeply. "Nothing. She won't talk to me. Hell, she won't interrupt her bourré game long enough to acknowledge my presence. My mother, on the hand, is in town and is talking to me, more than I'm used to. And then there's your brother, who took photos of me all through high school without my knowledge."

Michael entered the kitchen on those final words and halted at the threshold.

"Stalker!" Dewey said.

Tyler ran ahead and started rummaging through the bags Sandy had brought.

"Just the boudin balls," Michael instructed him, then turned to Dewey. "Photographer's prerogative."

"Through my bedroom window?"

Michael frowned. "You make me sound like a pervert."

"You have to admit, it's a little weird."

"Hardly." He crossed his arms. "You're a journalist. You know the best pictures are of people who don't know they're being photographed."

"But why didn't you ever show them to me?"

"Stop it, you all," Sandy said loudly, forcing them both to look her way. "I have a headache from hell and the last thing I need…"

"Do you know what he did, Sandy?" Dewey asked, while Michael grunted and looked skyward. "He took all these photos of me."

Sandy shut her eyes and stopped listening. So what? she wanted to yell. Michael snapped secret photos and Dewey stole one of his shirts that she kept beneath her pillow. Sandy would have thought the two of them would have figured out their love for each other when they finally advanced from best friends to performing like rabbits. Instead, they spent every waking moment making love in every possible spot in town, letting it blow up in a scene at graduation, with one splitting to Missouri and the other turning to alcohol.

"You know, we're all grown up here now," Sandy said through clenched teeth which were going to make her head explode, she knew it. "We've moved on, gotten jobs and turned out fairly decent considering our upbringings. Do you two think you could be civil, at least through dinner?"

"Boudin balls," Tyler said, tugging at Sandy's shirt.

Sometimes Tyler, with all his unfocused faults, could truly come to the rescue. Kinda like when Sandy was being bothered by pesky telemarketers or clothes salesladies. "Gotta run," was all she had to say and those trying to sell her something would look at Tyler or hear his protestations and gladly let her go.

"They're in the small bag," Sandy told him. "The larger bag has a tub of dirty rice, some fried chicken strips, catfish, French fries, remoulade sauce."

Michael sent Dewey a stern look he probably gave half his students and then went about the duty of putting plates on the table. Dewey retrieved the glasses and filled them up with ice and homemade iced tea from the fridge. The sudden silence made Sandy's head hurt even more. Or maybe she could finally hear the thumping going on in there.

"What's rom-a-laad sauce?" Tyler asked, gazing at the small container.

"Something your poor Aunt Dewey never gets enough of in Los Angeles," Dewey said with a smile. "As for boudin balls, she never gets any."

"How come?" The tyke shoved into his mouth one of the boudin balls, made of the same ingredients found in the sausage but rolled and fried.

Dewey shrugged. "Don't have them out there. Which makes your Aunt Dewey very unhappy."

Sandy was about to ask Aunt Dewey why she didn't move home and eat all the boudin balls she wanted, when Tyler continued. "Mom says your real name is Caroline. Why do you call yourself Dewey?"

Dewey sat down at the table, sipping her iced tea and enjoying a boudin ball that was the rage of the world-famous Cajun restaurant where Sandy worked. She closed her eyes in reverence as she took a bite, then smiled at Tyler. "When I was a baby, we lived in New York City."

"Aunt Dewey's a Yankee," Michael inserted.

Dewey sent him a look that could kill. "I'm not a Yankee."

"Where's New York City?" Tyler asked, oblivious to the hostility around him.

"Way up north where it's cold, food is bland and people are rude," Michael added.

Sandy wanted to stop this nonsense and set the boy straight, but she'd never been further north than Bunkie, about an hour upstate on Interstate 49. She really had no idea what New Yorkers were like.

"Anyway," Dewey said, sending Michael another cold stare, "my Lafayette mother was homesick and used to play Cajun music all the time. Dewey Balfa was my favorite musician and I used to say 'Dewey' when I wanted to hear more of his records. It was my first word, or so my mom claims."

"Isn't Dad supposed to be your first word?" Sandy asked.

Dewey's smile disappeared and Sandy kicked herself for the umpteenth time that day. Thankfully, Tyler came to the rescue again. "What was *my* first word?"

Definitely not dad, Sandy thought. Now that she thought about it, she doubted anyone in that room had seen a lot of their fathers when they were young. Sandy probably had the best record and she was the product of a second marriage, the daughter of a kindly but alcoholic man who had been the worst kind of father to Michael.

"Your first word was Mom," Sandy said proudly. Sometimes there is justice in the world.

"These are scrumptious," Dewey exclaimed between bites. "How do you guys manage to stay thin and work at Broussard's every day?"

Sandy loved good Cajun food but there were days when the smell of that restaurant could send her curling. Too much of a good thing.

"You guys?" Michael said with a smug grin. "I told you Aunt Dewey was a Yankee."

Dewey dropped her glass on the table a little too hard, obviously smarting at the reference. Michael used to call her that in school and it drove her crazy back then.

"Don't make me hurt you."

Michael threw his hands in the air, his eyes wild with fear, which made Tyler snort with laughter. "I'm shaking in my boots."

Dewey ignored him, reaching into the bag for something new to eat. "Jerk."

"Are you having some?" Michael asked Sandy when his audience disintegrated.

She had eaten way too many boudin balls and catfish for lunch, then wolfed down two pieces of leftover pecan pie in the afternoon right after Joe sent the temp flowers. The last thing she wanted was more Broussard food. "None for me. I'm not feeling well."

Michael touched her forehead, then gave her cheek a pinch. "Ah *chèr*, you need to rest. You look worn out."

Tyler giggled. He loved hearing Michael speak French expressions, even basic ones that everyone said. Michael recognized that laugh and launched into a lengthy discourse in Cajun French, which made Tyler giggle louder.

Pleased with himself and that no one else could understand him, Michael leaned back in his chair like he used to do in high school and grinned daringly at Dewey. "That, Yankee, is

Cajun."

Dewey leaned across the table, taking the bait. "So is *couillon, couillon*."

The legs of his chair fell down on the kitchen floor making them all jump. "That's the only word you know, Yank? Surely you can do better than that."

"What's a *couillon*?" Tyler asked.

"Nothing," Sandy said, sending them both a "stop it" look, hoping Dewey wouldn't take it further. There were worst words in Cajun French and Dewey knew them all, but Tyler certainly could wait a few years before picking them up.

"It's your Uncle Michael," Dewey instructed him, which made Sandy's blood boil.

"Dewey, don't teach him that."

"It means idiot, Tyler," Michael said. "Your Aunt Dewey thinks I'm an idiot because I tore up a letter a long time ago."

Dewey shook her head in astonishment. "Anyone in his right mind reads a letter first, then tears it up. You could have told the world you tore it up, but who doesn't read a letter first?"

"Who said I was in my right mind? Jesus, I was in jail."

"And whose fault was that?"

With the veins on his neck about to burst, Michael started to speak, but Sandy couldn't take it anymore. She leaped up from the table, one hand holding the side of her pounding head in case her brains came spilling out, and shouted, "Stop it!"

For the second time, everyone froze, but, she wasn't backing down and she wasn't giving them another chance. "I can't stand this anymore, you ungrateful, unappreciative bums."

Michael exhaled and reached for her hand. "Sandy…"

"No." She pulled away from the table, taking Tyler's hand and pulling the child to her side.

"For fourteen years I've had to listen to this insanity from both you *couillons*. Not to mention, all those years before when you didn't have the sense to tell each other how you felt."

This took them aback. She could see the wheels turning in their heads, which only made her madder. How could best friends fail to know they were mad for each other?

"I'm with Mamaw," Sandy declared. "Until you both get over this ridiculous feud and get married, I'm not talking to either one of you."

And with those final words, Sandy marched from the room, pulling a stunned and surprisingly quiet Tyler behind her.

Chapter Eight

"WHERE ARE WE GOING?" AS silly as it sounded, Emma was excited to be taken out at her age — by stuffy ole Patrick, no less, in his conservative suit and tie and unbending aristocratic manners. Or maybe she was just thrilled the two of them had finally moved beyond the follies of youth and the technicalities of parenthood and could now relax as rational adults by candlelight. It had only taken thirty years.

But the silence that followed made Emma wonder if that was possible.

"We need to talk, Emma," Patrick finally said, unsmiling.

Emma straightened her skirt, the one that showed enough of her long legs to incite interest but not enough to reveal what age and motherhood had done to her thighs. Equally flattering was her skin-tight red sweater that flashed a hint of the breast augmentation that cost her three years' worth of tax refunds. All in all, she still had it. And talking wasn't what she had in mind. But, what did she expect coming back here?

She sighed, her shoulders drooping and her gaze moving to the activity at the corner of Johnston. Boudreaux's used cars had opened a new office and employees were standing on the street dressed as giant crawfish, waving to cars that honked in return. Outside, a man stirred a giant pot that emitted steam from its top, no doubt a jambalaya or gumbo, while customers stood in line for a bowl. Put out food and Cajuns come running.

"I hope we're not eating there."

Patrick turned his head for a moment and a tiny grin flitted over his features before he sent it away. "I thought we'd go to Alesi's."

Someplace dark and quiet, Emma quickly surmised. A back booth where they could discuss what they always discussed. Somehow, over the past thirty years, the fabulous sex that had gotten them where they are failed to be an issue anymore.

Maybe it was the lack of sleep or her mother's disapproval — again — but Emma wasn't up for more lectures. She didn't want to discuss what she should have done thirty years prior, the poor choices she made in life or how she failed at motherhood. What she wanted was a romantic dinner, preferably with Louisiana seafood, followed by wild, unbridled lovemaking. Sneaking a side-glance at Patrick's burrowed brow and stern set of his jaw made Emma realize she would get none of that tonight.

When they pulled into the parking lot and Patrick set the break, Emma touched his sleeve. "Maybe this isn't a good idea."

He seemed to sense that coming, a smirk curling up the sides of his lips. "Not a good idea for whom?"

"Whom? Damn, you even talk like a principal."

"I am a principal, Emma, no thanks to you."

Yep, he wanted to drag up the past, relive days she couldn't bear recalling. Suddenly, she felt claustrophobic, her lungs constricting as if someone sucked the air from the car. They were only blocks from home. She could walk.

He touched her elbow as if guessing she might flee. "Please, Emma. We need to discuss this."

"There's nothing to talk about, Patrick," she whispered, her free arm grabbing hold of the door handle.

"There's everything to talk about." His tone grew louder as his grip on her elbow tightened. "She's my daughter."

Emma pulled free and left the car, wrapping her arms about her and heading west. She hadn't gotten past the restaurant's front door before Patrick grabbed her and turned her around, gripping both her arms in an effort to keep her close.

Which he did with aplomb. As he pulled Emma hard against his chest, she inhaled the heady scent of old English soup and some tangy masculine cologne, causing her head to spin even further. Dewey used to make fun of Patrick, calling him an old maid principal when she was in high school, bitching about his strict views on alcohol and sexual promiscuity, his square-looking clothes and membership in the Sons of the America Revolution. But, Emma knew better. Emma understood the power behind those massive, manicured hands and the expertise of those pedigreed lips. And she sorely missed the feel of them, the touch of a real man without an agenda relating to the Entertainment Industry.

"Please," Patrick said, his breath hot on her cheek. "I need closure."

Emma dropped her head against his forehead, still resisting the conversation but not wanting to leave the sensual fragrance of him, the strong grip of his hands on her. "There's nothing to talk about, Patrick. We've been through this a million times."

One set of fingers loosened on an arm and slowly slid to the curve of her back, pushing her even closer, while Emma swore he was absorbing the feel and smell of her as well. Oh please God, Emma almost uttered out loud, make this man want me tonight.

Instead, Patrick straightened, cold air filling the space he once occupied. "Then it has to be one million and one. Mamaw won't speak to us unless we settle this."

Emma couldn't help herself; she moaned. Loudly. "She's not talking to you either?"

He dropped his hands and looked away, which made Emma want to moan again. "Of course not. That's what this is all about, forcing her loved ones to get on with their lives. She's always been convinced my life is on hold because of you."

In an instant, Emma held hope. "Because of me or because of Dewey?"

Whatever flame of passion might have ignited between them disintegrated. His eyes turned cold. "I want a DNA test."

Emma ran a hand through her hair, wishing she had stayed on the set instead of risking her career, her daughter and her sanity for a trip to Louisiana. God, she hated coming home. "It's a waste of time. We've been through this before. We had the blood test done when she was three."

"Fine. Now let's do DNA."

"You'll need Dewey's approval."

"Of course."

So, that's how he saw it, as a simple test. Ruin a person's life, make them wonder of their parentage, think even less of their mother than they already do now. Dewey had been through enough, was still begging for approval from a man with ice running through his veins, a man Emma wished with all her heart was *not* her father. Now, Patrick wanted to further mess up Dewey's life.

Over her dead body.

"Screw you," Emma said, and began marching down the street toward home.

"You already did," he shouted to her back.

She didn't know why she paused and turned around. Maybe she was tired of men having the last word. Or perhaps she was sick of people judging her life, which had been ripe with disappointments and hardship. But she did, marching right back up to stand before him, her gaze boring into his soul. "We had a great time that Mardi Gras, Patrick. Best sex I ever had. But, Dewey is not yours and she never will be."

"She's not yours, either," he whispered so quietly Emma wasn't sure she heard him right, but the righteous look in his eyes confirmed it.

She pulled her hand back and slapped him hard across the face. "How dare...?" she said with blind fury, although by the time the final word was uttered, tears choked her speech.

He smarted from the contact; she could make out the shape of fingers in the red marks streaked across his cheek. Typical

Patrick Wagner, blue blood and all, didn't falter a bit. "Well," he said, "I guess I deserved that."

Something deep inside her lodged free, some long-buried pain broke loose and floated to the surface. Or maybe for once she wasn't going to let someone make her feel worthless.

"I don't care what you think of me. I don't care that you think I put myself first all these years, that I made choices for Dewey that only bettered myself. And I don't care that you think what I do is silly and insignificant, that a creative person does what she does for the hell-of-it, like a frickin' hobby."

The repressed hurt that finally broke free gave her strength. She could feel the power rage through her. "I am an actor and a damn good one at that, and there is no way I'm going to spend my life ignoring my talent and craft because you all down here think I need a real job."

He started to say something, but Emma was on a roll. This was her monologue and nothing was going to stop her from delivering it.

"But, let's get one thing straight, Patrick Wagner. Despite what you think about my mothering skills, that girl means more to me than any career and if you do one thing to harm her, to make her doubt her life, I'll kill you. Do you understand?"

To her surprise, Patrick smiled, albeit a guarded one. "Understood. So, are you still hungry?"

The rage retreated as fast as it arrived, making Emma feel lightheaded. "What?"

He took her face in his hands and kissed her lightly, another surprise. Even more shocking was how thrilling that simple gesture made her feel, considering everything that had transpired between them, both now and over the past thirty years.

When Patrick pulled back, he rested his head on her forehead, as she had done earlier, then exhaled and swallowed. "I still want to know, Emma. I need to know."

"Why haven't you gotten married?" Another long-buried question that rose up and snuck out of her mouth, like an unexpected burp.

He smiled grimly. "Who could ever match up to you?"

She didn't buy it — he couldn't possibly mean it — but he kissed her again and she didn't protest. It wasn't as steamy as their youthful escapades, but deep and purposeful and every bit as titillating.

The front door of the restaurant opened and a rowdy family emerged, all turning quiet when they spotted the necking middle-aged couple at the doorstep. Ever the discreet gentleman, Patrick withdrew, cleared his throat and offered out his arm. "Shall we?"

So much existed behind that simple question, and part of her demanded she run to the airport and hop on the next available plane heading west. Yet, they were here, now, together. And that tangy aftershave and the feel of those powerful lips permeated her senses, dulling her rational thinking process.

"I tell her," Emma said. "And whatever Dewey decides, you have to live with that."

Patrick's eyes dimmed, but he nodded. "Agreed."

"And just because you buy me dinner doesn't mean I'm going home with you." Finally, a smile broke through, the Patrick she once knew and adored. "Although if you kiss me like that again, I may change my mind."

Patrick's gaze shifted ever so slightly to make sure the family had moved on through the parking lot to their car. Then, with a smile still gracing his lips and that trademark dimple — that only special people were privy to — he kissed her again, this time not holding anything back.

Chapter Nine

RAIN FELL INTERMITTENTLY THROUGHOUT THE night, its drops sending waves of sound across the roof. Then suddenly, the temperature dropped a few degrees as the cold front followed, bringing a sharp chill to the room. Michael found himself reading the same page of the James Lee Burke mystery during the past ten minutes, but gave it up as he headed to shut the window.

He spotted Dewey on her back porch, sitting in the covered swing with a blanket around her shoulders. Pulling on a jacket, he headed out to warn her of Mamaw's failing heater, secretly grateful for a reason to talk to her.

The rain appeared to be moving off, the chilled wind blowing away the clouds that exposed a slice of moon. Finally, fall was arriving. If they were lucky, the cool weather would stick around for Halloween and not be pushed aside by encroaching warm air emigrating from the nearby Gulf of Mexico. There was nothing worse than a hot and humid night of Trick-R-Treating, especially if the popular costume that year was something thick and heavy, like Tyler's Minion outfit the year before. The poor kid had turned into a steaming mass of wet wool after three blocks.

Michael quietly exited the house, careful not to wake Tyler or Sandy, then crossed the yards between their homes, as he had done for countless years. When Dewey looked up to see him approach, she didn't appear at all surprised, maybe because walking up those steps was as routine as the bayou flowing behind their homes.

He climbed the steps to the deck, then leaned back against the railing, watching her rock the glider with the tip of her right toe. Even in the faint light of a crescent moon, she looked amazing, her Hollywood hair still sticking out at odd angles but so adorably sexy, her clothes a mixture of sweatpants and fashion, hugging her long, lean frame. He wished he had a camera.

"Don't let Sandy worry you. She'll come around eventually."

Dewey tipped her glass and knocked back the remnants of wine. "Do you want some?" she asked before realizing her mistake. "Oh God, Michael, I'm sorry."

Michael knew what the proper response was, but he was tired of pretending. Besides, this was Dewey. He leaned forward and retrieved her glass. "I'd love some. Thanks."

She opened her mouth to speak, but faltered. Michael took the opportunity to slip into the house and pour them both some wine, but not before checking out the label. Dewey had purchased some thirty-dollar Sonoma pinot noir, which pinched his pride a tad. How nice that would be to buy quality wine, the result of a hotshot Hollywood job. When he returned and handed her the glass, she eyed him curiously.

"Okay, confession time. I'm not an alcoholic."

She stared at him stunned, and he could imagine the thoughts floating around that head, crazy haircut included.

"I went a little nuts at LSU," Michael explained, realizing what an understatement that was. "I got drunk a lot. *A lot.* I practically flunked out of school. Wagner came up to Baton Rouge and dried me out, talked the administration into giving me another chance. He laid down the law and I knew he was right, so I straightened up."

Dewey absorbed this, nodding, but he could tell by that gaze she was still reluctant to believe him.

"He made me promise to attend AA meetings, which I did

and found amazingly helpful for dealing with my dad, but that's another story."

Michael took a long sip from his wine, savoring the fruity aroma and the smooth, somewhat tangy essence of grapes sliding down his throat without so much as a hint of aftertaste. "Wow, nice."

He sat down on the glider beside her, leaning back enough so he could do all the rocking and taking one of her feet into his lap. "I have no desire for alcohol, Dewey, besides the occasional beer on a hot day and glass of wine with a meal. I keep up the pretense because I teach teenagers and I'm a role model to them and the ole I-once-was-a-drunk-but-now-I'm-reformed is a good lesson for them."

She stretched back into the glider, pulling her other foot up and relaxing. When he spied that smile, he knew what she was thinking.

"Shut up."

"What?" Her smile expanded, much like it would in high school right before she erupted into hysterics. He could always make her laugh, like the time he wound her up before the school orchestra performance. As Wagner introduced the musicians and the auditorium drew silent, Dewey took the moment to start a laughing jag.

And, of course, they had gotten in trouble and Michael had been the one to blame.

"I'm sorry," Dewey said, trying to remove her smile but failing. "I have a hard time imagining you as a role model." She frowned, seemingly regretting the choice of words. "I mean, I can see you in that way — you're a terrific uncle to Tyler. Just not in that way, like a teacher. You know what I mean."

Sure, he did. He graduated from high school drunk, dragging his girlfriend into the janitor's closet at school and pulling off her clothes when all she wanted to do was "talk." Then the principal found them, who Michael punched in the face, and he got thrown in jail. Hardly the kind of person he wanted his kids to be.

"I've changed a lot since high school, Dewey. I'm not the man I used to be."

She absorbed this information silently, then whispered into her glass as she smiled slyly, "Pity."

The moment was ripe for flirtation and seduction and God knew he was ready, sitting there with Dewey's feet in his lap and that wine-induced glaze flitting across her come-hither eyes. But, he decided to focus on the subject at hand. "You think I'm in denial, right?"

She appeared taken aback by the question. "No," she said emphatically.

"A lot of alcoholics say they aren't alcoholics."

Dewey leaned back, gazing at him the way she always did, as if their minds existed on some alternate plane, always in sync. "You're not your dad, Michael."

Years of introspection and therapy had made Michael realize that, despite his dysfunctional upbringing and genetics, he was not his father, nor did he carry on his father's faults. But, it felt good to hear Dewey say it.

"No, I'm not," he reiterated, knowing that where he was now in his life was a direct result of that statement.

Dewey turned silent and Michael wondered if she had come to the same conclusion about her own father, or if she at least found some peace and wasn't spending her life waiting for his approval, as she had exhausted much of her youth. He started to ask but Dewey interrupted.

"Did you know my mother and Mr. Wagner are on a date tonight?"

Michael snorted in his wine. "No, really?"

"She hasn't come home yet."

Wow, the old man still had it in him. "And you're waiting up for your mother?"

"It's not funny, Michael. It's my mom and *Mr. Wagner*."

Michael fought back the urge to smile considering how Mr. Wagner used to worry about *their* sexual escapades, although it really wasn't that funny, considering, but Dewey didn't know that.

"They were a hot item in high school."

Dewey gulped down her wine and Michael wondered how much she had so far. "I guess."

"You guess? I've heard the tales. Surely, you've heard them too."

Dewey sent him a look. "I think I'm the one who told you."

"Then what's the problem?"

She shrugged and gazed off in the distance. "I don't know."

Michael had a clue, but he wondered if Dewey suspected. When Wagner had bailed him out of jail all those years ago, he bought Michael a coffee and spilled his guts about his relationship with Emma and how he always believed Dewey was his child. Wagner had sworn Michael to secrecy and, even though he and Dewey had kept nothing from each other, he felt honored to remain silent now. Besides, his friendship with Dewey had taken quite a beating over the years. When did he have a chance to even begin to tell her?

"Let the old folks have some fun," he said instead. "Besides, youthful passions are hard to forget."

Shit. What was he doing? They were civil for the first time since she arrived, why did he have to keep heading back fourteen years? Still preoccupied with her mother's sex life, Dewey didn't seem to notice.

"Are you still having stomach pains?" he asked, trying to get on another subject.

She looked over and noticed for the first time that he was rubbing her feet. In the pale moonlight, he swore he saw her smile. They used to spend many nights like this, sitting on Mamaw's swing, talking, or not talking and communicating just as much. And Michael always rubbed her feet.

"My stomach is doing much better, thanks. Surprisingly, considering all the spicy food I've been eating."

"Spice is good. It's everything else in life that will kill you."

"Is Sandy serious?"

So far that night, his sister failed to acknowledge his presence in the house. "'Fraid so."

"Has the world gone insane?"

From Michael's perspective, the world had always been crazy and he and Dewey in all their uniquely screwed-up ways had seemed like a midpoint of normalcy. "Well, it might work to our advantage."

Dewey smirked. "How's that?"

"Consider it. She's not *talking* to us."

Dewey laughed, the old belly laugh he remembered from high school, and it felt good to hear it.

"Now, I don't have to listen to the endless 'Why aren't you married' lectures from the two women in my life."

Dewey turned serious and leaned forward slightly. "Why aren't you married, Michael?"

"Oh God, not you, too."

"You're thirty-two."

"So are you? Why aren't *you* married?"

She reacted as if it was the strangest question and no relation to her own. "You're a good looking guy and Teacher of the Year."

"You're a good looking woman and a big shot in Hollywood."

Dewey laughed again. "I'm not a big shot. And I'm no way as handsome as you."

Michael tossed back the last of his wine. "Way," he imitated. "And you went to Cannes last year with some director. You write a blog that I hear is all the rage among foodies. You dated some famous body builder."

Dewey gasped. "What?"

"The question of the hour, *mon amie*, is why aren't you married and living in some mansion in Bel Air?"

Dewey relaxed and cocked her head in the most adorable way, still laughing as if someone said the funniest thing. "Mansion in Bel Air? I live in a closet that costs me a fortune."

"So marry the body builder and move up."

"What body builder? I haven't even had a date in months."

This tidbit of news made Michael sit up straighter. "Mamaw said you were serious about some well-built man."

"Jason," Dewey exclaimed, finally putting the pieces together. "I'm not serious about him; we went to the movies a couple of times. And he's a male model, not a body builder."

Now, it was Michael's turn to laugh. "A male model?"

She punched him on the arm.

"A male model?"

"Shut up. He makes a good living posing for romance novel covers."

Michael smirked and she punched him in the arm again.

"I heard you were dating Alice Fontenot from the Chamber of Commerce. Wasn't she covered in freckles?"

She was covered in freckles, but he wasn't about to admit that. Besides, they saw each a few times two years ago and quickly realized they had nothing in common. "Old news."

"Cary Bergeron?"

"She got married. And we only had dinner once."

"Patricia Talley, the P.E. teacher?"

Michael shook his head. Who needed the Internet when they had Mamaw? "Raymond Whats-his-name?"

"Way old news. Oh come on, surely you've heard about my last date, the actor from New York?"

"Cameron Stye. Not like it's a pretentious name or anything."

"Wow, you're good."

"What happened with him?" He really didn't want to know, wondered how they got on this distasteful subject, but he guessed anything was better than old stories about high school lust.

"He didn't last the night. He refused to eat anything spicy that might 'harm his instrument,'" Dewey said using her fingers as quotation marks. "And I refuse to date a man who eats bland food and shuns caffeine. End of story."

Michael smiled, thinking of that conversation.

"Besides, he was from New Jersey and kept making fun of me when I said 'you all.' That's when I started saying 'you guys,' for what it's worth. It's a preservation thing."

"Another reason for you to come home."

Shit. There he goes again. What had gotten into him tonight?

Dewey gazed into her glass, suddenly quiet and sullen, the squeak of the glider's chains breaking the silence. "Why would I come home, Michael?"

His first instinct was to be defensive, to counteract that question as if it were a personal insult. But, the way Dewey had uttered it made him think she wanted a real answer, something she could hold on to.

He draped an arm along the back of the glider, his fingers playing with a strand of hair flipped defiantly away from her face. "If I promise not to humiliate you in public again, will you come back?"

He couldn't believe he said those words, couldn't believe he was admitting that he wanted her home. Dewey leaned forward once more, a bit sluggish which made Michael realize she had too much to drink.

"You weren't the only reason I left, Michael."

Funny, after all those years, how one sentence from a certain someone could steal the breath from a person. He wanted so badly to ask for a full explanation, to find out at last why she had fled the scene all those years ago, but the words refused to come. He realized Sandy was right about his emotional constipation — although that was a picture he refused to imagine — for his attempt to ask Dewey why she had gone pecan failed to leave his lips, even though she stared at him as if she wanted him to ask.

Instead, he cupped his hand around Dewey's cheek, letting his thumb roam lazily across, savoring the feel of her soft skin and the image of her face in the moonlight. Then he leaned forward and kissed her, something chaste, unusual for the two of them, but so delicious and hot. Dewey leaned forward, expecting more, and Michael wanted to deliver with all his soul and other vital parts of his body. But she was hazy with wine, he had class to teach in the morning and having wild sex with Dewey — although, dear God, how wonderful that would be — was not the answer to their problems.

Michael pulled back, realizing the air had turned decidedly cooler. "Mamaw's heater is not working well. I came over here to tell you not to use it, because if you turn it on all it will do is stink up the house and pass cold air."

The clouds moved in front of the moon and it was difficult to make out Dewey's expression. "Okay."

Michael stood, his rational mind telling him to get out of there before he changed his mind, grabbed her up in his arms and headed for her second-floor bedroom. How many times had he had that fantasy, of making love to her in her own bed? And right now the urge was overwhelming.

"I have a break at ten thirty," he said, inching backwards. "Why don't you finish grading those papers and come visit the school in the morning."

Dewey pulled the blanket around her shoulders and stood, taking his glass from his hand. "Okay."

"And go to bed. Let your parents have some fun."

"My parents?"

He must be tired; he was divulging way too many things tonight. "Your mom. You know what I mean."

Michael needed to go home. He headed down the steps into the darkness.

"Michael," Dewey called out, which made him pause and turn around, her silhouette the only thing visible about her. "How much will you give me not to tell your students about Bad Ass Arceneaux?"

"I wouldn't do that if I were you."

"Oh yeah, why not?"

Michael inched closer to make out her playful expression, that sly smile beneath her cute little nose that was aimed skyward in mirthful defiance. He knew she was enjoying the banter, but he doubted she would appreciate the fallout or having to revisit old wounds at the scene of the crime. "I'm a bit infamous at the school, Dewey, because of my past. The only thing that seems to have faded away is who I was infamous with."

Dewey's gaze turned cold and she pulled the blanket tight about her. "Well, it's not like I was the only one," she said coldly and then marched into the house.

Michael watched the screen door slam shut, its noise reverberating across the dark quiet of night, and wondered who the hell she could possibly be referring to.

Chapter Ten

THE CELL PHONE BUZZED THROUGH the haze of sleep, but this time Dewey wasn't answering. She threw a lazy arm over the side of her bed to silence the phone but stopped when she checked the caller ID.

"Hey girl," she told Maggie, happy to be speaking to a friend and not her father.

"Hey yourself," Maggie answered. "Sorry this is so early but I'm helping put on a bridal breakfast and I won't be free for the rest of the day. You ready for tomorrow?"

Dewey had forgotten all about All Saints Day and her best friend from The Cajun Embassy. Maggie had been in New Orleans for a cousin's wedding and when she heard Dewey was in Lafayette she arranged to head over for lunch with a follow-up visit to her family's gravesite about an hour south. In South Louisiana, residents visited gravesites, cleaned them up and adorned them with flowers for the Catholic holiday on November first.

"Of course. I can't wait to see you."

Dewey meant that from the bottom of her heart. She needed a girlfriend now more than ever.

"Well, you won't believe this," Maggie continued. "But Lizzy heard about you and me being home and she's flying in tomorrow morning. I'm picking her up on the way over."

Dewey sat up in bed, excited to have the Embassy together again. "That's awesome."

"It's only for the day, unfortunately. I have to be back in Maine the day after tomorrow for a photo shoot with the magazine and Lizzy has some highfalutin function to go to. You know how those rich California people are."

Dewey laughed. "Only by association."

Lizzy hailed from south Louisiana but had worked not far from Dewey in a quaint town just north of Los Angeles. Lizzy had won the lottery through a crazy set of circumstances, an enormous amount that had ironically equaled her future husband's inheritance, both of which had happened when they had bumped into one another in a mini mart. Now wed, the two had no financial worries, to say the least.

Maggie's mother was Cajun, but she had grown up in Georgia, which explained her thick Southern accent. Also ironically, she had inherited part of Yankee Living magazine, a dream job that came with an equally dreamy husband, even if he was a Yankee.

For not the first time, the thought of her best friends blissfully happy pinched Dewey's heart. Would she find happiness like they did?

"But you got us for a very long lunch," Maggie concluded.

"You bet," Dewey said, pushing her unwelcomed jealousy aside.

The two conversed more about details, then concluded the call.

"Your father is a pain in the ass."

With slanted eyes, Dewey gazed through her open bedroom door to see her mother coming up the stairs. "Amazingly enough, that wasn't dad." When her mother didn't answer, Dewey added in a half-joking way, "Late night, young lady?"

"Uh huh."

When her mother headed toward Mamaw's bedroom, Dewey sat up and felt a slight rush of panic. "Do you want to talk about it?"

"Nope."

Emma entered the bedroom and started to close the door, then paused, gazing at Dewey from across the hallway. "Later, okay?" And with those final words, she shut Dewey out.

Dewey fell back on the bed, frustrated. The world had turned upside down. Her mother had always involved Dewey in her personal life, Mamaw was always a ready shoulder and Michael… Dewey touched her lips, recalling that brief but ever so sensual kiss he had bestowed upon her on the glider.

She leaned forward and gazed out the window, but Clotille was long gone. He had mentioned something about meeting him at school. The mere thought sent shivers up her spine.

"Damn," she muttered to no one. "Here we go again."

She took a long shower, trying to focus on Mamaw and calling her lawyer about her job situation, in case Ron got the promotion and she had to claim discrimination; it was obvious she was more qualified. Instead, her mind kept wondering back to what Michael had said on the porch, before and after that delicious kiss.

"Damn," she muttered as she rinsed the shampoo out of her hair. It was like high school all over again, seeing him in the hall, watching him walk through class, hoping he'd look her way. Then they would have their usual friendly time together and Dewey would return home, lying in bed wondering what it all meant.

"Last night means nothing," she said as she threw on clothes and a smidgen of makeup, "just like it meant nothing in high school." But she took special care with her looks, knowing she'd see him later. "I'm nuts," she muttered to her reflection. "Certifiably insane, like the rest of my family."

The nursing home opened at eight, so she strolled in for a quick visit with Mamaw. She kissed her grandmother's cheek, grateful the rest of the Holy Trinity still lingered over their morning dark roast.

"Hi Mamaw."

Her grandmother looked up from her chair where she watched *Passe Partout*, Lafayette's morning show. She appeared glad to see her and almost spoke, then caught herself and looked back at the screen where Cajun musicians Steve Riley and the Mamou Playboys were promoting a rock-Cajun crossover album.

"Look, you made your point," Dewey said, turning down the volume, since Mamaw was half deaf. "Michael and I have been talking ever since I arrived. I'm heading over to the school now to meet him during his break and we'll talk some more. Happy?"

Mamaw almost said something, but her lips pursed shut.

Dewey leaned over her chair, hoping to force eye contact. "Mamaw, even if we got married, it's a long commute from California."

She huffed and Dewey knew what that meant.

"Right, I should give up my high-paying entertainment job to move back to Louisiana."

Mamaw met her gaze then, frustration lurking in the French brown depths. "You think you so smart, yeah. You can't see happiness staring you in the face because all you think you deserve is this misery you've made for yourself."

Dewey was so stunned her grandmother spoke, she didn't have an appropriate comeback.

"The trouble with you, *chèr*, is you too busy chasin' things you ain't never gonna have."

"I'm not chasing..."

"You could have it all if you started looking in the right places."

Dewey wasn't sure what she meant, but at least they were talking. She started to continue the conversation, but Mamaw leaned over and turned the volume back up. Then she waved her hand, dismissing her as if to say, "Go back in the world and figure it out, then let me know."

Knowing it was fruitless to talk any further, Dewey left the home and headed toward school, puzzled how a ring on her finger tying her to emotionally repressed Michael Arceneaux — sweet kisses and all — was going to save her life. She carried her frustrations with her, not knowing she was mumbling to herself as she entered the high school.

"Flash from the past," she heard someone say.

Dewey looked up to find Mr. Wagner standing sentinel at the front entrance. "Hey Mr. Wagner."

"Hey, Mr. Wagner? Is that all I'm going to get?"

He opened his arms and Dewey knew he required a hug. She didn't mind giving it — she had never minded really — but it had always seemed so odd, the attention he sent her way. In high school Michael insisted Wagner was an undiscovered child molester. Dewey hadn't bought into that argument but she couldn't fathom why Wagner had been so attentive.

She walked into Wagner's embrace and he hugged her tight and for a moment she wished her own father would offer such bear-hugging affection. Mamaw used to say that in everyone's life, no matter their upbringing, they were always loved, that family comes in many forms and not necessarily those connected by blood. Dewey knew she could always count on Wagner in that regard.

He released her from his enveloping hug, gazing down with less affection than before, as if he sensed her hesitation and discomfort.

"Who were you talking to?" he said with a smile, trying to defuse what uneasiness lingered between them.

Dewey sighed. "The only person who will listen these days."

Wagner lightly placed a hand on her shoulder, as if this time he was being careful. "Don't take it to heart. She's not talking to me either."

This was news. Could it be what Michael had suspected all along and Mamaw had found out? No, it wasn't possible. Michael considered Wagner a good friend now. Not to mention that Wagner had slept with her mother only hours before.

That thought made Dewey slip away from his touch. "Seems to be an epidemic. My mother is suffering from it too."

Leave it to Mr. Wagner, steadfast principal who in thirty years never missed a day on the job, to not falter an inch at that remark. "I saw your mom last night."

"I heard." Dewey squinted as she gazed up at the tall man who still had his looks even with half a head of gray. "At least I saw her leave and then come home again at six thirty this morning."

Wagner surprised her. He tilted his head back and laughed, definitely not something Dewey was used to in high school. Usually when they talked at school, Wagner was sitting in his office with a scowl on his face, upset about Michael missing class or something inflammatory Dewey was printing in the school newspaper. In fact, the last time they had conversed at that dreadful school Wagner was hoping to convince Dewey to stop seeing Michael — a perfect example of a principal overstepping professional boundaries. Dewey had stormed out, after throwing a few choice words his way.

Well, that was the last time they spoke on campus until the closet incident.

"Wow, shoe is on the other foot now, isn't it?" Wagner said, smiling, leaning in close to add, "Only I wouldn't worry, sweetheart. Your mom's a big girl."

She rubbed the back of her neck, remembering how only a few days ago she was in Hollywood having a cold stone massage. Now, here she was talking with the principal of her high school about his love life with her mother.

"So, what is Mamaw mad at you for?"

She asked it to get the conversation moving elsewhere, but Wagner sighed and looked away. "Maybe we can have coffee and talk about it."

A woman called out to Wagner from the office and he nodded. "I have a meeting," he said.

"Sure."

"Do you know where Michael's room is?"

"Mrs. Bradley's old room?"

"Right. Do you remember how to get there?"

Unfortunately, she knew the place like the back of her hand. "How could I forget? It's right past the janitor's closet."

Damn. She really didn't want to bring that up, especially with him.

Wagner appeared not too happy to think about that incident either. He nodded, patted her arm and headed for the office.

"Coffee," was the last thing he said over his shoulder.

Dewey headed down the hallway where she enjoyed Mrs. Badeaux for English and slept through Coach Stevens for civics, a man who could describe the delicate intricacies of a two-point conversion but who failed to relay the importance of a three-branch democracy.

Around the corner was the home of the Courier, Paul Hébert's school newspaper and bane of Mr. Wagner's life — at least when Dewey ran it. Another hallway took her past Mr. Latiolais's advanced history class, her favorite, and the yearbook office, where she first learned pagination.

The dreaded closet existed a few steps away, next to the auditorium where Michael got stinking drunk for graduation. Dewey headed down an adjoining corridor that led to Michael's class so she wouldn't have to pass the closet, only the diversion caused her to get a little lost. She paused, looking around, hoping to gain her bearings when she heard a familiar voice. She turned toward the sound that once stopped her heart — which was doing a damned good job now — and watched in awe as Michael led his own civics class.

He wore his trademark khakis and polo shirt that, as Dewey now realized, matched the uniforms of the kids. Even though the weather had turned nippy, he chose short sleeves that accentuated well-toned muscles in his upper arms and shoulders. What in the world was he doing these days to be so buff?

Dewey leaned in further. Michael's eyes grew passionate as he described the lesson of the day, his voice rising and falling to emphasize whatever it was he was passing on to future generations. Dewey cautiously approached the hallway window, gazing past Michael to see almost every face riveted on their teacher, several girls in the front row with stars in their eyes. One guy seemed preoccupied with doodling, but Michael nonchalantly walked past his desk, lightly touched his shoulder, which made him jolt up self-consciously, and asked him a question. Then, while the surprised boy attempted an answer, Michael headed to the board and began writing.

Dewey didn't hear the answer, but the class laughed. Michael smiled as he scribbled something to do with term papers and continued talking, while the doodler now seemed as enraptured as the rest.

"Amazing," Dewey muttered as she leaned in close to make out what he was writing, still enchanted by the confident educator before her. He had always been passionate, but this specimen of intellect and humor thrilled her in ways she never thought possible. He had become the kind of teacher, the kind of leader — hell the kind of man — she would have idolized in high school, completed every homework assignment for, worshipped. He was with it, together, cool. And God help her, so incredibly sexy.

But this was Michael. When had he become so…grown up?

Michael's handwriting took him further to the right, so Dewey stretched in that direction and nearly lost her balance. Michael spotted her through the glass and headed her way, never faltering in his lecture and never breaking eye contact with his class until he reached the door.

"Sorry," Dewey whispered, "just stopping by."

Michael gently took her arm and pulled her inside. "Class, we have a guest."

She started to object, but Michael pulled her toward his desk, where he released her and sat back on the edge. "Perfect timing. We're discussing the media's role in government." To the class, he said, "This is Caroline Hennessey. She's a Paul Hébert graduate who's now a journalist in Los Angeles."

All teenage gazes turned her way making her feel uncomfortable.

"We just talked about the media being the Fourth Estate to the three branches of government," Michael said. "Maybe you want to comment on this for the class?"

Dewey hadn't a clue what to say. Investigative journalism and all that hard news stuff wasn't her forte, despite the fact that she spent four years at Columbia's fine journalism school. "Fourth Estate?"

Michael smiled slightly, never faltering from his role as teacher. "We were actually talking about the Pentagon Papers."

Dewey pulled her curser through her brain's computer trying to pinpoint that Supreme Court case. "Nixon and Vietnam?"

"The government's restraining order against the New York Times regarding Nixon's involvement in the war in a top secret document that the Times obtained."

Dewey leaned back against the desk as Michael had done and exhaled. "Right."

Wow, he was articulate as hell. He could take her right there on that desk, minus the thirty pairs of eyes.

Wherever her dirty mind had traveled, Michael's had remained right there in that classroom. And he was looking for her to make some astute comment about freedom of the press. Dang it all, but she couldn't think of a thing to say.

"I'm an entertainment journalist," she finally said, looking out at the classroom. "I work in Hollywood so Woodward and Bernstein aren't my specialty."

As soon as she uttered her confession, she realized Watergate wasn't connected to the Pentagon Papers or The New York Times. Maybe she could make a polite excuse and go wait in the teacher's lounge.

Michael continued the thread by discussing how the media keeps a check on government and big business, such as the entertainment industry, when a hand shot up.

"Yes?" Dewey asked.

"Do you know Chris Pratt?"

"Not personally."

"Have you met him?" an excited female asked from the back.

"Sort of." Does bumping into a celebrity in a coffee shop count?

"What's he like?" asked the girl in front with a dreamy look in her eyes. Funny how some things never change. There always has to be celebrity idols in every generation.

She shot Michael a look, hoping he wasn't angry at the turn in subject matter. "Uh, cute?"

This started a rumble of conversation among the class and Dewey winced, knowing she had started something that would be hard to bring back to order. She gazed sideways at Michael, who studied her with an intense gaze that seemed to have nothing to do with the media's role in government. "Sorry," she whispered.

Michael straightened. "Any other questions you want to ask Ms. Hennessey about *journalism*?"

A hand shot up. "Have you ever met Daniel Radcliffe?"

Michael rubbed the back of his neck and Dewey knew she had usurped his class. "Harry Potter? I covered him at a press conference. *Very* cute. And making very interesting films."

Suddenly, half a dozen arms reached skyward and Dewey raised her hands. "Folks, I'm an editor at an entertainment trade magazine. I really don't see that many celebrities."

"You went to the Oscars last year."

Dewey turned, amazed to find that last comment from Mr. Arceneaux himself. "Who told you that?"

Who else?

Michael said nothing, staring silently, unsmiling, while teenagers around them begged for questions. Something in his stare unnerved her. She wondered if he, too, wanted to make love right there on that desk.

The bell rang, breaking the tension that had developed between them. Michael shouted out an assignment while kids gathered around Dewey, still asking questions, which she offered to the best of her limited celebrity knowledge.

Finally, a skinny kid in glasses with a smirk on his face asked her about something she actually knew. "So, what was Mr. Arceneaux like in high school?"

To his credit, Michael never paused while passing out handouts to the kids hauling out the door. Her old wild streak, the one lying dormant after years of trying to become a hard-nosed career woman emerged, ran up her spine and flew out her mouth. "We used to call him Bad Ass."

The skinny kid laughed. "That's what we all heard."

When Michael sent her a warning gaze, Dewey felt empowered. "He used to give all the teachers a hard time. And civics, if I remember correctly, was not his best subject."

The front row girls giggled. Another thing that never changed: Women in love with bad boys.

"Of course, the guy who taught civics back then thought the Fourth Estate was where the president went on vacation."

Michael started herding the class out the door. "You all have classes, remember?"

"Was he as good looking?" asked one of the lovesick girls.

Dewey hated the thought of teenagers idolizing her Michael, but she had started this nonsense. "Uh huh."

Michael called out the girl's name, the one who asked the question, and nodded in the direction of the door. The girl got the message, pulled her books tight against her chest and left. He went to do the same to the others, when the skinny one blurted, "We heard he got drunk at graduation."

Suddenly, Dewey didn't want to play anymore. The frown on Michael's forehead proved he wanted these kids gone now as well.

"Rumor," Dewey muttered.

"Carl, get to class," Michael ordered.

Carl headed toward the door, but paused and leaned in conspiratorially to Dewey. "At least tell me if what they say about him hitting Mr. Wagner is true."

"Carl!" Michael was losing patience.

The kid exhaled, clearly disappointed that time ran out and Dewey wasn't talking.

"Okay, Mr. Arceneaux," Carl said, heading toward the door, "but one of these days I'm going to find out who the 'Dewey' is in regards to the 'Dewey Closet' down the hall."

The bell rang again, this time screaming in Dewey's ear. Michael paused in the middle of the classroom, hands on his hips as he watched the remnants of kids rushing to class. He closed his eyes for a moment, sighed and looked her way, his gaze a mixture of sympathy, anger and regret.

"Shit," Dewey said softly. "They named the damn closet after me?"

Chapter Eleven

MICHAEL HAD BEEN ON EDGE all morning, more than likely because he hadn't slept the night before. The afternoon conversation with Dewey in the shed had started the ball rolling, then intensified when she started discussing high school over the kitchen table. Having Sandy blow up hadn't helped. Then there was that kiss.

What the hell was he thinking?

Fourteen years. He had mastered control over his emotions for more than a decade, harnessing all that wild anger and rage of his youth and now she waltzes in and stirs it all up. He had tossed and turned every night since she had arrived.

Michael forced a deep breath as Dewey stormed out of his classroom. He wasn't going to let it slip now, heading back to his high school days when punching walls and emotional outbursts were the norm. He wasn't going to dwell on how hot Dewey looked in those skin-tight jeans or the way her well-defined breasts filled out that sweater. Or how his body had reacted when she walked into his classroom, making him want to drag her back into the closet infamous for their past indiscretion.

"Get a grip," he told himself, then followed Dewey into the hallway where he grabbed her arm and led her toward the teacher's lounge.

"What are you doing?" she asked, pulling her arm free.

He turned to find her standing defiant among the throes of teenagers, creatures who *should* have raging hormones. He leaned in close to keep their voices from carrying. "Let's get out of the hallway so we can talk."

Still smarting, Dewey moved her head close to his ear as if to whisper something. "It was your idea. And they named it after *me?*"

Michael winced when she shouted the last word, but took her arm to keep her from fleeing. "Let's get out of the hall," he said between gritted teeth.

Dewey must have been surprised at his tone — hell, so was he — but she obeyed, following along as he maneuvered their way through the crowd.

"You're a piece of work, you know that?" she said.

The anger festering in his middle, like coals smoldering for fourteen long years, burned up his spice. "*I'm* a piece of work?" When he opened the door to the lounge, Dewey pulled free. "From all the moans you were giving out, I don't remember you objecting to our lovemaking."

Michael didn't know if it was the choice of words or the fact that he was shouting — dear god, was he shouting? — but every teacher in the lounge turned and stared. He closed his eyes and forced a breath. Why was it that he had conquered the ghosts of his childhood, dealt calmly daily with the emotions of raging teens and hyperactive nephews, but Dewey could really burn his ass?

He opened his eyes and found them all gaping while Dewey moved to the window, arms crossed around the package she had brought with her, gazing off into the traffic of Congress Avenue. "Sorry," Michael muttered to his coworkers.

Dewey ran a hand through her crazy haircut and turned, but refused to look at any of them. "Sorry," she added.

"Actually, please don't stop," said Arlene. "It's nice to see that Mr. Smooth over there has a boiling point." To Dewey, she extended her hand. "Arlene Savoy."

"Caroline Hennessey," Michael offered.

Dewey reached a hand and shook Arlene's. "Just call me Dewey, like the closet."

Michael rubbed the bridge of his nose, wondering when the horrid nightmare would end. "And Mamaw wanted me to marry you?"

Again, there was that tone. Damn it all, the woman was driving him insane, causing him to lose his cool.

"Michael getting married? That's an inspired thought." Jack McDonald joined the group and introduced himself.

"We never thought it would happen," added Shelton Breaux.

Shelton and Missy Hargraves offered their hands and Dewey shook them all, looking somewhat spry and grateful to have allies.

"Our grandmother offered this ridiculous ultimatum," Michael said in his defense. "She isn't talking to us until we get married." How had he morphed from being a confident, self-assured teacher to being on the defensive? And why was the whole world insistent on him getting married?

"Your grandmother?" Jack asked. "Doesn't that make it illegal?"

"She's *my* grandmother," Dewey explained. "But she adopted Michael in an act of charity."

"She's more mine than yours. At least I'm here." Wow, now he was reverting back to elementary school.

Dewey gritted her teeth. "If you had just gotten married in the first place."

"What the hell is that supposed to mean?"

"It means you're over thirty and not married and now my grandmother won't talk to me."

"And I suppose your not being married doesn't have anything to do with this."

Arlene raised a hand. "Kids. Calm down. Let's talk about this rationally."

"Rationally?" Dewey asked as if the idea came from outer space. "They named the damned closet after me."

Michael was sure the rest of the teachers had heard the infamous tales about his youth at Paul Hébert. He was also convinced they had heard people refer to the janitor's closet in that way, as well. Now they had a face to the name, one with the idea of marriage attached. All four teachers gathered around like tomcats surrounding a wounded bird.

"Maybe it's best we discuss this later," Michael said to Dewey.

"Want some coffee?" Jack asked.

"We have donuts," Missy added.

"I'd love some," Dewey said, falling into a chair and making herself comfortable.

"You work for *That's Entertainment*, right?" Missy asked.

"Yes ma'am," Dewey answered.

Missy settled into the chair directly across. "Please don't call me ma'am. I'm not your teacher and I'd like to think we aren't that far off in age."

Dewey nodded, braving a smile and relaxing deeper into the armchair and making Michael realize he should try to chill as well. For the life of him, his anger still surged, as if a dam opening had been lifted and the rushing water prevented it from being closed again.

"You know, high school's a tough time," Arlene continued. "And it's hard to get past all that, even when you're grown."

Jack handed Dewey her coffee and placed a small container of milk and sugar on the ugly, secondhand table in front of her. Gazing back at Michael with a sly grin, just before he sat down next to Dewey, he added, "That was the last of it, Michael, but if you want to make another pot…"

His coworkers were having a good laugh at his expense. If they weren't insisting on him getting married, they were always complaining about how well he kept his cool. As if they wanted him to join them in their misery, to arrive at school wrinkled and exhausted like the rest of them, with Cherios in his pockets and throw-up on his shoulders.

It wasn't that he was against having kids and getting married, quite the opposite. He just needed the right girl.

Watching Dewey smile and make small talk gave Michael pause. Was she the reason he had never married all these years? He honestly hadn't met the right woman. But maybe that was because the right woman was sitting before him and no one would ever come close.

No, Michael commanded himself as he paced toward the windows. Dewey made her choice. He wasn't the one who fled the scene when all hell broke loose. Maybe having her name attached to the damn room was justice to what she did to him.

"Breathe," he told himself inside his head. "You're beyond this, remember?"

"You know high school can really stink," Arlene said from behind him. "Things happen that can stay with you the rest of your life."

"Tell me about it," Dewey muttered. Michael grabbed the edge of the nearest chair and squeezed.

"Blame the hormones or the inability to rationally think things through because of a lack of maturity, but the time is ripe for emotional outbursts that will wound you for life," Arlene continued.

"Speaking from experience, darling?" Jack asked.

"Hell, yes," she said with a laugh. "I've been self-conscious ever since Elaine Waguespack made fun of my homemade dress in eighth grade, the one I spent three weeks working on and used two yards of lace."

"Lace?" Shelton asked, stifling a smile.

"It was the eighties. Lace was in. Remember Prince?"

Arlene waved him off and continued. "Then Jessica Landry, the most popular girl in high school, told me I was a nerd who knew nothing about fashion."

"You are a nerd," Shelton injected with a laugh. "And we all wish we were as smart."

"You're absolutely right," Arlene said, tossing her head back with pride. "And Jessica works at the mall now, although she looks amazing doing it. And it still smarts when I realize my shoes don't match what I'm wearing or I can't find the right earrings."

"Crazy," Jack said. "Women worry way too much."

"You're right," Dewey said confidently, which made Michael turn. "Why should I care that generations of kids know that I made love with their drunk teacher in a dirty janitor's closet after the high school graduation ceremony."

A shocked pause settled on the group and Michael winced. Dewey stood, placing her coffee cup on the table. "Sorry, tactfulness was not my strong point."

"Think about what I said," Arlene added.

Dewey handed Arlene the packet she was holding. "These are the graded papers for the pregnant English teacher's creative writing class. And thanks for the coffee."

With those final words, Dewey headed out the door. All four teachers turned toward Michael, their gazes saying, "What are you waiting for?"

What was he waiting for? They would be mad at each other for eternity unless someone stepped up to the bat. He rubbed the back of his neck. If only he wasn't so mad.

"Crap." Michael followed Dewey into the deserted hallway, catching up with her in a few strides.

"I need to go home," she muttered, not turning around. "I'm going to get my bowl of gumbo and get on the next plane."

How could he deal with this? The woman fled whenever anything turned sour. "Go, then," he said, his anger evident. "That's what you're so good at."

Dewey stopped walking and turned her steel gaze his way. Anger, resentment and years of pain shone in those eyes. "Yeah, Michael? Well, you left me a long time ago. Before the damn closet."

She stormed off, her lower lip trembling as if she fought off tears or anger — or both. This time Michael wasn't following. He was too busy trying to figure out what the hell she was talking about.

The door slammed, rocking the entire house. Even the windowpanes by Emma's bed rattled, making her wonder if it was an earthquake.

"You're in Louisiana now, idiot," she mumbled to herself and fell back against her pillows.

But the noises continued. Either Dewey was in the kitchen searching the cabinets for something — obviously having trouble since she was opening and slamming each one — or the house was infested by giant rats that needed immediate sustenance.

When the refrigerator door slammed, Emma groaned and got out of bed. It was for the best anyway. The day was closing in on noon and she needed to call her director before the man panicked, not to mention having to visit her non-communicative mother, for what that was worth.

"What are you looking for sweetheart?" she asked Dewey upon entering the kitchen. "You probably would have gotten it sooner and with less noise had you gone to the Winn-Dixie."

Dewey gazed up, clearly agitated, but then her daughter lived in an agitated state when Emma was around. To the rest of the world, she was more than likely Snow White, but to dear ole mom, Dewey remained a rabid teenager.

"Where are the damn coffee filters?"

"Ah, caffeine." Emma walked over to the glass shelf above the sink that held three pots of herbs in used coffee cans, a Mary statuette and a placard that read, "No matter where I serve my guests, they always like my kitchen best."

"No wonder you're in a rage," Emma said, pulling out the filters from behind the basil. "Make a big pot, will ya?"

Dewey stared. "Late night, Mom?"

Yep, here it comes. Best to get it over with, Emma surmised. "Yes, sweetie. Mommy was out fornicating."

To her credit, Dewey didn't falter. "With my principal, no less."

"With your principal?" Emma took the filters out of Dewey's hands and started her own pot of dark roast. "God, what are we, still in high school?"

This unnerved Dewey, for some reason. She didn't think her daughter could be more irritated, but she suddenly looked like a skunk had run up her dress. Now, if she were upset about the paternity issue, then Emma would have understood the sour face.

"We have to talk, sweetheart."

"Why? Have they named the back shed in my honor as well?"

Emma had no idea what she was talking about or why Dewey was so incensed. She figured it best to ignore her daughter's protestations and keep going. "I'm going to have to go back to the shoot today, so if you have a moment…"

"You don't remember the shed, do you, Mom?"

The shed behind the house, the one the cute neighbor was using as his darkroom? "What about it?"

"Or that Wagner had this ugly incident with me right after graduation?"

What on earth? "I heard that graduation was beautiful. That's what mother said."

Dewey shook her head in disbelief. "Right. You wouldn't know. You weren't there."

Here we go. Whatever was eating her today, it was all because Emma had "disserted" her at Mamaw's house when Dewey was twelve, failed to be at her graduation, forgot to call precisely at eleven forty-three a.m. on one of her birthdays, the exact time of her birth, which, of course, meant that Dewey's arrival in the world had meant absolutely nothing to Emma, that Emma was a regretful mother who only cared about her career.

Emma flicked on the coffeemaker switch. "Why don't you tell me what's eating you, unless it's one of your usual guilt trips you're so good at inflicting. That you can spare me. I've traveled down that road before, thank you."

This took Dewey aback. Emma was surprised at her candor as well. Usually, the guilt of the past thirty years had left her spine the consistency of a rubber band.

Maybe she should get laid by Patrick more often.

The thought of the previous evening set her cheeks on fire, including one particular moment where he performed something delicious and earth shattering. How long had it been since a man did *that* to her?

"Must have been good."

Emma found Dewey staring again, probably amazed that her mother had a love life. The girl could be a real pistol.

"It was, thank you very much. And if I can find time to come home again, I'm going to grab that man and do it some more. Now, do you want some coffee so we can sit down and talk?"

Shocked, her daughter said nothing and sat down at the metal table that looked like something straight out of a fifties diner. Emma sat at the other end, admiring the simple piece of furniture that had taken her parents months to buy on layaway that could now be sold in a retro "antique" store in L.A. for twenty times that amount.

"If she's going to stay in assisted living from now on, we should haul some of this back to the Coast and sell it. It will help pay for all her new expenses."

"That's what you want to talk to me about?"

Emma looked up, wanting desperately to touch her. "What's the matter, sweetheart?"

Dewey stared down at her hands. "Everything."

Great, and here she was about to explain her paternity. "Do you want to tell me about it?"

Dewey looked out the window. "It doesn't matter. It's not like you'd know what I was talking about."

"I see." Emma got up and made them both cups of coffee, adding plenty of cream and sugar. "Does this have anything to do with that good-looking guy next door?"

"His name is Michael." The way she pronounced his name, Emma knew she had hit her target.

"Michael. Does this have to do with him?"

Dewey gave her that evil eye Emma detested. "You don't remember him, do you?"

Another dose of guilt was on the way. "No, Baby, I don't.

Except that I met him yesterday."

Dewey shook her head. "Do you at least remember Mamaw calling you in a panic that I was screwing a guy in high school, that she found us making love in the back shed?"

That, Emma remembered. The phone call had filled her with dread that her daughter might make the same mistake she had. "Of course I remember."

Dewey's gaze turned cold. "I was going to go to LSU. With Michael. You talked me out of it, said I shouldn't waste my life in Louisiana when I had been accepted to Columbia. You sent me a plane ticket for New York so I could spend the summer with you and dad. Remember?"

The guilt finally found home, settling in Emma's heart like an anchor. "Yes, but I think you're confusing me with your dad..."

"I didn't want to leave Michael but for the first time in my life my parents were taking an interest, how could I refuse? Then Dad went to Europe with Donna and you got a part in summer stock in Montreal. And I spent the summer in New York by myself, in dad's empty apartment, waiting for Michael to call. Which, of course, he didn't because he was pissed I left."

With those final words, Dewey hung her head, tears pouring down her cheeks. Emma reached out a hand, but Dewey pulled away.

"Baby, I had no money. Summer stock was the first job I'd had in months. I tried to get something in New York. And I took the train down every weekend. You remember that much, don't you?"

Dewey said nothing, wiped her runny nose with the back of her sleeve.

"Your father is a jerk. I won't make excuses for him."

Emma's brain ran through all the possibilities, trying to find some assurance that Dewey had made the right move. "I'm sure going to Columbia made all the difference in your career — look what you've done. And it's not too late to make up with Michael. He doesn't look married. I think that woman living with him is a relative."

Dewey covered her face with her hands and leaned her elbows on the tabletop. "You don't get it, Mom. You ruined my life."

Any other day, Emma might have crumbled inside and agreed. This morning, however, she refused to play the role. She gingerly removed Dewey's hands from her face, forcing her to look her in the eye. "I love you, sweetpea, and I'm not perfect by a long shot. But I did not ruin your life."

Dewey gave one of her typical sarcastic grimaces that most daughters grow out of by college.

"I got pregnant with you by sleeping with your father during Mardi Gras and yes, I was happy that he lived in New York and agreed to marry me, which got me out of Lafayette."

She paused, taking a sip of coffee for reinforcement. "I didn't love the man and he didn't love me. Hell, we barely knew each other. But we faced our responsibility and agreed to make a go of it. I won't say he wanted children or that he was pleased with having you, because I honestly doubt he gave a rat's ass about either one of us. Which is why I left him."

Dewey huffed. "You left him for that film job in Hollywood. And you left me here, for that matter, so don't try to tell me you left dad because he didn't care."

"Why do you always stick up for him? After all this time and all the disappointments?"

"Why do you always make it sound like you never had a choice but to leave me on Mamaw's doorstep?"

Emma folded her arms about her chest. She didn't know where the strength was coming from, but she was going to clear the air if it killed her. "I'm an actress, Dewey. I have always been an actress. When I lived here, I acted in community theater and worked as a cashier during the day. The job was the only one I could get and I did it poorly."

She exhaled, trying to calm her rapidly beating heart. "I won't say I wasn't glad to go to New York, but if you think I neglected you, you need to have your memory serviced. I never worked a day in New York until you were in kindergarten. Then I took classes most of the time — only when you were in school, I might add — and I never worked much in theater because I couldn't be away from you at night. So, don't you dare tell me I didn't care about you or that my career came first or that I had a choice in anything."

Emma found her heartbeat racing. "That job in L.A. was the first real money I got acting and it was a chance for me to start my career and get out of a loveless marriage that was killing me. You were twelve, a good age to be without me, and I wanted you to have a chance to experience my home state."

Dewey started to object, but Emma knew what was coming next, so she raised her hand to stop her. "I loved it here. Why did you think I played all those Cajun songs for you when you were little, *Dewey*? Despite what you may think about me wanting to get away, I cherished my Cajun upbringing, where family means something, and I wanted you to experience some of that too."

Emma sighed, taking her daughter's hand once more. "Mamaw is a much better mom than I'll ever be. Look at the rotten advice I gave you in high school."

A lone tear rolled down Dewey's face. "He's never forgiven me."

"Who?"

When Dewey gave her the evil eye again, Emma sighed. "Oh yeah, Michael."

"Wagner caught us screwing in the janitor's closet at school. We weren't actually doing it yet, but Wagner was furious and Michael hit him, got thrown in jail and I split that afternoon to New York City."

Her voice trailed off and Emma could only imagine how lonely she must have been that summer, her parents far away and the phone never ringing.

She squeezed Dewey's hand. "He'll come around."

Dewey shook her head. "I don't know if he ever loved me."

At this, Emma smiled. "I've seen the way he looks at you. And those photos. Are you kidding?"

Dewey looked up, gazing at Emma like a friend, which warmed her heart like nothing else. "Mamaw won't speak to either of us until we get married. Married!"

At this, Emma laughed. For one, it was a ridiculous request. For another, it was so mother.

"It's not funny," Dewey said.

Emma stood and grabbed the coffee pot, refilling both their cups. "Actually, it is. She wants me to do the same."

"Marry Michael?"

Was it possible her daughter made a joke? They both grinned at each other.

"By the way, I didn't get the promotion," Dewey said. "It's more than likely going to some inept man with a brown nose. And they named the closet after me, the one Wagner found us in."

Emma had forgotten about Patrick. "Speaking of Mr. Wagner," she said, taking her seat gingerly. "There's something else I need to tell you."

Dewey ran a hand through her hair and groaned, but she still smiled which gave Emma hope. Until she blurted out the words.

"What? That he's my dad or something?"

Chapter Twelve

SANDY HEARD DEWEY SCREAM THE minute she pulled into the driveway. She rushed into Mamaw's house to find Dewey standing in the kitchen, cellphone in hand, jumping up and down like a crazed woman.

"What happened?" Sandy asked.

Dewey stopped her Cheshire Cat grin long enough to lean her head back and howl, arms outstretched in ecstasy. "My post went viral!"

Sandy should have kept up the cold shoulder, but the pure joy on Dewey's face was contagious. "That's great, Dewey."

Dewey continued dancing, arms flailing through the air with glee. "You have no idea how long in coming this has been."

Honestly, Sandy didn't. "So, this means they are going to publish your food blog?"

Dewey sobered slightly, a grin still consuming her face. "No, it means I now have several top food advertisers wanting to join *Louisiana Simple*. And my agent thinks I can get a book deal."

Didn't make much sense, but Sandy nodded. "And this is great news?"

Dewey laughed. "It's more money but more importantly, it's recognition of my hard work as a food writer."

"Cool. Then you can quit your job and move home."

Dewey paused and tilted her head. "Are you talking to me, now?"

"Hell, no." Sandy ran a lazy finger along the kitchen table's design. "I'm going to tell you about this party and then I'm going back to not talking to you."

Suddenly, Dewey looked panic-stricken. She touched Sandy's arm as if to keep her in place. "I found out something today. Something strange."

What could be stranger than Mamaw asking her to marry Michael or her mother dating Wagner? Like a lightning bolt cascading down a dead cypress, Sandy knew what had spooked Dewey. "Does this have anything to do with Wagner?"

All the blood in Dewey's face drained out some unseen hole. "You know about this?"

Sandy winced. Michael had confided in her about the paternity question and she had sworn the fact to secrecy. "Uh, depends on what we're talking about."

Dewey's eyes narrowed as she wrapped her arms about her chest. "You know what I'm talking about, don't you?"

Sandy tried to crawfish, backing up toward the door. "I heard Wagner and your mom were a hot item in high school, that's all."

"Right." She wasn't buying it. "And that he and my mom got it on nine months before I was born?"

Sandy swallowed hard. "I think I heard that too."

The groan that followed was louder than the scream. "Damn it, Sandy. Why didn't anyone tell me?"

Now it was Sandy's turn to cross her arms. "And when were we supposed to tell you this, Boo? The two days you're here at Thanksgiving or the long weekend around Mamaw's birthday that you managed to sneak in every year?"

"That's not fair. I come in twice a year, which is not bad for someone who lives *two thousand miles* away. Besides, I'm over thirty, Sandy, I think someone could have found the time."

"Wagner never told anyone, for what it's worth," Sandy said, inching toward the door. "He confided in Michael the night he bailed him out of jail. And he swore Michael to secrecy. Michael told me on one of the rare moments in his life when he actually exhibited some emotional depth."

"Jesus." The blood came rushing back into her cheeks. "Michael knows?"

Double damn. This won't go down well, Sandy thought with dread. "Of course, he does. He and Wagner are friends. What did you think?"

"That he and I were friends first? Jesus, Sandy."

Dewey appeared as if she would hyperventilate. She placed her hands on her knees and bowed over.

In that moment, Sandy ached for her friend. Felt truly sorry, not to mention being worried that Dewey's ulcer might be kicking up again. But that didn't change the fact that she and Michael needed to get over their juvenile spat or that if they had made up before now, Dewey wouldn't be freaking out over Wagner possibly being her dad. If she had come home more often, realizing the extent of her family as Mamaw always hinted, she might have done the DNA test long ago and had a real father to show for it.

"Are you doing the test?" Sandy asked, still not sure if she wanted to return to being Dewey's good friend until she and Michael made amends.

Dewey nodded, but remained bent over. "I talked to Wagner a few minutes ago. He said I have to visit Lafayette General and do a throat swab."

Sandy doubted Wagner was that matter-of-fact. All a person had to do was mention Dewey in conversation and that man lit up like a Carnival float. She wondered if Dewey knew how much he loved her.

Dewey straightened and took a deep breath. "Thank God that agent called. I might be dead by now from all these revelations."

Sandy gritted her teeth and gazed skyward.

"What?" Dewey asked. "Are you going to tell me I haven't had a week from hell?"

Sandy looked her in the eye, feeling more together than she

had in a long time and unusually confidant that she had the smarts to say what was needed. "You have the world's finest man in love with you. The finest. They don't get better than Michael. All he needs is a push and a shove and a chance to tell you how he feels and he's yours. And God knows, you feel the same. Otherwise, why else would you get Mamaw to buy photographs of his every Christmas and send them to California without Michael knowing about it? How many Michael Arceneaux photos do you have on your walls now anyway? Ten?"

"You know about that?" Dewey asked.

Sandy rolled her eyes and paused, swallowing, choosing her words carefully because Sandy was done being the happy sister who listened to these fools.

"You have the world's greatest grandmother, someone who loves you dearly and who has filled in any gaps your mother might have left. It doesn't get any better than Mamaw. For all her faults, she's the wisest woman I know.

"And then there's your mother. Not the most stable person or the best maternal figure, but she loves you dearly. And she's so *interesting*. Most people would give their right arm for a mother like that but you constantly put her down because she dropped you off at this wonderful woman's house so she could make a living. And if your mom hadn't of dropped you off, you wouldn't have known Mamaw the way you had or met me. Or met Michael, who you're in love with if you'd only admit it."

"That was a long time ago," Dewey said in her defense.

"Damn it, Dewey." Now, Sandy was furious all over again. "You won't forgive anyone so it might as well be yesterday."

"That's not true."

"What's true is you have it all!" Sandy exhaled. "At least, if you allow it to be that way. And now, you might have the world's best father figure. I guess that's a problem too?"

Dewey stared out the window, biting her lower lip.

"I'm going now," Sandy said, leaving the flier on the table. "Michael likes to take Tyler around on Halloween, but I know you want to, too. I'll have him ready at five if you both think you can be civil in his presence."

Dewey didn't turn. "Of course we can."

"Good. There's a party at a coworker's house. Y'all are welcome to join me afterwards. The flier has all the details."

Sandy headed out the back door, pausing on the threshold. "You know, Dewey. If this DNA test proves that your father is your father, which is what I think, it doesn't change anything."

Dewey continued the assault on her lip, but she gazed back at Sandy.

"You dad will still be an asshole who doesn't give you the time of day and Wagner will still love you as his own. But maybe it's time you figured that out."

And with those final words, Sandy headed back to her house, hoping something — anything — she had said would make a difference.

"Momma," Tyler squealed as Michael drove up to the house.

Michael pulled up behind Sandy's beat-up Toyota in the driveway. "Yep, Momma's home."

Michael had just managed to unlock Tyler's car seat when the boy jumped down and tore out of the car.

"Whoa, Tyler," he said, reaching for the tyke, but the boy had already turned the corner of the house and run up the back stairs. Michael heard the screen door slam and a young voice yelling for Sandy coming through the open windows as Tyler ran down the inside hallway.

Michael let the truck shutter to a stop. Clotille desperately needed a tune-up, but he never could find a couple of hours to do the job. Sandy thought it ridiculous for him to do it himself, but getting his hands inside an engine and making things right was the greatest stress reliever he knew.

That and sex.

He rubbed his thumbs at his temples. He really didn't have a headache, but it helped some. Trouble was, it wasn't his head that was pounding.

The screen door opened and slammed again and Sandy poked her head around the corner of the porch, more than likely wondering why he was still lingering in the truck. What had she done to her hair? She held up ten fingers and Michael nodded. He had ten minutes before he would take the little guy into the neighborhood for an obscene amount of sugar.

Michael grabbed his briefcase and headed for the house. He stared at his stepsister, amazed at the transformation. Gone was the rainbow atop her head, replaced by a deep auburn color and a smart haircut. She was dressed as Mini Mouse in a puffy short skirt, tights and a cleavage-showing top. Michael was about to inquire what or who had caused such an outfit but he had to know first. "Are you talking to me?"

Sandy slammed the door in his face. "Nope."

"Momma said we can go to a party later," Tyler said as Michael entered the kitchen, then handed him a flier with a map and details.

"Is this that nerdy guy at work who keeps asking you out?" he asked Sandy, hoping she was kidding about the non-talking part, but she didn't answer.

"Can we go?" Tyler asked, grabbing Michael's hand.

"I need to take a quick shower. Get your costume on and I'll be right down."

The boy didn't waste time. He bolted out of the room, rushing up the stairs, his feet pounding out every inch of the way. Ever since Michael had brought home a copy of the Pixar animated film *The Incredibles*, which Tyler had watched repeatedly, the young boy had planned his costume in intricate detail.

Michael followed, although much slower and a lot quieter, as if a weight rested on his shoulders. Yes, a cold shower was just what he needed.

Ten minutes later, fully dressed, his hair still damp and mussed, Michael failed to see an improvement in his mood. For one thing, the water was damn cold. For another, it failed to relieve the nagging desire that was consuming him ever since Dewey paraded into town.

"Damn," he muttered. It was high school all over again, where the mention of her name used to make him hard. Trouble was, he wasn't sixteen anymore and she eventually would head back to L.A. He didn't need this.

Tyler screamed for his attention, so Michael threw on the tweed coat and fedora he had used in a school production of a Noel Coward play, when the acting club had begged for his assistance after an adult teacher had dropped out. He thought he looked ridiculous, but Sandy said it made him look like Cary Grant, which had to be good. For some insane reason, he wanted to impress the brat who lived next door.

"Who are you supposed to be?" Tyler asked, sitting next to the back door, bag in hand, ready for action.

Michael leaned over and studied his nephew in his bright red suit with a big "I" over the chest. "Wow, a kindergartner used to live here. But now, we have one of *The Incredibles*!"

Tyler giggled and placed his fists on his hips, super-hero fashion. "I'm Dash!"

Just then Dewey opened the back door.

"Outstanding," Michael said in his best Cary Grant impression. "You can protect me from the evil witch who lives next door."

Tyler looked up at Dewey who was dressed in a way-too-tight sweater and a way-too-short skirt for Michael's comfort.

"Cute," Dewey said. "And who are you? Professor Higgins?"

"Yeah, Uncle Michael. Who are you?"

Why did he have this insane idea to dress up, Michael thought. He wanted to tear the clothes off until Tyler grabbed his hand.

"I know." He jumped up with excitement. "You're the man who helps out Mr. Incredible when he loses his job."

Works for him. "That's me."

That thought long gone, with his hand still clutching Michael's, Tyler pulled him out the back door. "Let's go."

Michael went along for the ride, picking up an extra bag on the counter that Sandy must have left. He passed Dewey on the way out, catching something sweet and enticing in her scent. "You coming?"

She, too, grabbed an extra bag and followed, Tyler practically running toward the street.

"Whoa, Tiger. Slow down." Oblivious to anything but candy, Tyler ran ahead, rushing up to their neighbor's door and knocking. Michael waited on the sidewalk as Dewey reached his side, arms crossed, eyes narrowed. He could almost feel the frost emanating from her.

"What do you care what they named the damn closet? It's not like you come home often enough for it to bother you."

She sent him a harsh glare, then brushed past him to follow Tyler running to the next house. When they paused again at the next home's walkway, Dewey kept her back to him.

"I can't believe you're so upset about this."

Dewey turned and sent him an icy stare that could have frosted his eyebrows. "The closet was minuscule compared to the news I got this afternoon."

Michael's mind whirled trying to figure out what she could have unearthed that was worse than being infamous at their high school. The fact that he failed to know infuriated Dewey more. She leaned in close, her gaze now burning frosty holes in his head. "Patrick Wagner might be my father and you never thought to tell me this?"

Now, it was Michael's turn to heat up that ice. "When was I supposed to tell you? As I remember, you were gone pecan when I got out of jail."

Tyler ran down the walkway, yelling for them to follow, which they did in silence. Michael felt the familiar anger, so long buried and controlled, firing up his temper. He couldn't even look at her. The memory of that night, when Wagner bailed him out, informing him that Dewey had split and handing him that letter, still pissed him off royally. He screwed up; he knew that. But she left him on the worst night of his life. Friends didn't do that to one another.

They said nothing for the rest of the trek, making a long loop around the neighborhood until they arrived back at the house, Tyler tired but full of candy.

"Are we going to the party?" Tyler asked both of them as they walked to the back porch where Sandy waited, beer in hand.

"Of course they are," Sandy said.

"Yeah." Tyler did his hyper happy dance. Despite all his faults, the boy had unbridled, unlimited enthusiasm.

"I have things to do," Dewey began, but Tyler interrupted, begging and pleading.

The last thing Michael wanted to do was go to a party. He decided to give Dewey an out. "Actually, the debate team is meeting in the morning so I need to stay and work on our program."

Sandy rolled her eyes, then handed them both a copy of the flier. "They're both going, Tyler, don't worry. Michael is coming with us — he's driving because mommy is going to have fun — and Dewey has her own car. Right, Dewey?"

Staring at his sister and her newfound assertiveness, Michael took the map and found himself agreeing, and they all climbed into Clotile. Through the dashboard, Michael saw Dewey sigh, then pull out her own keys and get into Mamaw's car. For a moment, the pissed-off part of him wished she would stay put. But then those deep-seated urges bubbled to the surface and he found himself glad she was coming. The contradiction of emotions angered him once more.

"Shit."

All conversation ceased and Sandy sent him a dirty look. He really needed to regain his control.

"Sorry."

They pulled into the upscale River Ranch subdivision and up to one of the larger houses of the exclusive, planned community built alongside the sleepy Vermilion River.

"Kevin lives here?" Sandy spoke his mind.

Just then, the man of the hour came out, dressed in nerdy attire, and welcomed them. He paid particular attention to Tyler, which meant he passed test number one in Michael's book.

"Who are you supposed to be?" Tyler asked him.

He laughed. "Steve Jobs?" When the child said nothing, Kevin added, "He created *The Incredibles.*"

Suddenly, Kevin was god in Tyler's eyes.

"He's a director?" Sandy looked confused.

Kevin, passing test number two, smiled without being condescending to Sandy's limited education and led them into the house, explaining how Steve Jobs created Apple computers and Pixar, the company that makes animated movies. Sandy even looked interested. Maybe there was hope she'd fall for the right man this time. One with a brain and a heart.

The house was packed and a zydeco band was playing in the back yard where the crowd, mostly other geeky types, had costumed up and were busy dancing, their bodies pulsing to the rhythm like a giant heartbeat. Michael picked up a Coke and watched Kevin introduce Tyler to his cousins and show them all some cool video games on a giant TV. He didn't seem to mind that all three kids were bouncing on his designer couch.

Just then Dewey walked through the door, glancing around nervously. She asked the first person she met something, then headed down a hallway. Michael was curious so he followed, losing track of her somewhere near the massive game room that housed a state-of-the-art entertainment system. From there, the house seem to branch out in all directions, so he paused outside what looked like a hall bathroom, leaning his head against the wall and sighing, trying to keep his mind off of her and that sexy sweater.

Suddenly, the bathroom door opened. Michael's gaze met Dewey's while she froze in the doorway, one hand still gripping the handle. No one said a word as they gazed at one another. No one moved.

Then, as if hormones guided him forward, Michael straightened, wrapped an arm about her waist and pulled her hard against his chest as he moved them back into the bathroom, kicking the door shut with one foot. With one hand he deftly locked the door, then plunged his mouth on to hers.

Chapter Thirteen

IT ALL HAPPENED SO FAST, Dewey hadn't had time to breathe, let alone object as Michael pulled her back into the bathroom, locked the door — how the hell did he manage that? – while kissing her madly all at the same time. But then, why would she object? Dear God, it was the sexiest thing anyone had done to her in a very long time, not to mention those searing kisses and the feel of that long, tough body against her. Besides, this was Michael! She knew what was coming and her body sizzled in anticipation.

She heard her brain screaming for logic, but she simply shut that door and silenced the voice. She wanted this. Heavens, but she wanted this.

Michael wrapped the other arm about her, then slid one hand up the backside of her sweater, pulling her tight against him and deepening the most delicious kisses she had ever known. She didn't know how he did it — the sensual, pulsing movement of his tongue, the way it explored the inner reaches of her cheeks, the nipping of his teeth against her lips, the way his mouth consumed hers without being overpowering like some men. Dewey melted like an August snowball at noon on the hood of a black car.

She backed up to the massive vanity, allowing Michael better opportunities to press into her and he instantly took the bait. She raised one leg around his and he moaned, which made her that much hotter.

Their hands fumbled wildly, touching, caressing, grabbing. Dewey longed to have those massive hands — with his inquisitive, imaginative fingers she remembered all too well — on her bare skin so she pulled back and tore the sweater off, leaving nothing but skirt to contend with. Michael paused, absorbing the fact that she wore no bra, then swallowed deeply and continued his assault on her lips. Only this time, his hands drifted to where his eyes had just feasted.

Dewey broke away from his ferocious kisses in an attempt to inhale air as his hands massaged her breasts, resting to roll her nipples between his fingers. When his lips and teeth took their place, Dewey arched her back and stretched to give him room, her head bumping against the mirror. Could they just for once pick a spot to make love in that included beds?

Bathrooms had their positive points, however, especially in someone else's home with dozens of people milling about. In one cool motion that rivaled Michael's, Dewey reached over and turned on the faucet, then let escape a deep moan that emanated from the deep recesses of her soul and her agonizing months of celibacy — hell, her years of separation from Michael's expertise.

While Michael savored her breasts, and Dewey reveled in the experience, the sensations roaring through her, she slowly shifted on to the vanity until her legs wrapped around him, bringing that viral manhood as close as she could get him. Michael never faltered in his actions, sliding a hand up her thigh without breaking a beat. Mother of Pearl, the man was talented.

When he finally looked up, ready to take command of her lips again, Dewey quickly grabbed the hem of his shirt and lifted, pulling the button-down garment off in one motion with only one button flying. She was fairly talented herself.

Until she saw the tweed jacket on the floor that he apparently discarded during those talented kisses. She smiled. If there were an Olympics for this sport, the two of them would take the gold.

He seemed to read her mind for he smiled as well. Still, they said nothing, resumed kissing while Dewey took the opportunity to run her own hands across his bare chest while Michael slid his hand further up her skirt.

Trouble was, she was sitting on that vanity.

Dewey pushed him back, then slid her own hand underneath her skirt and began to remove her panties. While she struggled in her seated position, Michael pulled a wallet out of his back pocket, removed a condom, then tore the package apart with his teeth.

They both flung their possessions aside at the same time, grinning at their accomplishments.

Then they began again. It all happened so fast, Dewey felt consumed in a haze of passion. Their hands explored each other madly, their lips tasting, biting, savoring. Then Michael had his hands on her bottom, pulling her skirt up and delving inside. In a heartbeat, Dewey was complete, as Michael entered and they both moaned together.

She secured her feet on the opposite wall and the familiar dance began. He knew every pulsating motion that brought her pleasure, every wavelike movement that could make her body sing. No one could work magic like Michael, his hands teasing her breasts, his lips nipping at her shoulder, all the while pushing deeper and deeper.

Dewey felt the rush instantly, and with each motion the pressure built, making her dizzy with pleasure. She leaned her head back, letting the waves of passion wash over her, waves that got bigger and bigger until finally they swallowed her up. Just before she surrendered, Dewey reached a hand over and flushed the toilet, then tilted her head and moaned loudly with pleasure as she drowned in a sea of passion.

"Oh my God," she muttered, as Michael continued, bringing another round with him. She didn't think it could get any better, but she shivered with another roll of passion and closed her eyes to savor the unique experience.

In the darkness she heard the toilet flush again and Michael moan, then opened her eyes to see him close his, while he shivered with his own climax.

He smiled, resting his head against hers, both of them attempting to resume a normal breath, a regular heartbeat.

"We need therapy," Dewey finally said, when she was able to speak.

Michael smiled, his eyes still hazy. "Yeah."

They grinned at each other through the aftermath of love, slowly sobering as the knowledge of what they did sunk in. Just before Dewey could witness regret on Michael's face, she pulled him close, resting her chin on his shoulder, praying he wouldn't apologize. She closed her eyes, waiting for the inevitable.

To her surprise, Michael pulled her closer, wrapping his arms tight about her waist. Dewey did the same, snuggling deeper into his shoulder until they were tightly wound.

They held each other for several moments, neither saying a word, Michael's hand sliding up and down her back in an affectionate motion while he refused to relinquish the tight hold he had on her. Dewey breathed in his scent, still the same after all these years.

The sweetness of the moment, the distance between them that had finally been breached, lodged an emotion deep inside Dewey that came springing forward with alarming speed. Before she had time to react, the emotion burst out of her mouth in one loud sob.

Shit, Dewey thought. Please don't let me cry.

But she couldn't help herself. More emotions followed, so long buried, bubbling to her lips like hot gases pouring forth from the bowels of the earth.

Michael touched her hair, still holding her close, which made tears well up and stream down her face, further embarrassing herself.

Suddenly, Dewey had to get out of there. She needed to escape. Panic followed the sobs, now lodging in her throat, cutting off her air.

"Michael, you're killing me," she whispered, before pushing

him away and grabbing madly for her clothes.

She felt his hand on her arm and him calling her name, but Dewey could only focus on getting her clothes on and fleeing.

"Dewey." Now, the panic was in his voice, as it had been all those years ago. This was crazy, she thought. What had they been thinking doing this again? In a bathroom, no less.

"I need to go." She pulled on her sweater, straightened her skirt and snatched her purse and panties off the floor.

Whatever comfort had existed in his voice was now long gone as he called out her name again. Michael grabbed her arm one last time, turning her around, but Dewey refused to look at him. "I have to go," she muttered and rushed out the door, passing a surprised partier waiting in the hallway.

With the panic still clutching at her chest and the tears pushing at her eyes, Dewey ran out the house and into Mamaw's car. She wiped her eyes and nose clear with one slide of her sleeve, then pulled out of the driveway before Michael could stop her. Or worse, she would witness the fact that he wasn't coming after her.

Dewey rushed home to shower and change into her regular jeans and sweatshirt, then immediately headed to the home, pushing open the doors seconds before the nurse with a set of keys could raise her hands to the lock.

"I need to see Mrs. Guidry. It'll only take a moment. It's important."

Despite the alarm in Dewey's voice or the tear streaks on her cheeks, the nurse set her steel gaze upon her and crossed her arms. "Visiting hours are over, young lady."

"It'll only take a moment. I promise."

The nurse wasn't relenting and panic rose again in Dewey's chest, while her ulcer took the moment to rear its ugly head. She pleaded with Nurse Ratchet, to no avail, until someone called out and the nurse headed down the hallway.

"Stay there," the nurse commanded, pointing to an invisible spot on the floor. "I'll be right back."

Fat chance, Dewey thought and headed toward Mamaw's

room. She found her grandmother immersed in a late-night show, laughing at some off-color remark about politicians, convincing Dewey once more that Mamaw hadn't lost one ounce of her faculties. Her grandmother looked up and spotted Dewey. She didn't hesitate, understood completely and held out her arms. Dewey wasted no time rushing forward, letting the matriarch of her life envelope her in her embrace.

While Mamaw's arms wrapped her in a safe cocoon as they had numerous times over the years, Dewey let the emotions loose, weeping in her grandmother's chest while she patted her hair and spoke comfort in a language that was slowly disappearing.

"Ah *chèr*," Mamaw said after several minutes. "You finally admitting you love this boy?"

The tears abating, Dewey paused, wondering if that was at the heart of all this. Meanwhile, Mamaw shook her head.

"So hardheaded, you."

Dewey straightened, wiping her eyes. "What?"

"You been *boudeting* ever since you arrived," Mamaw said, using the Cajun expression for pouting. "Then you come in here like this, but you still don't know why?"

Dewey knew why. She just wasn't ready to admit it. She chewed on her lower lip, wishing Mamaw would hold her tight again.

"You know Michael had a drinking problem, *hein*?"

Dewey nodded, wondering how much Mamaw knew about that. Likely all of it. The woman knew everything, including the next Pope.

"He went to this AA thing. Steps, they said. First, you admit you have a problem, then you fix it. But you can't fix it until you admit you got it. Get it?"

Dewey slid backwards until she found the nearby chair, then sat on its edge. "Yeah, I get it."

Mamaw's eyes narrowed. "Do you?"

Did she? Was she still in love with Michael? Hell, of course she was. Who was she kidding? Certainly not Mamaw, Sandy or half the residents of Lafayette Parish.

Dewey rubbed her eyes, mentally kicking herself for running away. What did Michael think of her now? More than likely the same thing he thought all along, that she was a coward who would rather run away than face up to her problems.

She really wasn't that weak, only where Michael was concerned. There was still that one enormous question looming: Did he love *her*? Had he during that lustful month of high school? Those unanswered questions frightened her all the way to her toes.

Just then, Dewey realized something else; her grandmother was speaking to her. Mamaw seemed to understand the same thing, just as Nurse Ratchet arrived.

"I'm sorry Mrs. Guidry, but visiting hours…"

"It's okay, Gertrude. My granddaughter is just leaving."

Dewey obeyed, rising from her chair and kissing Mamaw's cheek. "Does this mean you're talking to me now?"

True to form, her grandmother resumed her haughty stance, arms folded against her weary bosom, eyes glued back on her show and its humorous commentary. "Nope. Not until you get a ring on that finger."

Sure, Dewey thought, she'll return to the party and ask Michael to marry her. After all, they already had the honeymoon. She was sure he'd jump at the chance.

Dewey paused on the threshold, remembering another horror the day had brought. "Oh, by the way, thanks Mamaw, for telling me about my other dad."

This got her grandmother's attention. She looked up through her thick glasses, her lips parting as if to say something, but Dewey smiled grimly and left the room. Maybe the next time she visited, Mamaw wouldn't be so silent.

Thinking of the man in question, and not wanting to go home where Michael might be, Dewey headed to Wagner's house. The closer she drove, however, the more she considered it a bad idea. Retreating from one emotional nightmare to another wasn't going to help things. She was still conflicted over how she actually felt about the situation.

His house came into view the same time she realized the street dead-ended in a cul de sac. She would circle and go home, find some way into Mamaw's house without seeing Michael. But, Wagner was in the yard pulling toilet paper from a tree and he spotted her instantly and waved.

Dewey grunted, then pulled into his driveway. Her former principal and maybe soon-to-be paterfamilias walked over and leaned his head into her open driver's window.

"Hey." Despite her expensive communications degree from Columbia, she had a hard time expressing herself verbally.

"Hey babe." As soon as the words emerged, Wagner frowned and looked away. In that second, Dewey understood the conflicts plaguing him all those years. And she thought he might be a child molester! Guilt assaulted her and she wanted to lay her head on that steering wheel and disappear. Instead, she tried a different approach. Stupid small talk.

"That's terrible about your trees."

Wagner glanced back at the toilet paper now lying in a neat pile on the lawn. "Nah. I go to dinner every Halloween and give them a chance to have fun. Gets it out of their system."

"You do this on purpose?"

Wagner shrugged. "Kids have a lot of steam they need to let escape. Better than having them set fire to the school."

Guilt pressed heavy on her heart. "Or make love in the janitor's closet." This time, she did let her head hang forward.

Wagner opened the door and took her hand. "Come on. I have some single malt scotch and leftover steak from Evangeline Steakhouse. It's calling your name."

"Is it saying, '*Couillon? Couillon?*' " Dewey mumbled from the wheel.

"Come on, Dewey. We need to talk."

There it was, that principal's voice, authoritative and commanding yet gentle. The perfect father's voice attached to someone who could make the perfect father, if she thought about it. Only Dewey never thought about it. She wouldn't have suspected in a million years that the bane of her teenage years shared similar blood in his veins. She truly was an idiot.

But she left the car and followed, avoiding Wagner's eyes.

"I don't understand," he said quietly as they entered the house. "I figured you'd be mad as hell at either me or your mom, most likely me."

She turned to offer up some poor excuse — that she and Michael had a fight, for instance — but when she met his gaze and witnessed the sadness and desperation shining back, she folded like a Cajun musician's accordion. Dewey stepped forward gingerly, touching his lapel and wondering…

Wagner stretched out his arms, also tentatively, and they slowly entered an embrace, hugging each other as if each was constructed of brittle glass, the kind artists create into miniature statues that snap like a twig when pinched. They held each other like that until finally Wagner laughed nervously.

"This is crazy." And with that statement, he pulled her close and gave her a proper hug, the kind she was used to, the type of affection Southerners offered on a daily basis. She leaned her head into his shoulder, breathing in a memory scent to carry back to L.A. and reveling in how wonderful a father — one who cared and showed it — could feel.

"Ah *chèr*."

Wagner hadn't grown up in Lafayette; he hailed from some English area north of New Orleans, the piney woods near Britney Spears' hometown. Even though he spent dozens of years in Acadiana, Dewey never heard him speak French or any of the expressions Cajuns and Creoles were so fond of. Hearing him speak endearments now made the moment that more special.

Dewey was the first to move away, more out of embarrassment for her state of dress. She pushed a nervous hand through her still damp hair, hoping she didn't look as bad as she imagined. She felt as if she always did in Wagner's presence, a child guilty of something, caught by the principal. Wagner was like the eye of Sauron, always watching, always knowing.

"I'm sorry," he said. "Maybe we should take this slower."

Dewey realized he misread her distance. "It's not that."

Wagner wasn't buying it. He moved to the kitchen where he produced two glasses and poured them both a scotch. "You don't have to do the test, Caroline. I'll understand if you don't want to."

Following him into the kitchen, Dewey paused at the family photos on the wall, searching for familiarity. Everyone had light-colored eyes, fine hair, an English heritage kind of look. One older woman in the photos even looked like Queen Elizabeth. "It's done. I did it this afternoon."

When he handed her the glass, he appeared surprised.

"Is this your mom?" She pointed to a slightly overweight woman with a generous smile.

"Yes, she died last year."

"I'm sorry."

"Thanks." He titled the scotch back and drank the entire glass. This was a first, watching the Wagner knock back alcohol. "She struggled with cancer for about five years, then the cancer finally won."

"I'm so sorry." Dewey cringed, wishing she had something better to say.

He grinned sadly. "It's okay. We all have to go someday."

"And your father?"

"He died about ten years ago. Heart attack."

Dewey nodded and took a seat when Wagner offered her a chair. He headed back to the kitchen counter, talking as he heated up the leftovers.

"One of the reasons I wanted to do the paternity test was because you should know about the health issues in my family." He shifted nervously. "If we're related, that is."

"What if I am?"

Wagner turned, studying her. "What do you mean?"

"What happens then?"

The microwave beeped, startling him. He took the plate out and placed it before her, than sat in the opposite chair. She stared, frozen, at the juicy steak before her, wondering what the next comment would be.

Wagner took her hand. "It changes nothing."

Before Dewey could react, or inquire what exactly that meant, he got up and headed for the living room. "I'll be right back."

The smell of the steak and the accompanying potato got the best of her. She realized it had been hours since she had last eaten, too much stress in one day to remember to eat. No wonder her ulcer pinched at her side.

Wagner returned with an old photo album, then opened it to the first page. A Polaroid of he and her mom dressed in outrageous clothes was the first photo Dewey saw.

"Wow. I knew my mother wore funky clothes once, but look at you."

"Hey, it was the eighties, what can I say?"

"You're sorry?" She smiled and Wagner seemed to warm up immensely.

"Yeah, well, this is the two of us in high school. I guess you know we were a hot item then."

"I've heard. Tell me you did it in the janitor's closet and I'll be happy the rest of my years."

Wagner smiled like a principal, a grin wide enough to emotionally connect with the student but still cautious. Dewey leaned forward and placed a hand on his forearm. "Please. You'd make my night if I knew I wasn't totally off base in high school."

He laughed. "Are you kidding? Do you have any idea of the number of students who leave high school as parents these days?"

This hit home. "I guess I'm one of those products, huh?"

Wagner straightened in his chair. "Absolutely not. I was in college and your mom was working and studying acting. We were both adults. If we hadn't been so drunk that Mardi Gras we would have been careful."

"Drunk?" Dewey giggled. It was one thing to see her mother tipping the bottle, but Wagner? And the lack of birth control surprised her. Her mother, despite her Catholic upbringing, belonged to the "Be Careful, Always Have Protection" school of sex. She was still handing Dewey condoms.

After filling her stomach with the potato, Dewey sipped her

scotch, hoping the ulcer wouldn't notice. Maybe her mother was the way she was because she gave birth at twenty, halting her career chances and forcing her to marry someone she didn't love.

"Why didn't she just marry you?"

The moment she asked the question, Dewey regretted it; Wagner's face blanched with a pained expression. To his credit, he straightened and shrugged. "We had a fight. And the last thing Emma wanted was to be married to a schoolteacher in Lafayette, Louisiana."

Her greatest fear took control of her heart, but Dewey refused to let it settle there. She wasn't going to believe that her mother married for money or for a chance to move to New York and a vibrant acting community. Not after the conversation they had that morning. She had to have some feelings for Dad, had to believe that marrying him would have benefited Dewey somehow. Still, Dewey couldn't stop wondering what life would have been like had her mother picked this kind but stern man before her.

He appeared to read her mind. "She would have hated it."

Dewey smiled grimly. "Yes, she would have."

He turned the pages of the photo albums, showing more of the couple, then Emma pregnant in New York City. At the bottom of one page was a grinning Wagner, holding a newborn.

"That's not me, is it?"

Wagner leaned forward, pride evident in his smile. "Your father couldn't be there, had to attend some business function in Europe and you came early. Your mother called me in hysterics and Bernice was too scared to fly, so I took the first flight up and got there just in time. Poor Emma was in labor for over a day."

Dewey stared at the photograph, studying every detail, every inch of Wagner's broad smile. She couldn't remember her father looking so pleased in the few baby photos she had.

Then she remembered the baseball game and the photos began to blur.

"There was a relative who used to come visit me when I was little," Dewey managed to say as a lone tear trickled down her cheek. "My mom said I made him up, but he took me to a Yankees game and Ron Guidry was there signing autographs."

Wagner shook his head, while taking her hand and squeezing. "How could you possibly remember that? You must have been three, four. 'Louisiana Lightning.' I see Guidry around town sometimes."

"You had him autograph the ball and he spoke to me in French."

Wagner squeezed harder and nodded. "I still have that ball."

Those memories her mother denied, they had all stopped at an early age. "Why did you go away?"

Wagner looked down and swallowed. "I was being difficult, demanding things. We had a blood test done. It proved I wasn't the father, but your dad started suspecting things. She didn't want to make problems for you."

Like the fresh winds blowing away the L.A. smog after a winter storm rolls off the Pacific, suddenly everything became clear. No wonder her father had been distant all these years. He felt he'd been had.

"I got roses for my sixteenth birthday and my dad seemed surprised when I thanked him. Were they from you?"

Wagner looked down again, staring at their adjoined hands. "Your dad doesn't realize what he's got."

Whatever guilt plagued her before with thoughts of molestation and years of battling him at school, it replicated tenfold. "And the graduation present?"

Wagner looked at her then, wiping the tears from her face. "Like I said, the test changes nothing. You have always been like a daughter to me and always will."

In that instant, Dewey wanted to cast aside her father and his stuffy New York relatives, glad to be rid of the pain associated with his demanding, uncaring relationship. She wanted to agree to Wagner being her dad, DNA test or no. But something held her back.

Wagner sensed her indecision. "Eat your dinner. You look pale."

"Yeah, well, it's been an interesting day."

He rose to refill his scotch. "Where's Michael?"

Dewey closed her eyes, wishing she could go to sleep and have the day start again. It was too much for one heart to absorb.

After refilling her glass, Wagner sat and faced her again. "Did I ever tell you about the time his father came to see me?"

She shook her head and pushed the plate aside.

"It was during one of his sober periods. Michael was home with him at the time and he was trying to be a good father."

Dewey vividly remembered those days, Michael being shifted back and forth between his father when he was sober and his Uncle Peter when his father was not.

"Frank Arceneaux told me a lot of stories," Wagner continued. "The man had a really tough time fighting the bottle. Started when his wife died. I guess you know about the car accident when Michael was only a baby and her swerving to save Michael's life, taking her own."

Dewey nodded. She'd heard the story from many sources, of Julie Arceneaux's ultimate sacrifice for her child, although Michael would never talk about it.

"She was the love of Frank's life," Wagner continued. "He had a hard time loving Michael because of it. When Michael was little, he would follow his dad around begging for his attention and saying, 'I love you, Dad,' all the time."

This made Dewey look up. She had never heard Michael utter that phrase to anyone. Not even Mamaw or Sandy. Not even Tyler.

"One day when Michael's father was intoxicated and Michael was following him around begging for his love, the guilt got the better of him and Jack slapped Michael hard across the face."

"Dear God." The words stung Dewey as much as the physical act must have done.

"Michael didn't say a word or even cry, his dad said. He just retreated to the back yard and started playing with his baseball."

"He used to do that when we were young," Dewey inserted. "Throw the baseball against the side of the shed when he was mad, over and over again."

"His dad told me he thought he had wounded his son for life. He felt really bad about it."

"He should have felt bad. What a jerk."

Like the calm, collected teaching administrator that he was, Wagner gave her one of those "now, now" looks. "Don't judge people too harshly, Caroline. You never know their history, their faults, their weaknesses."

"Judge? He probably did wound Michael for life."

"And he lived a wounded existence himself. The man couldn't stay sober to save his life. Literally."

Dewey grunted, not buying it well. How hard could it be for a parent to offer up a little love once and a while? She gritted her teeth, thinking of her own dad, who couldn't be bothered to send her flowers on her sixteenth birthday.

Wagner took her hand. "Michael says he has come to grips with his father, but you and I know better. And if anyone can save him, it's going to be you."

At this, Dewey laughed. "I doubt that."

But Wagner didn't relinquish her hand, staring at her like he did when he wanted to carry home a point. "Dewey, don't leave Louisiana without making peace with him. He needs it as much as you do."

She wiped another tear away with her spare hand. "Kind of hard to do when we're fornicating in a bathroom at a Halloween party."

To his credit, he didn't falter nor appear shocked at the news. And somehow, it felt good to reveal it. "Promise me?"

"It takes two…"

Wagner shook her hand, continued staring. "Promise me," he demanded this time.

"Okay, I promise."

"Good." He smiled. "Want some ice cream?"

Dewey wanted to remark how odd that question was, how they had just finished discussing her paternity, years-long secrets and new indiscretions made in River Ranch bathrooms, but there was no rhyme and reason in this world. She needed to forsake any form of rational thinking and move on.

After all, this was Louisiana.

"Sure. Got any praline pecan?"

Chapter Fourteen

MICHAEL GRIPPED THE BASEBALL MAKING the veins bulge in his hand and forearm. It took everything in his power not to fling the damn ball at the shed. No doubt his neighbors would love hearing that in the middle of the night. Old man Thibodeaux from across the bayou used to yell whenever Michael played catch at unreasonably hours as a child. Back then, it felt good to pour his anger into a pitch. He wondered how it would feel now as a grown man.

He sighed, hoping to relieve some of the anger and frustration. How long had it been since he had felt this way, like he wanted to rip something apart?

Damn her, he thought. Damn her for waltzing back into his life and stirring up old feelings he never wanted to relive.

Michael walked down the back steps and began pacing through the darkened yard, flexing his hold on the ball. Admittedly, he instigated the tryst in the bathroom, started the old passion again. She had looked so sexy in that tight sweater and skirt, and with his blood boiling over knowing what lurked beneath, all resolve had disappeared.

He paused, took aim and flung the baseball at the side of the shed, hitting the wall so hard it left a dent in the side of the aluminum. At the same time, he heard a gasp at his back.

"Shit, Michael, you scared me to death."

Michael released the breath he had been clenching through his teeth and turned. "Where the hell have you been?"

The sexy skirt had been replaced by jeans, a loose fitting sweatshirt and tennis shoes and Dewey's hair was mused as if she had hastily taken a shower and her hair dried odd. He couldn't make out her eyes in the darkness with the porch light only extending to the edge of their driveways, but Michael detected they weren't exhibiting signs of being glad to see him.

"I didn't know you were my mother. Why are you shouting?"

"It's two o'clock in the morning."

"Okay, I'm grounded. Can I go to bed now, Mom?"

She turned to head toward her own back porch and panic seized him. They couldn't leave it like this.

"I didn't hear you drive up."

She paused and turned, studying him intently. "I parked on the street so I wouldn't wake anyone up. Why are you throwing baseballs at this hour?"

"Why do you think?"

This made her pause and he detected an emphatic look. For a moment they were best friends again, when Dewey knew everything about him and his insecurities. He missed that. God, how he missed that unique connection. No doubt he was the reason it had all changed; he had consciously drifted away from her the moment the police had visited the house and told him of his father's death. He couldn't explain why, just needed the safety of a solitary darkness. Michael finally reached back when she had visited him the night of the funeral, when sex had replaced their years-long friendship. What was left now? he wondered.

Michael rubbed his eyes. "Are you okay?"

She inched forward enough so that he could make out her tired and wary gaze. "Yeah, just dandy."

"Where have you been all this time?"

Dewey crossed her arms over her chest. "Visiting a non-communicative grandmother and a man who could be my biological father. All this after finding out I'm infamous at school and having a fling in a stranger's bathroom. Can I be excused now? It's been an exhausting day."

He was stung by her dismissal and he wanted to retort that leaving was her trademark, why didn't she waltz back out of his life now, but Dewey wasn't moving. She stood there on the boundary of their yards, almost daring him to make her stay.

Michael inched closer. "Look, I've been thinking. If you need to get back to your job, I'll take care of Mamaw. In a month I'll be off for the Thanksgiving holidays, will forgo my freelance photography assignments this year and come out to L.A. We can talk somewhere neutral, where we don't have all this history staring us in the face."

Michael had practiced this speech waiting for Dewey to come home. It was the only thing that made sense, he reasoned, could help them move forward, although when the words emerged from his lips he realized he couldn't bear seeing her leave. Or waiting another month to talk again.

Dewey absorbed the idea, nodding, but tears welled up in her eyes. "Fine."

When she moved to leave, Michael blurted, "It's just a thought. I'm not saying that we have to wait until then."

She gazed heavenward as if collecting her thoughts or fighting back tears, he couldn't be sure. "What are you saying, Michael? For once in your life, tell me what you want."

The force of her question stunned him. "What I want?"

She moved closer, enough so that he could see the tears. "Yeah, Michael, what do you want?"

Panic rose up in his chest, like gasping for air when emerging from under water too long. He couldn't compose himself fast enough, couldn't think of how to put it in words. What did he want? Her, of course. Yet something old and moldy lingering in the shadows of childhood held those words tightly inside.

Dewey shook her head, wiping away a lone tear. "You're right, Michael. It's time for me to go. My friends are coming in tomorrow, I'm getting a big bowl of gumbo and heading west."

This time, she moved away, heading toward the back steps of her house.

"Fine," he shouted at her back, using the one emotion he felt comfortable with. "Leave. That's what you do best."

She spun around so fast Michael didn't see it coming. Stars flew across his vision as her hand forcefully slapped his left cheek. It caught him off guard, this right hook in the dark, so it took more than a moment to regain his composure. Ignoring the sting on his skin, he grinned slyly while rubbing his jaw. "Wow. You pack quite a punch."

"Screw you, Michael Arceneaux."

Michael grabbed her arm to keep her in place, then pulled her close so their bodies touched. "We're past that stage, don't you think? Been there, done that."

She relented some, softening in his grip, but when he leaned in close to attempt a kiss she shoved backwards freeing herself, wiping away another angry tear. "This is nuts. I'm going home."

"Right," he shouted, feeling the anger rise at her dismissal and toward himself for doing something so stupid as trying to bring on the passion — again. "Home is anywhere on the planet but the one place where people love you."

Dewey paused, staring at him with such pain and hurt he almost couldn't bear it. She doubted him, he was sure of it. Yet how could that be? She was the closest person to him in his life. She had to know that. She had to.

Michael grabbed her shoulders, pulled her close and breathed in the scent that still kept him awake at night. "What happened to us?" he whispered heatedly. "We used to tell each other everything. Now, you're looking at me as if you don't know me."

Tears fell freely this time as she sadly shook her head. "I did all the talking, Michael. Only I chickened out once and put it all down on paper."

The old panic resurfaced, coupled with fourteen years of fear and regret, but Michael was determined to clear the air, to not let this chasm between them linger longer than this night. He swallowed hard and cupped her cheek with his hand. "What did you say in that letter, Dewey?"

He saw the same emotional dance occur in her eyes and knew she wanted to retreat someplace safe as well. Weren't they a pair? Two dysfunctional children raised by emotionally retarded fathers who couldn't express their love. And now, despite all the love and support they had given each other over the years, they could barely speak honestly to one another.

Dewey swallowed and raised her eyes to his. "I fell in love with you back then. Only I didn't think you felt the same way. And I couldn't bear having you reject me like everyone else that I cared about, so I left. My scholarship to Columbia came through. My mom had sent me a plane ticket to New York the week before graduation so I could spend the summer with them."

She sighed and gazed off into the darkness. "I thought it'd be best for both of us if I went to New York, give us time to think. It was all planned before the, you know, closet incident. I wanted to tell you then but you had too much to drink, were so angry at the world."

A sharp kick to the groin would have felt better than Dewey's explanation. It was everything he had feared and worst. She had loved him, all those years ago. If Michael had known that, if he had read the damn letter...

Michael shut his eyes, hoping to stop the tearing of his heart. If he had only an inkling of what was going on in her mind, he would have moved heaven and earth to get to New York City. Nothing could have stopped him.

But he hadn't gone. Like the rabid adolescent idiot he was in those days, he had torn the letter up in a rage and ignored the one person he truly loved. God only knew what pain she suffered waiting for him to call, as he drunk himself into a stupor blaming her for all his problems.

When he reached up to pinch the bridge of his nose, grimacing with the anguish of fourteen wasted years, he felt Dewey slip away.

"It's okay, Michael," she said defensively, wrapping her arms about her chest and inching backwards once again into the darkness of her yard. "It was a long time ago."

Michael instantly grabbed her arms and pulled her hard against him, his face buried in her hair. Hell and Louisiana would freeze over before he'd let her escape again. "Don't go," he demanded harshly.

At first, Dewey remained stiff in his embrace, but as he reached up to caress her hair, wishing with all his soul that she could read his thoughts, she slowly relented. At first, she slipped her arms about his waist cautiously, but Michael wasted no time tightening his hold. Within moments, they were wound, Dewey's tears wet on Michael's neck, her head resting on his shoulder.

"I'm sorry," Michael whispered. "For so many things."

Dewey pulled back abruptly, threading a loose strand of hair behind an ear and frowning. "Sorry for...?"

Michael cupped her face, letting his thumb roam free to enjoy the feel of her soft skin. "I've thought about that night after my dad's funeral a million times, Dewey. Running it over and over in my mind. As much as I should have, considering what it did to our friendship, I've never regretted one moment."

Instantly, Dewey relaxed in his arms, exhaling deeply. She even attempted a smile, which gave Michael so much hope he kissed her again and again until his lips were seductively traveling down her neck. Yet at that moment it wasn't sex he was thinking of. After he absorbed the taste and smell of her, he wrapped his arms about her shoulders and held on tight, burying his face again in her hair. Dewey, in turn, snaked her arms around his waist and claimed fists of material in her hands, as if she wasn't about to let him go either. Neither one spoke and neither would release.

They might have remained that way forever, entwined in the darkened backyards of their youth, had it not been for Madelaine Thibodeaux sticking her head out of the familiar window.

"Are you two going to be at this all night?" she bellowed from across the bayou. "Some of us have to work in the morning."

He could feel Dewey smile against his cheek and they both

inched away from each other. By the time she moved into the penumbra of the porch light, Dewey's brow twisted in that familiar way, as if she sensed something bad was about to happen and she contemplated fleeing before it did.

Michael instantly grabbed Dewey's hand and starting pulling her into his embrace. Just before his lips were on hers, she balked.

"Michael, it can't always be about…"

Michael grabbed her by the waist and kissed her soundly, stopping all conversation. He groaned enjoying the taste of her, so sweet and luscious in the moonlight. His Dewey. The only woman he had ever loved.

But things had to change and certain desires had to wait.

"I know," he whispered when he came up for air. Then he turned her around and pushed her toward home.

"*À demain*," he said to her back.

"See you tomorrow," she answered as she turned slightly and gave him a hesitant smile, then climbed the stairs to Mamaw's house and disappeared into the dark, the screen door slamming shut in her wake.

"God, please tell me you don't regret this."

Sandy glanced across her pillow, amazed at how different Kevin looked without glasses, a Clark Kent kind of transformation. She wondered if he'd be insulted if she suggested contacts.

And those pajama bottoms — what was the pattern, *Star Wars*?

"Uh, I have to go, Kevin."

He grabbed her arm as she swung her legs across the expensive bed linens. Now that she got a good look at his bedroom, it was quite impressive. And huge. The only thing she'd caught on the hurried trip to the bed after Michael offered to take Tyler home was the feel of the lush carpet beneath her feet.

"Don't go," Kevin was saying seductively behind her back, but her focus was on the flat-screen TV attached to the wall at the foot of the bed like a prized painting. And there was this intricate electrical box next to a Blue Dog, an original oil on canvas. The man owned a George Rodrigue painting? And one sporting the trademark Blue Dog next to a boy who looked like a younger Kevin, meaning Kevin must have known the famous Cajun artist.

"Where am I?" she muttered with a laugh.

Somehow, Kevin managed to pull her back on to the bed. "You're in my bed, in my house and I'm not letting you go."

He kissed her soundly, making her forget for a moment the trials of her life, the money problems, the man at work she had crushed on and broken her heart, the hyperactive child who was no doubt getting ready to wake up and start yelling her name. But she did remember.

"I have to go," she whispered, savoring the way he consumed her lips. Geeks sure knew how to kiss.

"It's not sunrise yet," he continued in between nips.

"It will be soon and I can't let Michael deal with Tyler alone."

"Why not? He doesn't seem to mind."

"It's not fair. Tyler's a handful and he's mine."

Kevin pulled back then, taking her chin in his hand. "Let me have you for twenty minutes more, then we can go pick up Tyler and I'll take you both to breakfast."

Sandy leaned into his chest, enjoying the light, fresh cologne he wore and the way his hands caressed her arms. She wanted another twenty minutes so bad. But Tyler, in a restaurant?

"You don't know what you're asking."

Kevin kissed her soundly while his hands slipped beneath the sheet she held to her chest. "Your son is great and I know exactly what I'm asking. Remember, I suffer from this too. I used to be hell on two legs." His hands found a tender spot and squeezed, making Sandy gasp. "I don't mind at all."

Okay, so she could blame her reaction on what his hands were doing, surely, but his last words were the most seductive thing any man had said to her since her baby's birth.

"You really mean that?"

He paused, grabbing a nearby remote control and aiming it at the control box, which provided both soft music and a faint light from some recessed sconces along the wall. Then he stared down into her eyes with both passion and conviction. "I like Tyler a lot, Sandy, hyperactivity and all. And I've been in love with you forever."

Sandy inhaled, so overcome with that news. But before she could react, Kevin captured her lips once again.

"Besides," he said, taking a breath, "I haven't taken my medicine yet. Let me show you the finer points of being ADHD."

For the next twenty minutes he did just that, and the world as Sandy knew it, disappeared.

Chapter Fifteen

"**W**ILL YOU TWO BEHAVE? WE have less than a week to prepare for this thing?"

If he didn't know better, Michael would have thought something outrageous, like "Was I ever this disruptive in school?" He understood the wild teenage mind better than most people, but today he felt like the elderly couple sitting next to them in the coffee shop, staring at the group of teens as if they had never seen such behavior. Funny, how you live it and then the events sort of disappear from your memory. And yet, didn't he commit the same act last night as he had in high school?

Michael cringed, rubbing his temples. So many things from the past had come lose from their chains and old desires had gotten the better of him. He hadn't meant to lose control, start the old cycle with Dewey once more. But, heaven help him, like so many times in the past, he didn't regret one moment.

"Are you okay, Mr. A?"

Michael sobered. "Let's go over this again."

All four members of the Paul Hébert High School Debate and Speech Club groaned. Then Stephanie Dugas began listing the program of the competition, who would speak in what order and who needed to work on what. While Tony Attales reviewed his speech, Michael's attention drifted toward the door, where a noisy group of women were entering, all talking at once.

"Nothing a strong cup of coffee won't fix, Sweetpea," announced the loudest of the group, a cute dark-haired woman dressed in fashionable clothes. Another chatty woman followed — a bit mousy and dressed in plaids and khakis — both turning to link arms with Dewey after they stepped over the threshold.

"Don't you worry about nothing," the lead one said. "The Cajun Embassy is here to fix things."

The Cajun what?

"Mr. A?"

Michael turned back to Tony. "Read your introduction for me."

The kid grinned like a teenager catching his teacher being distracted. "I just did."

"Oh." Michael shifted, more from knowing Dewey was heading his way than for being unfocused. "Um, let's hear the arguments, for and against, then."

As Tony discussed the many facets of multi-culturalism in mainstream American society, Michael heard the hyenas cackling behind him at the counter, although Dewey's laugher was absent among them. Just as he turned to see what they were up to, Dewey looked over and their eyes met.

Her back stiffened and Michael forced himself to swallow as he sent her a nod. She looked like she had every morning since she arrived home, as if sleep had eluded her and life had been unkind. Yet, gazing at that crazy haircut and those sweet lips reminded him of how she had felt in his arms again, of that delicious scent she carried about her. She was so damn cute.

Dewey shivered as if trying to shake off his gaze. Then she turned toward the counter and ordered, but not before the hyenas witnessed their interaction. He heard one of them ask, "Is that the next-door neighbor?"

Michael turned back to the kids, angry that their past was public knowledge to her friends. He had managed all these years to remain silent, even when other teachers inquired as to who the Dewey was in the Dewey closet debacle. And here she was spilling her guts to the world.

"Harry, you go next," Stephanie instructed and Harry began recounting his speech plans. At the corner of his eye, Michael saw the pack sit in a grouping of leather chairs by the front door.

"Excuse me, Harry, but I need an extra sugar."

Michael headed to the bar that offered cream, sugar and coffee cup lids. The shoulder-high counter buffered casual coffee drinkers in the front from those who wanted more privacy and quiet in the back, like his students. Today, it offered him concealment from the Cajun Embassy.

"He's dreamy," the mousy one with a Southern accent was saying. "If he speaks French, I'm grabbing him for myself."

The mouse laughed like most women do when they really don't mean it but Dewey shifted nervously from the other side of the bar. Thankfully, her back was to Michael. "I don't think Colin would appreciate that, Maggie. Let's talk about something else."

"We saw how you reacted just now," the dark-haired one said. "We're not talking about anything else."

"Look, I had a week from hell and I've hardly slept…"

"Have you talked to him?"

"Yes, Lizzy, I have talked to him."

"And?"

Dewey paused and Michael knew what she was thinking. Sometimes words could be replaced by something infinitely better. Yet, Michael also knew that the main problem between them was a severe lack of communication.

"And nothing."

"What's he like in bed?" Maggie asked, making Michael spill his sugar all over the counter.

While he scooped it up with his hand and slid the powder into the trash, he heard Dewey laugh. "Now you all, you know I don't kiss and tell."

"Like hell?" Maggie said with a snort. "We know all about that male model and actor in L.A."

"Oh yeah?" Lizzy asked. "I must have missed that."

"Nothing to report about either, especially the actor," Dewey answered.

Maggie snickered. "Something about him not performing well."

Both girls giggled and leaned forward, waiting for an explanation. Michael found himself doing the same.

Dewey hesitated, and then sighed. "He never wanted to have sex or do anything to interfere with his workout routine or his scheduled vitamin intake. For instance, we went to this incredible romantic restaurant on the Pacific Coast Highway and there was this lovely B&B next door and they had an opening. We could have had wine on the deck overlooking the ocean and spent the night but he wanted to go home so he could get up early for a long-distance jog."

What a *couillon*, Michael thought.

"But was he worth it in the end?" Lizzy asked.

Michael leaned closer as Dewey's voice whispered, "What difference does it make if they don't want to make love all the time. I mean really?"

The girls giggled.

"And he only wanted to date me because I worked for the magazine. He thought I'd pass his name on to some hot-shot director."

"What was the model like?" Lizzy asked.

"I don't remember," Dewey said. "Because the minute it was over, he started talking shop."

Maggie shook her head and pointed a finger at Dewey. "I remember at Columbia when you went out with that guy from Duluth."

Dewey nearly choked on her coffee. "The guy who thought I'd gotten to grade school by pirogue, fighting off alligators all the way down the bayou?"

"And then you fed him alligator," she added with a hearty laugh.

Dewey smiled slyly, pulling her legs underneath her and sliding a lock of hair behind an ear. "And what's wrong with that?

Alligator is good eating."

The two women cringed, which almost made Michael laugh.

"Y'all have been living outside Louisiana way too long," Dewey said.

"So how does cutie pie over there rank up?" Maggie had to know.

Dewey paused and turned slightly, making Michael duck behind a palm tree.

"My problem, Maggie, is I'm either crazy or I date the wrong men. I mean, really y'all, aren't men supposed to want to make love all the time. I practically have to throw myself at these guys."

"You're avoiding the question," Maggie said.

Michael peered over to see Dewey shift in her seat, smoothing out the invisible wrinkles in her lap. Maybe she hadn't told them much.

"I've just been spoiled at an early age, I guess."

Lizzy started to speak, but Dewey held up a hand. "Enough, ladies. Let's talk about something else. Pa-Lease!"

Maggie started to object just as Tony called out Michael's name. "Shit," he muttered under his breath, hoping the Cajun Embassy hadn't caught sight of him shamelessly eavesdropping.

He sauntered back to the group, slipping in his seat and gazing back to see if the hyenas had caught him spying, but they seemed entranced in something new Dewey was explaining.

"That's the woman who came into class yesterday," Tony said.

Michael looked at the program lineup. "Did we work on the pros and cons of Tony's speech yet?"

"Mr. Arceneaux, we're on to the third speech now," Stephanie said smugly, arms folded across her chest like Michael would do when kids weren't paying attention. "You seemed kind of busy over there so we just kept going."

"I was getting sugar."

All four students grinned. "For like what, ten minutes, Mr. A?" Tony asked.

Michael fell back in his chair. Busted.

"She's cute," Stephanie added.

"You knew her from high school, right?" Juanita asked.

"She's got fine legs," Harry said.

"Watch yourself." Michael sent him a look, but it only made the others laugh.

"Yep," Tony said, pleased with himself. "He's crushed."

"Crushed?" Michael asked. Give it to high schoolers to say something, well, juvenile.

"Yeah, man, when's the wedding?"

Now, teenagers were saddling him up, just like everybody else in town.

"Although," Tony inserted, "she was giving you a harsh glare when she came in."

Michael took a sip of his now cold, very sweet coffee. He settled back in the heavy leather, thankful for the comfort and the change of focus. He wasn't in the mood to get these students ready for district. And coming off Halloween, neither were they. Might as well run with it, he thought. "She's mad at me."

"Why?" asked Stephanie.

"You don't want to know."

Stephanie looked like she really did.

"Let's just say we had a falling out in high school and we can't seem to get past it."

Harry leaned forward, pushing his glasses up his nose. "Did you all date?"

This made Michael laugh. Dating wasn't exactly what he'd call it. "We were best friends."

"But you got in an argument."

"You could say that. Things got a little crazy. My fault."

The moment the words left his lips, Michael visualized the days leading up to graduation. Emotions so raw and hot burning his veins that he barely recalled getting through each day. Dewey was his saving grace, his outlet, his savior. His mind had shut down, forcing out the pain of his father's death.

The one thing he was able to focus on was her. He had to have her. All the time. Had to feel her body pressed against his, breathe her scent, caress her soft skin. Sex or no sex, Dewey was his oasis in a world that had gone stark raving mad.

Trouble was, all he could remember was the sex. Surely, they had managed to find time to talk during all their ravenous trysts?

Doubtful. All these years he worried he had transferred all that rage at his father and life into his wild lovemaking with Dewey. But then, she hadn't complained. Still, something was going on inside that quiet brain of hers. And if he hadn't been such an ass that night after graduation, he would have read her letter. To this day, he wondered desperately what she had written.

"You need to talk," Juanita said flatly.

Understatement of fourteen years.

"I think you should call her up and ask her out on a date. Do you have her digets?"

A lightning bolt traveling through the coffee shop and hitting Michael smack on the head would have been tame compared to Juanita's last statement. Suddenly, everything became clear.

"Of course," he whispered.

"I mean it, like a date," Stephanie continued. "And bring her flowers."

This could work, Michael thought, feeling clarity permeate his brain like a Buddhist monk achieving nirvana. He knew just what to do.

"Thanks, guys."

Harry stood, slapping his hands on his knees. "Now that we settled your love life, can we go?"

"Sure." Michael grabbed the materials before him. "Let's just do this one more time next week. How about Tuesday afternoon?"

Conflicting plans, extra curricular activities and "I have to ask my mom" immediately floated up in a chorus of four, but Michael's ear focused on the clanging of the coffee shop's front door bell. He looked over to see the Cajun Embassy filing out, all offering hugs to Dewey.

When he looked back, all four students were gazing at him, waiting for an answer. If only he had heard what they had said.

"Never mind," Harry said, standing. "We'll let you know on Monday, Mr. A."

"What did I miss?" Michael asked.

Stephanie grinned smugly again and Juanita patted his arm as they joined Harry. "Good luck with Ms. Hennessey."

"Are we meeting Tuesday?" he asked to their retreating forms, but Stephanie only waved.

As the kids filed out the front and headed to Tony's car, Michael saw Dewey standing alone by the front window, watching her friends disappear. An intense loneliness gripped his soul. Is this the way they would live out their lives? Polite interactions and sudden arguments over incidents that happened years before? Quickies in bathrooms and backyard sheds, ending in cold shoulders once more?

He picked up his satchel and headed for the front. Not if he had anything to do with it.

As he approached her, he witnessed the sadness and fatigue gracing the lines around her face, knowing damn well he was mostly the cause of it all. He would make amends, but now wasn't the time. He had a plan and he was going to stick to it.

But as he passed her at the door, he couldn't help relaying one last thought. "You were dating the wrong men," he whispered to her, then exited the coffee shop.

He paused at Clotile, unlocking the truck's door the old-fashioned way — with a key — and throwing in the satchel. When he looked back up, Dewey was gone.

Didn't matter. Michael had her digets.

Feeling saddened that her friends couldn't stay longer than a few hours, Dewey drove around town, if nothing else than to clear her thoughts. She was dreadfully tired, but not ready to return to an empty home just yet. Stopping by the home was a waste of time since Mamaw wasn't talking; she had visited that morning and the cold shoulder was back. She couldn't stop thinking about Wagner and all the revelations of the night before, but she wasn't in the mood to talk about it.

Her father continued to call early in the morning, although Dewey ignored him today. She didn't ignore her agent who was over the top with her blog success, begging her to return to Los Angeles to meet with advertising executives. Even with that news, thoughts of leaving Los Angeles and returning to Lafayette kept popping into her brain, God help her. The blog was, after all, about Cajun and Creole cooking.

She shook her head. Maybe she just hadn't had that bowl of gumbo yet.

But then there was Michael and what occurred in Kevin's back bathroom.

"You're dating the wrong men."

Dewey closed her eyes at the red light, trying to push off his last comment and the delicious way he smelled as he passed her to his truck. Not to mention, Michael had heard their conversation!

"Jerk."

The car behind her honked, making it seem like the universe was slapping her hand for such a comment. After all, she hadn't objected to their bathroom tryst the night before. And then there were all the things Wagner had said about Michael's father, making her feel guilty for not making up after all these years.

They really needed to talk, needed to settle things once and for all.

Dewey drove into Girard Park, a centralized rural space of walking trails, ponds and playgrounds. She and Michael had made love there by the water one night, on a blanket on the truck bed of Clotille. It had been steamy, crazy, yet somehow innocent and sweet. Afterwards, though, he had seemed distant, starring off into the darkness, his eyes wild with some thought that didn't include her.

Dewey pulled Mamaw's old car into the same space and watched the children feed the ducks by the water's edge. The sun was setting behind her, casting sparks across the pond like diamonds thrown to the wind, while the mosquito hawks passed overhead eating the endless swarms of dinner that hovered over the area.

Was it the pain of his father's dying that had kept him so distant, even though they had made love every chance they could? Or was it just teenage lust?

She slid further in her seat to let sleep wash over her, to escape the endless thoughts about Michael flitting through her brain, but the cell phone invaded her plans. At first, she ignored her father and agent, but after the third ring, she figured she'd better check the number just in case. Her L.A. neighbor, Sammy, for instance, had been watering her plants in her absence and collecting her mail, and someone from the office may need information, like her computer password.

But, the number on the screen was not of the West Coast, but only one door down from her current residence. Dewey hit the talk button. "Sandy?"

"Uh, Hi," came the male voice. "I'm looking for Miss Caroline Hennessey."

It sounded like Michael, but surely…

"This is Caroline."

"Hi, Caroline. This is Michael Arceneaux. We knew each other in high school."

Totally clueless to what this was about, Dewey responded with dead silence.

"You might remember me as the boy next door," he added with a laugh.

The phone remained at her ear but her mouth gaped open, unsure of what to say next. What was he doing?

"Caroline?"

"Yes." Well, she managed one word. Was this a joke?

"I heard you were in town and I figured you might be hungry for some Cajun food."

He wants to cook me dinner? Dewey was so confused.

"Are you still there?"

"Yeah."

"I thought if you were, I could take you out for a meal at this hip new place in Grand Coteau. It's a town not too far from here."

"I know it." What a brilliant conversationalist she was. But he wanted to take her out? Like a date?

"They have this fabulous dish I want to introduce you to, since I heard you write a food blog. And the Pine Leaf Sisters are playing. I figure we could eat first, listen to some music, dance if you want to and then walk around town, now that the weather has turned nice."

This was a date. Wasn't it? Again, Dewey found no words to say.

A pause ensued, until she heard Michael laugh. "No gumbo, though. I don't want to give you an excuse to leave."

He wanted her to stay. In so many words, he was asking her on a date and admitting that he wanted her to stay. This time Dewey had trouble answering from the emotions lodging in her throat.

"Um, do I take that as a yes?" he asked the silence.

Dewey shook her head, and then realized how ridiculous that was. "Yes," she finally managed.

"Great. I'll pick you up at six tomorrow then."

Still perplexed by the conversation, Dewey said nothing.

"Miss Hennessey?"

"Yeah. Sure. Six is fine."

"Great." He sounded so jazzed, like a real suitor. Could they really pull this off? "See you then."

"Okay." Pull yourself together woman! "Six it is."

Michael made his goodbyes and hung up the phone.

"Six it is?" she asked the encroaching darkness. "The man finally asks you out properly and that's the best you can do?"

But was that what happened? He asked her out?

She couldn't be sure what the hell he just did, but her instincts hinted that he wanted to make amends. For the first time in days, maybe months, a warm glow started in Dewey's belly and spread until she had no recourse but to smile.

Like a lovesick teenager.

The cell phone burst to life as Melody applied the eyeliner to Emma's tired, fifty-something eyelids, the makeup artist never flinching as the chorus to *Phantom of the Opera* filled the air. As the music of the night continued, Emma commanded her heart to be silent. They had only minutes before her next shoot and Melody had more magic to create on Emma's less than youthful skin.

"Do you want to get that?" Melody asked.

She really did. It could be Dewey with news about mom or her agent informing her of an upcoming movie deal — both calls that took precedence over anything. Yet, God help her, neither one caused her heart to flutter as it was now.

"Can you look at the phone number," Emma asked. "It might be my daughter."

Melody dropped her artist tools, wiped her hands and glanced at the cell phone lying on top of Emma's bag. When Melody announced the Lafayette number Emma had committed to memory, Emma sighed, relaxed in her chair and grinned at her reflection, one that didn't look so bad after all these years. She still had it.

"Shall I answer it?" Melody asked.

The production assistant tapped on her trailer door and announced that it was ten minutes to her shoot. She needed to finish her hair, after Melody was done.

"No need," Emma said with a wide smile.

Just knowing he called was enough.

Chapter Sixteen

PATRICK THOUGHT HE WAS IMAGINING it, until Michael strode by for the third time. When he poked his head out of the office and spotted Michael lost in thought by the water fountain — just standing there – Patrick knew something was up.

"Do you need to see me?"

Michael turned and smiled as if he paced Patrick's office every day. "Why do you ask?"

"You're wearing out the rug."

Michael looked down at the linoleum. "What rug?"

"Come in," Patrick said with a sigh, wondering what happened to the art of sarcasm and imagery.

Michael followed him into his office and Patrick closed the door. "What's up?"

At first, Michael presented his standard smiling exterior that masked any emotions he might have lurking inside. Then, he sighed and dropped into one of Patrick's chairs. "I have a date tonight and I'm not sure what to do."

At this, Patrick laughed. "You're asking me for advice. The old maid principal."

Michael turned silent, the smile long gone. "It's Dewey."

"Oh." Patrick sat down in his chair behind the desk, letting that news sink in. "Oh."

"That's all you're going to say?"

"Did you say date?"

"Yes."

"As in pick her up and drive her somewhere to eat, maybe a movie."

"Uh huh."

"Not like a school closet or a back bathroom kind of thing?"

Crap, Patrick thought. Dewey had told him about the bathroom, but not Michael. His eyes grew large at the realization that Patrick knew. "Uh, she told me," Patrick quickly inserted.

"Great," Michael said, standing and pacing the office, sarcasm alive and well. "That's just great."

"We had a long talk on Halloween night about…well, everything. And naturally you came up."

He paused and turned back, hands on his hips and the masking smile firmly in place. "And she just happened to mention that we made love in a bathroom?"

Sometimes youth can be so deft, Patrick thought, especially the prime young man before him and the woman in question. So defensive, always in denial. Can't bother to talk to one another after all these years but they can manage a quickie in some dark and isolated place.

Even so, it was in that very office that Patrick had warned Dewey about Michael and his womanizing ways in high school. And he had been so wrong.

Still, he wasn't wrong now. He saw the look in her eyes two nights before. Old flames never extinguish. And if Michael's anxiety was any indication, these two were still very much in love.

"Did you ask her out?"

Michael still bristled from the bathroom revelation, but he nodded.

"Are you taking her someplace tonight?"

"Grand Coteau."

"Good choice. So what's the problem?"

Michael fell back into the chair, but his spine remained rigid.

It felt like an eternity before he finally answered. "I don't know what to do."

Patrick forced himself not to laugh. Michael was not one to be shy with women. "Of course you do."

A large exhalation escaped him as he relaxed deeper into the chair. "Not with her. There's too much there between us. Too much we never resolved. And now we have a bathroom to contend with."

That image whisked across Patrick's mind but he instantly sent it away; not something fathers wanted to think about where their daughters were concerned. Even if Dewey wasn't his daughter.

"You two were best friends once. Try finding that again."

Michael opened his mouth to say something but couldn't find the words. It was then that Patrick realized this was, indeed, a dilemma considering that both of them were still angry, and the man before him rarely found the words to express his emotions.

"Okay, try this." Patrick leaned forward and Michael did the same. "You haven't really spent much time together in fourteen years. A lot has happened to the both of you during that time, correct?"

Michael looked like this was an obvious point, but he shrugged anyway.

"So, go about it like you're meeting her for the first time since high school. Ask her what she does, what her job is like, who her friends are."

"She hangs around with this group called the Cajun Embassy."

It was an unusual piece of information, and Michael spoke of it like a teenager grasping at straws to impress a girl. But hey, whatever worked.

"Good. Ask her about them."

Michael looked at Patrick like he was missing something. "That's it? Ask her about her friends?"

"Jesus, Michael. No. You're not fifteen. Surely, you know how to act on a date."

With one burst of raw energy, Michael stood and began pacing again. Patrick could almost feel the heat emanating from him, as if repressed anger, frustration and loneliness sizzled off his skin like a bad sunburn.

"I know how to act, Patrick," he said with the most emotion Patrick had witnessed since he found him drunk at LSU, "I just don't know what to say to *her.*"

Michael gripped the edge of the neighboring chair and hung his head. As much as Patrick hated seeing the boy in pain, he knew this display of emotion was restorative. He walked to Michael's side and placed a paternal hand on his shoulder, grateful that despite all his shortcomings and his own loneliness, Patrick had at least two wonderful children he was very proud of. Now if he could only get them heading toward the light – preferably together – his life would be complete. Well, and getting Emma back into his bed.

He shook his head of that persistent longing and focused back on the issue at hand. "Why don't you try twenty questions?"

This got Michael's attention. He looked up with a twisted smile and Patrick knew the old hard-shelled Michael had returned. "What?"

"You heard me. Start with 'What's your favorite holiday movie coming out?' and work your way up to 'Why did you leave me all those years ago?'"

The smile quickly disappeared when the old pain was mentioned, but Michael appeared to be absorbing this advice.

"Seriously."

"Ask her about her favorite movie?"

Patrick rolled his eyes. Youth was wasted all right. "Or whatever. The point is ask her questions, get her to ask you things. Find out stuff about each other, like any normal person would on a date."

This made Michael laugh. "We're the last two people you'd call normal."

Funny thing about dysfunctional kids, Patrick thought, was that they felt unique. If one was to add up all the "dysfunctional" families of the world, "normal" would be unique.

"Fine, then ask her to marry you."

It was meant as a joke, but Michael didn't laugh. For a second, before Patrick deemed it absurd, he actually believed the boy was considering doing just that.

"Twenty questions," Michael finally said.

"Twenty questions."

The bell rang and they both groaned. Now that his principal guard had been let down to the friendship level, Patrick let an emotion slip. "I hate sixth hour."

Michael looked up surprised, a mischievous gleam shining in his eyes, like a schoolboy catching a teacher using a cuss word.

"I have to babysit a couple of unruly classes and the district asshole is coming to check up on them. And me."

A new look descended upon Michael, one of sober amazement, making Patrick want to punch him in the arm. "What? You didn't think I had a boss?"

"I thought you were god."

Patrick did punch him then, and they both laughed.

"Thanks." And with that one, final word, which Patrick knew covered so much more territory, Michael headed off to teach the world about American history.

As Patrick watched him go, he wished his own life could be that simple. Twenty questions. Hell, she wouldn't even answer the phone.

Dewey pulled each new outfit from the Dillards bag and held them high. After she had sped to the mail, obtained the clothes and got a new haircut in record time to make her date, she stopped by the home hoping to get needed advice from her grandmother.

But Mamaw wasn't talking.

"No thoughts on which outfit looks best, huh?"

Nothing. Dewey dropped her arms.

"What did you expect?" Claudine asked from their game of bourré. "Are you married yet?"

She and Jeannette giggled and Dewey suddenly sympathized wholeheartedly with her mother. She wondered if her mother had put up with this all her life.

Mamaw didn't laugh, though. She studied her through thick glasses over the top of her cards. "I'm leaving Sunday," Dewey announced, looking her grandmother in the eye, whether she acknowledged her or not. "Despite all this wonderful fun I'm having, I have to get back to work."

This silenced the two cackling crows.

"When are you coming back?" Jeannette finally asked.

"Why should I come back? No one's talking to me."

Dewey didn't wait for an answer, didn't bother to tell Mamaw she had a date with the man in question or to again ask which of the outfits she had purchased at the mall would be appropriate. She simply strode out of the room and out to the car, unable to stem the tide of tears rushing down her cheeks.

"Damn it," she mumbled, which made the nun at the door look up. But she didn't care. She was taking one step forward that day — at least she hoped so — and Mamaw had pushed her two steps back.

By the end of the week she was heading back to Los Angeles. She really should be heading back in the morning; her agent insisted as much and she was pushing the patience of her employers, assholes though they may be. But she needed a little more time. What she would do tonight and in the next few days she wasn't sure, but it had to be an improvement over the past fourteen years.

Still, she had so wished Mamaw would have changed direction. She needed girl advice.

When she arrived at the house, she bounded up the stairs and placed all of the new clothes out on the bed, then held them up for inspection.

"So, casual in jeans, dressy in a dress or just cute in a miniskirt?" she asked her reflection, gazing at the choices before her.

The jeans and the comfort they allowed beseeched her and the lacy white dress reminded her too much of church, although it was the most elegant of the three. The short skirt with its matching sweater appeared the logical choice, but was it too sexy? It did emphasize the ample curves of her breasts, which in most cases she was only too happy to show off. Her chest was her finest feature, helping to de-emphasize the extra weight lingering around her hips — thanks to her blogging job — and her uninteresting waistline. The sweater was angora and the skirt suede but was so short she'd have to wear leggings. The shoes she bought to match were adorable and she couldn't wait to try them out.

"Okay, the skirt then."

She pulled them up to her body and stared hard in the mirror, still unsure.

Of course, the shoes would look just as well with the sweater and jeans.

"Why is this so hard?" she yelled at herself. "It's just Michael."

Of course she knew that answer. As Dewey fell on the bed in frustration she wondered why grown, accomplished, educated women never leave high school.

Just then the phone buzzed and her heart constricted. After all these years, she still lived in fear of her father's disapproval. He would be the last one to approve of her dating Michael.

It was a West Coast number.

"Hello."

"Dewey, baby. How are things?"

Her mother sounded unusually happy. "Oh fine, Mom, just dandy. What's up with you?"

It wasn't the answer her mother wanted and she sighed. Now that Dewey thought about it, she had heard the same sound hundreds of times throughout her life. Had she always been such a bitch to her mom?

"When are you coming home?"

Where was home? Dewey thought. Right now, she felt as if she floated between two distinct, both equally crazy galaxies. "Sunday. I get in late."

"I should be done with my scene by then. I'll pick you up."

"Okay."

"Okay."

Silence followed, and Dewey searched her brain for something to say, something her mother wanted to hear and not her usual sarcasm. "How's the shoot?"

This worked. Her mother seemed genuinely pleased Dewey asked about her job. "It's good. Things are going very well, the director's pleased. He wants me to audition for his next film, said he really wants to use me."

"That's great, Mom." And Dewey really meant it.

"My agent has another project lined up, as well. A leading role in a Lifetime movie."

"Wow, things are taking off for you."

"Yeah, feels that way." Her enthusiasm nearly burned a hole in the cell phone.

"I'm happy for you, Mom."

After a pause, Emma asked, "Are you really, sweetie?"

Dewey gaped at the question. Despite everything, she always wanted what was best for her mom, always wanted her to be happy. "Of course I am. If anyone deserves some good luck, it's you."

She wasn't sure what made her mother cry, but Dewey had a strong feeling it was her daughter admitting that her mother had feelings. And that she had worked hard and was finally succeeding.

Dewey felt guilty for the crap she had laid on her mom all those years, for being so self-centered and myopic, for adding fuel to the fire when Jeannette or Claudine complained of her mother's parenting skills, choice in men and lack of dress etiquette.

"Mom," Dewey whispered through her own tears, "I do love you and I think you're wonderful. The greatest friend I've ever had. I only wish the best for you."

This brought on a flood between them, until finally Dewey laughed and Emma joined her. "Aren't we a pair," her mother said, blowing her nose.

Dewey then told her mother everything, about the tryst in the bathroom, the Cajun Embassy coming to visit, Michael over-hearing their conversation and the phone call announcing he wanted a date. The last comment perked Emma up considerably.

"So, what are you wearing?"

Speaking of high school…

"Gosh, gee, Mom. I thought I'd wear my poodle skirt and Oxfords."

"Don't be a smart ass."

That all-too-familiar hurt lingered between them once again and Dewey kicked herself. She was a smart ass, wasn't she? Her father once said she was too intelligent and too cynical, a deadly combination. Then he had laughed and commented at how alike they both were in that regard.

But, he was the last person she wanted to emulate.

"Sorry, Mom, it just sounded funny, you know. Like two teenagers talking about a date."

Emma laughed once again. "Okay. I guess you're old enough to figure out what to wear."

She started to say her goodbyes and Dewey panicked. "Uh, actually I could use some advice."

Dewey spewed off the three choices, explaining the pros and cons of each, while Emma laughed. They then switched to Skyping so Emma could see the different outfits. After twenty minutes of more girl talk that left Dewey feeling infinitely more confident and happier, Emma got off the phone to perform her final scene of the day, adding that she would meet Dewey on Sunday at LAX.

Time was ticking so Dewey threw on the skirt and sweater, adding the cute shoes and accessories, and headed off to the bathroom to apply makeup. She knew just what to do, having had the expert direction of a fifty-something woman who could pass for Dewey's sister.

Two minutes to six. Dewey rushed downstairs to get a look at herself in the mirror, panic striking as soon as she gazed at her reflection.

What if Michael's dressed in jeans and a T-shirt like he always does?

Did I overdo the makeup?

Will he like this new haircut?

She thought to change earrings — something more discreet — when the doorbell buzzed at the front door, the formal entrance that no one used. Just what she needed, Dewey thought, Jehovah's Witnesses or carpet suckers advertising specials. Best to get rid of them quickly and then rush upstairs to make adjustments, she surmised.

But as she flung open the door, ready to dismiss whoever was selling something, Dewey spotted Michael standing on the threshold. He was dressed in jeans, all right, and a tie, dress shirt and jacket. In his hands were flowers, and his eyes seemed to dance at the sight of her.

All the saints be praised, Dewey thought, as she grinned like a sixteen-year-old being picked up for the prom. She was totally, completely, helplessly in love with this gorgeous man in front of her.

Chapter Seventeen

MICHAEL COULDN'T STOP STARING. GONE was the flighty haircut and the hip California clothes, replaced by something similar she used to wear in high school, something cute yet sassy, with a sweater that really highlighted…well, he didn't need to go there.

"You look great." Michael handed her the flowers. Daisies. Her favorite. He had driven to three flower shops to find them.

"Wow." She gazed down at the bouquet, her simple haircut now framing her face. She appeared stunned by the gesture and the fact that he had knocked on the front door. He wasn't even sure the damn thing opened!

"Wow," she repeated, still grinning like a teenager. Now that he thought about it, so was he.

They stood like that for what seemed an eternity.

"Let me put these in water." Dewey self-consciously twisted a lock of hair behind her ear, then sauntered off to the kitchen. Michael could hear her pulling a vase from a cabinet and the water running.

"You know, I was worried you might…"

She appeared around the corner, flowers in hand. "What?"

"Well, you did seem confused on the phone last night."

She placed the flowers on the hall table, still grinning. "I made some calls around town and realized you were legitimate."

"Cute." Michael wiped his sweaty palms on his jeans. "Then we're all set?"

Dewey grabbed her purse and headed out as Michael held the door open for her. They said nothing as they both maneuvered through the rickety old porch that no one used, laughing awkwardly when one of the railing boards snapped off when Michael leaned against it.

"Don't tell Mamaw," he whispered.

As they arrived at the truck, Dewey attempted to climb into Clotille on her own when Michael reached around quickly and opened the truck door. She blushed and thanked him, then climbed into the passenger seat. Chalk one up for him, Michael thought as he headed to the driver's side. He just made Dewey Hennessey blush.

They mumbled small talk until they made the interstate, then silence fell between them. Time to initiate Patrick's plan, Michael thought, hoping the damn thing worked.

"Um, Dewey, do you remember the old game of twenty questions?"

Dewey looked at him sideways, curious. "Yeah."

"Feel up for a game?"

Her eyes narrowed. "Huh?"

"It's Patrick's idea. He thinks it's a good way to break the tension between us."

"Who's Patrick?" She grinned as she added, "And no, that's not my first question."

"Mr. Wagner."

"Oh." Her smile disappeared. "My so-called dad gave you dating tips?"

Maybe this wasn't such a good idea, considering, but Michael decided to come clean. "I'm not very good with words. He thought maybe this might…"

Dewey didn't refute that fact, and he was grateful for it. Instead, she straightened her skirt and smiled. "Should I start with the first question?"

"Absolutely."

She starred out the window. "Wow, what to ask first."

This really might be a bad idea, Michael thought with a panic, thinking of all the territory she had to explore. After a moment's silence, Dewey looked at him sheepishly, as if she dreading starting this game, as well.

"Okay." She took a deep breath and Michael tensed. "Who did you sleep with in high school?"

At first, he laughed. Then he realized she was serious.

"What do you mean, who did I sleep with?"

She crossed her arms. "Just what I said."

Michael had a difficult time maneuvering around an eighteen-wheeler and a slow-moving Toyota while gazing over at Dewey to make sure she wasn't pulling his leg. "Who did I sleep with in high school?"

"Right."

"As in sex?"

She passed him the evil eye.

"Well, *chèr*, we never slept."

This clearly made her uncomfortable — something Michael was afraid the game might do — but he had to know what on earth she was talking about.

"Before us." She picked imaginary lint from her skirt, then smoothed out the leather with the heels of her hands as if her own palms were leaking. "If there was somebody during, I don't want to know."

Michael couldn't stand it anymore. Besides, they had reached Grand Coteau. He drove down the exit ramp and pulled into a nearby gas station parking lot, raising the emergency break so Clotille didn't roll away, as she was accustomed to do. He leaned an arm along the side of the seat so he could get a good look into her eyes. But what he saw shining back from those baby blues was hurt and resentment.

"Jesus, Dewey, I made love to you."

"There were rumors that you slept with half the school."

"What rumors?"

"Lots of them."

"And you believed them?"

"Even Patrick warned me about you?"

This stopped Michael cold. "Patrick said I was sleeping with half the school?"

Dewey twisted the strand of pearls at her throat, the ones her father had given her for her sixteenth birthday. Late, of course, unlike the dozen red roses Patrick had made sure she received that morning. Shit, if Patrick had warned her about Michael's womanizing, he must have been convinced as well.

She exhaled, and then looked him in the eye. "Did you?"

Michael let his own breath out. "Wasn't it obvious you were my first? I was a bumbling idiot."

Her frown deepened, creasing a line between her eyes. "No," she said loudly. "It was obvious it was *my* first."

"I was all thumbs. I went too fast."

She shook her head, either to make sense of something not fitting right or determined to believe some silly rumor she had heard. "You were fine. In fact, you were great."

They both backed up at the same time, staring at each other with puzzled expressions.

"You were the one in the shed after my father's funeral, weren't you?"

Dewey punched him on the arm.

Michael hated remembering that first awkward time when he rushed everything in his desire to fulfill his need. "I made you cry," he said softly, turning his gaze to the parking lot where a couple laughed as they returned to their car, arms entwined.

Silence fell inside Clotille's cab but after a moment, Michael felt her hand take his. "Did you think I was crying because you hurt me?"

Of course he did.

"Michael," she said, tugging his hand so he would look at her, "I was crying because afterward you gave me this look, like you were sorry for what had happened. I was crying because I was afraid you regretted it."

Michael cupped her face with his other hand, letting his thumb roam free to enjoy the feel of her soft skin. "I've thought about that night a million times, Dewey. Running it over and over in my mind. As much as I should have, considering what it did to our friendship, I've never regretted a thing."

She attempted a smile, but something still held her back. "And there were no other women…?"

At this, Michael laughed. "Darlin', you came back from New York one summer wearing one of those tube things around your chest, those tight things that show off everything underneath. And you must have grown several, what do you call them?"

Dewey relaxed, eying him suspiciously. "Cup sizes?"

"Whatever. In the course of a couple of months, you suddenly sprouted. And suddenly my whole world revolved around your breasts. There were no other women in the world, as far as I was concerned."

She began to smile, making Michael hopeful, because he couldn't believe he was spilling his guts about all this. "All anyone ever had to do was mention your name and I got hard."

At this, Dewey's eyes grew large. Funny, how the two of them copulated in just about every spot in Lafayette Parish but failed to mention that one little fact. But then, they didn't speak much in those days.

An eighteen-wheeler hauled past, upsetting the dust around them and causing them both to look up. Dewey continued staring at the cloud the truck left behind, lost in thought.

Michael released the break and started heading toward town. "Anyway, there was no one else, despite whatever rumors you might have heard."

They passed the town's first stop sign and curved toward the main street where the restaurant, antique shops and the Academy of the Sacred Heart Catholic School made up the tiny town. As the sun set behind them, a deep orange twilight created halos on the live oak trees offering their Spanish moss like ghosts beneath them. They rode in silence until finally pulling into the restaurant parking lot.

Dewey sent him a glance, then whispered, "Your turn."

Michael grimaced. This was going to be a long night if nineteen more questions followed along the lines of that one. He decided he needed a break.

"What holiday movie are you looking forward to seeing?"

She gave him one of those "Are you crazy" looks, a familiar gesture he was used to receiving in the old days, when they told each other everything, including how the other one was nuts. And in familiar fashion, he punched her on the arm.

"Jerk."

"Yankee."

"Coonass."

His eyes widened as she breached the unforgivable territory. She knew how much he hated that derogatory word for Cajuns. She laughed, then quickly opened the door and fled the truck. Michael was hot on her heels. Before she could reach the door, Michael grabbed her from behind, pulling his arms about her waist and yanking her backwards, while she protested, laughing.

But the scent of her disarmed him. He stopped playing, soaking up the feel of her against him, breathing in the smell that was all Dewey.

"What are you wearing? You smell like you did in high school."

Dewey relaxed against him, moving her head slightly so he could nestle her neck. Then when Paul, the maitre'd, opened the door and looked their way, she giggled and pushed him aside.

"Almond Suave. The cheap stuff. My turn."

He started to object, but she was already in the restaurant. As he followed, he could hear Paul offering up his own twenty questions to her: "Where did you meet this guy?" "Known him long?" "You must be special, he reserved our best table and I've never seen him do that before."

Michael sent him a look and Paul cleared his throat, grabbing two menus and heading toward the back, but not before Dewey spotted Michael's photographs lining the walls and stopped to admire them.

"These are yours, aren't they? Wow, they're gorgeous."

It was how Michael was affording such a meal. The owner had sold two photographs of his of the nearby Atchafalaya Basin. Tourists loved the swamp photos and Michael was only too happy to hand them over.

"I love the one of Geno Delafose," Dewey said, clearly pleased at the photographs before her. "Is that him playing zydeco at Sid's?"

"Yeah, they're mine and yes, that's Geno. My turn."

Her mouth opened in protest, then she laughed, but she left her gallery stroll and took the seat Paul was offering by the front window that opened before the hundreds-year-old Jesuit Spirituality Center. Paul handed her a menu and Dewey said with a smirk, "I'll have what you're having."

"What?"

"Your next question is 'What do you feel like eating?' Right?"

Michael grabbed the menu from her hands. "Nope. Still my turn. But I will order for both of us."

She tried to appear annoyed by this, crossing her arms and pouting somewhat, but a smile lurked underneath. When Paul brought out his pad, Michael ordered everything from the wine to dessert.

"How did you know what kind of wine I liked?"

"You keep trying to take over this game."

"But..?"

Michael leaned his elbows on the table and gazed into her eyes. "Do you like L.A.?"

A myriad emotions crossed her face, making Michael wonder if she really knew what she wanted these days. Before she could muster up a false front — something Michael knew how to do all too well — he took her hand in his. "Answer yes or no. Quickly."

"No." The answer surprised them both.

"Then why…?"

She pulled her hand away. "My turn."

Michael leaned back, pulling his hands through his hair. She was too good at this stupid game.

"Do you really think you seduced me that night?"

On second thought, she was failing miserably. Her questions were outright ridiculous. "The night of my dad's funeral?"

"Yes," she practically whispered while blushing profusely.

"Uh…didn't I?" he asked with his trademark seductive smile he used on women when he wanted something. She shook her head, which made Michael laugh and panic at the same time. "I didn't?"

Thankfully, Paul arrived with the wine, pouring a small amount in Michael's glass to taste. Michael downed it in one gulp, nodding to the waiter, his inattention causing him to completely miss the point of that ritual. The bottle could have been vinegar for all he knew.

Dewey sipped her wine, and then folded her hands in front of her. "Do you remember the bridge incident?"

"In middle school?"

"Yeah, when I first moved here and everyone was making fun of me because I pronounced everything wrong and said 'you guys' instead of 'you all'?"

"Yankee."

"Shut up."

"What about it?"

"You were a shit, too."

"You were a snob."

"I was not."

Paul came back with a basket of bread, allowing Michael a chance to rub his eyes and clear his head. "What does this have to do with…?"

"The kids dared me to jump off the Vermilion River Bridge."

"And you actually were going to do it."

"I take dares seriously."

This made Michael grin, remembering all the dares he had thrown her way for that very reason.

"You joined me on that bridge that day, said you'd jump with me."

"I hated junior high and those assholes. They used to torment me too."

Dewey leaned forward, her fingers laced around her wine glass. "But you climbed over the edge with me. You were going to jump too."

He honestly didn't remember much about that time except that he liked Dewey from the moment she arrived at Mamaw's house, even if she was a little snob from New York City. Plus, she hadn't grown up with the knowledge of his father's drinking, or even cared when she found out. And she hadn't looked at him with pity like everyone else loved to do in those days.

Besides, Dewey was different, interesting, unique, creative. He wanted her as a friend. Not to mention that he had seen the cops coming and knew they wouldn't go through with jumping off that bridge.

"*Mais*, it was no big deal."

"It was to me. You said, 'If you're going to jump off bridges, it's best to be holding on to someone's hand.'"

She blushed again, her words emerging with a catch in her throat. "You could have asked me to fly you to the moon after that and I would have."

"So, let me get this straight." He took another long sip of his wine. "Because of that incident, you let me seduce you?"

Paul arrived and placed salads before them, giving Dewey a chance to sit back and regroup her emotions.

"That was my tube top moment," she said when he left. "I was crazy about you from that moment on."

This was news. Big news. "Since junior high?"

She grimaced, and then began moving cabbage slices around on her plate. "Actually, the steamy thoughts started happening one day in high school when you were washing Clotille with your shirt off."

Michael felt a smile split his face. Up to this point, he thought the cold showers belonged to him alone. "You had carnal thoughts about me back then?"

Dewey blushed so much he thought she might choke. "I used to watch you from my window."

"No."

As quick as she flushed at the conversation, Dewey turned pensive and quilt-stricken, a look of pure pain crossing her features. "I was doing that the night of your dad's funeral. Staring at you from my window, watching you sitting on the porch."

"I don't get it," Michael said, taking her hand. "What does this have to do with me...?"

She wouldn't look at him.

"Dewey?"

She glanced up briefly, then quickly looked back at her salad. "I seduced *you*," she whispered.

Like the earlier question, Michael wanted to laugh, but he had learned this game could produce some wild confessions.

"How is that possible, *chèr*?"

"You were grieving and vulnerable and I wanted to have what I thought the rest of the school was getting. Didn't you think it was odd that I came down with almost nothing on?"

Michael raked his brain to recall exactly what happened that night. All he could remember was the giant black hole of guilt and anger that had opened up and was eating him alive when Dewey appeared at the porch steps, touching his cheek, offering comfort, solace and kisses. A bright light to shine him home. He had immediately pulled her to him, devouring her instantly and running a hand up her nightgown to grasp what he had longed to feel for years. Then he took her hand in his and led her to the back shed where they had instantly consummated their passion.

Their passion.

"Holy shit."

Dewey took a long drink of her wine as the realization hit him full force. "Your turn," she whispered, avoiding his eyes.

He was beginning to dislike this game immensely, although he could now see why they had failed to communicate all those years. And he was beginning to resent how she had the upper hand. He hadn't meant to rush through to the punch line, but the question flew from his lips without thinking.

"Why did you leave?"

She looked at him then, eyes as big as blue marbles, and something inside of him snapped. He didn't want to know, didn't want to hear her lame excuses for flying off to New York while he fumed in that nasty jail cell. If she was willing to give him the moon, why couldn't she wait twenty-hour hours to leave town? All the long-buried anger came rushing forth, singing his skin, and he waved his hand in front of them. "Forget it. Forget I asked."

But Dewey wasn't forgetting anything. She leaned forward, anger brewing inside her as well. "The thing is, Michael, you already know the answer to that question."

The trouble was, he did. After he — or hell, she — had opened the door to their lovemaking, he had gone crazy. The black hole continued to suck him in daily and he grasped for Dewey like a drowning man lunging at a lifeline. He thought she had understood all that, knew what he was thinking, was feeling during those dark, horrible days. But after the past twenty minutes, nothing made sense anymore.

"I drove you away, is that it?"

She sat upright in her chair, emotionless, her posture perfect and still, her hands in her lap. As quick as it had arrived, the anger and pain disappeared replaced by something Michael couldn't read.

"I don't know."

"You don't know?"

"Yes. No." She looked at him, unsure, tears suddenly welling up in her eyes. "I don't know. It all happened so fast. It scared me."

Dewey was right. He had known the answer, a painful revelation he didn't want to hear. He longed to explain, but for the life of him couldn't express what had been going on inside his mind back then. Except that he loved her.

So tell her, his mind demanded. For the love of God, tell this incredible woman in front of you how you feel!

As usual, the words refused to come.

Paul arrived with the restaurant's signature dish, layers of different seafood piled on top of each other, with a massive Gulf shrimp perched on top like a ballerina, and accented by a rich Creole sauce. They both laughed at the monstrosity before them, Dewey taking a photo with her cell phone for her blog and they delved into the entrée. The questions continued, such as what was Michael's favorite subject to photograph and what Dewey found the most interesting in her job, but the atmosphere had decidedly changed, vital questions left unanswered.

When they arrived back at Mamaw's house, Michael felt they had made significant progress, although the old hurt of that graduation afternoon remained, lingering between them like unfulfilled promises. He asked Dewey for another date the following day and she agreed, thanking him for dinner and offering to pay the next time.

"Absolutely not. You can pay when I visit you in California."

"Will you?" Her eyes brightened at the prospect and Michael wondered where all this would lead. Would she return to the Coast and they would both go about their lives, Mamaw returning home or at least talking to them again? Or would they call each other now on a regular basis, email, talk about their day, their jobs, their love lives? Would they become friends once more? Or had Michael, in succumbing to the most primal desire, despite who initiated the infamous seduction, ruined the finest friendship he had ever known?

"Sure," Michael said, brushing the hair back from Dewey's face and savoring the sight of her in the defused light emanating from the porch. Truth was, he didn't want to hear about Hollywood actors and male models. He couldn't go back to being friends. He loved her too much.

And Mamaw was not one to back down. Hell would freeze over before his adopted grandmother talked to him again without a ring on his finger. He knew that Cajun stubbornness well. Too well.

Then there was disapproving Sandy, his lonely sister struggling to raise a learning disabled child, a spurned woman who had ever right to be pissed at them both for throwing love away so casually.

No matter what happened in the next few days, Michael was doomed to lose the three women he adored. And for the life of him, he couldn't figure out how to fix things. Except…

"I had a great time," Dewey said, no doubt to fill the sudden silence.

"Me too."

Resisting the urge to kiss her in the truck that had more than its fair share of carnal history, Michael left the driver's side and headed over to open her door. She laughed when he held out his hand, but a date was a date.

"I get off around three tomorrow, so think about what you want to do, where you want to eat. You only have a few days left to get your fill."

Dewey smiled, pulling the key out of her purse as they walked up the rickety steps. "It's going to be hard to beat what we had tonight."

"I would have included gumbo, but I didn't want you moving up your flight."

It was hard making out her face when she turned to unlock the door, but Michael was sure her smile faded. "Do you want to come in for some coffee?"

He wanted to do more than drink coffee, but he had school in the morning. Plus, he had made a promise to himself to take this slow. Do it right this time.

"Thanks, but I need to get up early."

She turned, her eyes glistening in the darkness. "Thanks for everything."

Uneasiness permeated the distance between them, but it didn't stop Michael from leaning forward to give her a goodnight kiss. Dewey reacted, rising from her toes slightly to close the height gap. The movement made them both come together too fast, causing the kiss to be deeper and more forceful than the caste one Michael had in mind. But he took the opportunity to savor it, brief as it was.

When he pulled back and her feet touched the ground, an

aching emptiness followed that filled him with longing and melancholy. Like the black hole returning.

Hours later, when he would lie awake in his bed pondering that moment, he would blame it all on that kiss and the dark chasm that it opened. Because for once in his life, he opened his mouth and words came out that he never expected.

"Last question," he said with a grin. "Do you want to get married?"

Chapter Eighteen

IT WAS A TYPICAL HOME visit. Mamaw said nothing while Dewey fidgeted or stared out the window, always wondering how long the silent treatment would last. This morning, however, Dewey didn't care. She had way too many issues pressing on her mind, mainly the fact that Michael had proposed the night before.

She replayed the tape in her brain, trying to remember his exact words and what had led up to that moment, but the sound bite had been tiny, her response equally brief.

"Do you want to get married?" he had asked her sincerely.

And not knowing where the words had come from that emerged from her lips, Dewey had agreed. She had actually said yes!

Dewey began to pace Mamaw's room, while her grandmother continued knitting someone — Dewey, most likely — a sweater for Christmas. Had Michael been serious? Had he been playing a joke on her? Was he laughing now, thinking back on her reaction?

He had certainly not said the three words she had been hoping to hear. After her painful confession in the back yard, Dewey was hoping for some form of declaration. Instead, she got a marriage proposition after a titillating kiss.

Dewey turned away from Mamaw to pour herself a glass of

water, touching her cheeks to see if they were, indeed, on fire. She closed her eyes and sighed, reliving how only Michael could make her feel the way she did, or react the way she had. Dear God, Dewey thought, closing her eyes as her body tingled with the memory, that Cajun man could work magic.

Dewey sobered, hoping she hadn't moaned out loud in her brief trip back to ecstasy. What was she thinking last night? Dewey had looked into those chocolate brown eyes she had adored since high school and muttered agreement like a lovesick teenager.

"Yes," she muttered out loud incredulously. "I said yes."

He had smiled when she acquiesced, but not one of triumph. When she starred at him in astonishment, he quickly added that the license alone might make Mamaw come around.

Before Michael had left the porch, he explained how it took a couple of days to get a marriage license in Lafayette Parish, that he knew someone at the courthouse who could speed it through before her plane left on Sunday. Then they could present the license to Mamaw before Dewey headed back. Mamaw, naturally, would insist on a Catholic wedding and those took time, so things would be better between them all until Dewey could return at Christmas. What happened then was the question Dewey had failed to ask.

It was a start, Michael had said, a way to get their grandmother back in their good graces.

"We don't have to go through with it," he had added.

But as crazy as it seemed, even now in the light of day and away from those sensual Cajun lips, something primal and innocent deep inside Dewey wish they would.

She shook her head, hoping to knock sense into her brain matter. "I must be losing my mind," she muttered aloud again.

"You done lost it, *chèr.* Who you talking to?"

She should have been surprised that her grandmother had uttered her first sentence to her that morning — and glad to hear it — but Dewey had too much to think of. She ignored the comment and continued pacing, as much to digest what had happened between she and Michael as to drive her grandmother nuts. She turned toward the window, watching the people with jobs heading toward work and could almost feel her grandmother bristling at her rudeness. It felt good having a moment of being in the driver's seat.

"Who lost what?" came a familiar voice behind her, a voice that once stopped her heart cold and was doing so now, especially when images of their lovemaking came to mind. Dewey tried to ignore the goosebumps skittering up her arms and the fact that she may one day be marrying this man.

She swallowed hard, then turned and faced Michael, who was bending down to plant a kiss on Mamaw's face. Mamaw, back in character, offered a cold cheek.

He straightened and then pushed his hands inside his jeans. "It's so comforting to know that some things never change."

Dewey grinned at him, hoping it wasn't one of those giddy smiles she felt coming on last night. She tossed her head nonchallantly. "What are you doing here?"

His eyes still held that come-hither appeal from the night before which made Dewey shiver. "Looking for you."

"Shouldn't you be at school?" Now that she thought about it, Michael was dressed way too casually. "You're dressed normal today."

"It's an in-service day." He squinted, as if remembering something. "What do you mean, normal?"

"Didn't know preppy was your usual style."

"Preppy, if you mean uniform, happened because of something I said to my kids." He leaned against the old wall radiator, crossing his legs in front of him, looking every bit as delicious in his "Make Levees, Not War" T-shirt and jeans. "They were complaining about having to wear uniforms and me, teaching civil disobedience and all that, said I would join them." He shrugged. "Solidarity thing."

"Ooh, such large words."

"Smartass."

She started a rebuttal with her Cajun derogatory vocabulary, but his eyes grew large as if daring her to even try. So, she chickened out. "Why are you here?"

"Looking for you. You weren't answering your phone."

He mentioned calling her that morning, which was one reason why she felt this license business had all been a joke; he hadn't called. Until she realized she had turned her cell off. In an effort to be free of her father's calls, she forgot about Michael.

"Dang, I turned it off. My dad keeps calling in the early hours. He can't remember I'm not in the same time zone."

Mamaw mumbled something about letting fools know what time zone they were in.

"She speaks," Dewey said with a laugh.

"But she's right," Michael added. "Why don't you tell him to stop calling you so early?"

She had told her father this, but it did no good. The time was convenient for *him*, although she could have made a stronger point about it. Talking back to Walter Hennessey was not an easy task for Dewey. It was a chink in her armor and she resented the two of them pointing it out.

Besides, she was afraid to talk to him at all these days, afraid to discuss the promotion. Or lack of one.

"Who's side are you on?" she asked Michael.

He shook his head. "Not on your dad's, that for sure. You let that man walk all over you. Always have."

Something resembling anger, but most likely shame, brewed inside her, especially when Mamaw made another comment about Dewey's inability to stand up to her dad.

"Fine," she said to Michael softly, "jump to her side and I'll tell her what happened in a certain River Ranch bathroom Halloween night."

Michael held up his hands, grinning. "Do whatever you like with your dad, Dewey. No business of mine."

She folded her arms and sat on the window seat, trying not to laugh. Mamaw glanced briefly at them both, trying to read what had been unspoken, then returned to her knitting as if she couldn't be bothered with either one of them which, they both knew, was a lie. In fact, having the two of them in the same room was probably making her day. Now she could study their interaction, witness firsthand if marriage was in their future.

Michael met Dewey's gaze, seeming to understand where Mamaw's thinking was headed. "I doubt she would care, anyway," he whispered, smelling of that tangy after-shave he loved to use. "As long as we were careful."

Dewey laughed, thinking back on the morning after Michael's father's funeral, when Mamaw had caught them emerging from the shed. She had slapped Michael for being so careless, then whisked Dewey off to a G-Y-N. Mamaw then lectured Michael about responsibility and handed him a pile of condoms while telling him a good Catholic would never use them. Michael had laughed, for which he received his second slap of the day. Neither cuff deterred him. He and Dewey were back at it the following evening in the back of Clotille, the condoms well used.

"These days, I would think she would want us *not* to be careful," Dewey whispered back.

Michael laughed. "Well, I'm not taking chances. I'm not getting slapped again." He rubbed his jaw glancing her way. "Seems to run in the family."

Dewey ignored the comment, trying not to rehash all that was spoken on Halloween night. "You sure were Johnny-on-the-spot in that bathroom. What do you have, like a ready supply in that wallet?"

"Only when you come to town."

Her heart did a little dance. "And such talent. I loved the way you ripped that baby in half with your teeth."

They started laughing then, really laughing, the kind that quickly evolves into hysterics, like a cigarette being thrown from a car, resulting in a brush fire, out of control.

Michael leaned so close she could feel his warm breath on her ear. "I was particularly impressed with the way you orchestrated those toilet flushes."

Dewey closed her eyes in embarrassment, still laughing. "I didn't want anyone hearing us."

"Oh, I think they heard. The neighbors were talking about it all night."

She punched him in the arm, he faked pain and the laughter erupted again.

"Like I said," she managed between bouts, "we need therapy."

Mamaw threw her knitting down in disgust, making them both look up. She took her cane and stood. "I'm going to bingo. You two can sit here and laugh all day, if you want."

Dewey wanted to do just that but Michael stood and held out his hand, pulling Dewey up when she took it. "We're on our way out, too, Mamaw."

Her grandmother huffed and left the room, Dewey and Michael following.

"Where are we going?" Dewey asked when they saw Mamaw safely into the dining hall surrounded by fellow bingo players.

He stretched a hand on the doorframe, studying her. "Court-house. Did you bring your birth certificate?"

He was serious. Or was he? "Did you?"

In a flash, Michael pulled a document from his back pocket.

Well, that answered that question. Still, the whole thing was absurd. She was about to tell him so when her hands moved independently of her brain, pulling out her own birth certificate from her purse — she had found one in Mamaw's document drawer — and paraded it before his eyes.

"Great. Let's go."

Dewey couldn't be positive, but Michael seemed as skeptical about her intentions as she was about his.

"Why are we doing this?" she asked him once inside Clotille as they made their way downtown.

"It's best not to think," was all Michael said, offering up his trademark seductive smile, the one that used to melt her heart and was doing so now.

He had a point.

Neither said a word until they reached the clerk of court's office and Randy Wisner stepped forward, greeting Michael like an old friend.

"You're getting married?" Randy practically shouted. "I can't believe this? I never thought I'd see the day."

Randy glanced at Dewey to view the miraculous woman who had snagged the devoted bachelor Michael Arceneaux. She smiled, hoping she filled the shoes well. When Randy started asking questions, Michael changed the subject, offering up the birth certificates and remarking that he had to get back to school. His friend looked a tad insulted, but Michael assured him he would explain later.

They signed a series of forms, produced birth certificates and driver's licenses.

"Is this happening soon?" Randy asked, handing them the finished product.

Michael and Dewey starred at the clerk at a loss for words, then looked at each other hoping the other one might say something.

"I have to get back to Los Angeles on Sunday," Dewey finally said. "We don't have a date yet."

Randy grinned broadly and leaned over the counter enthusiastically. "I have a friend who got one of those Internet ordainments. She's actually really good. She'll go anywhere and perform any kind of ceremony you want."

Again, Michael and Dewey starred dumbfounded until Michael uttered, "Uh, thanks, Randy."

Still grinning, Randy held up his index finger. "Wait, I have her card here somewhere."

Michael glanced over to Dewey and shrugged. "Guess it wouldn't hurt to have it."

Dewey swallowed hard while her heart skipped a beat. "No," was all she could manage.

Business card and marriage license in hand, the two left the courthouse in silence while Michael drove Dewey to her car in the home parking lot. When he pulled in front, neither one spoke or moved.

Finally, Michael looked her way. "You okay?"

"Yeah. Besides being totally confused."

He ran a lazy arm along the back of the seat, grabbing a strand of her hair with two fingers. "I have to get back to school to my kids. I promised them I would help with their speeches, but I'll be home around three. We can talk then if you want."

So many issues had been aired the night before but other painful memories remained hidden in shadows. She still didn't know how Michael felt, either in high school or in the present, and now they had a marriage license. Where would they go from here?

"Sure. I'll see you then."

He must have known what she was thinking, for he stared at her pensively, the sensual smile and laughter long gone. When he started to speak, some explanatory sentence that began with "Dewey, I...," she threw herself forward, grabbing him in an embrace, holding him close and hoping for the life of her that one hug would solve everything.

Of course it didn't, but when Michael pulled her against him, the world briefly disappeared. Maybe Michael was right. They should forgo thinking and use their hearts instead. If only she knew what was truly in his.

A car honked behind them, jerking them back to normal.

"I need to go," Michael said. "Teens aren't patient people."

Dewey tried to regain some ambivalence. "Apparently, neither is the guy behind us." She grabbed her purse. "Okay, Teach. See you back at the ranch."

She opened the door, but Michael quickly grabbed her hand and pulled her back toward him, delivering a quick but powerful kiss. The car honked again, but Michael ignored it, savoring the moment. Dewey reached up and touched his cheek, then slipped off the seat and exited the truck.

And nearly ran into her mother.

"Wow, that was some kiss."

If Dewey hadn't heard her voice, she might not have recognized Emma, decked out in sunglasses, scarf and a slick pair of scarlet jeans. The way she smiled into the sun, wearing bright red lipstick that matched the paisley scarf and pants, made Dewey laugh.

"You look like a movie star."

This pleased Emma, who shook her head to dangle the curls cascading over her shoulders and leaned forward slightly, arms extended, as if she were taking a bow. "I'll take that."

"What are you doing here?"

"What are you doing kissing that man?"

"Me first."

Emma tossed back her head in Hollywood fashion one last time, then grabbed Dewey's elbow and led them both toward Mamaw's ancient car. "Stopping in on Mom, who's as talkative as usual. Took a cab over."

"Did she even look up from her bingo card?"

"Nope. Stubborn as the devil."

Dewey pulled out the keys. "She actually spoke to me today, said I should tell my father to go to hell."

"I doubt she said those words and yes, you should."

Dewey turned and leaned against the passenger side door. "Do you want a ride or not?"

Emma held up her hands. "Now who's stubborn?"

"Me, but I don't think you have the right to discuss my paternity at the moment."

To her credit, Emma acquiesced. "Point taken."

They climbed into the car and headed west. Dewey hadn't a clue what her mother had in mind, but in Lafayette, Louisiana, on a weekday around lunchtime, it was either home, shopping or a great meal.

"And that guy? Is that Michael?" her mother asked. When Dewey groaned, Emma quickly added, "Baby, you know I'm terrible with faces."

"Yes, Mom. That was Michael."

Emma tapped Dewey's arm, squeezing her affectionately like she did when Dewey was young. "So, is this like, love?"

Funny, how marriage was on the table but that simple word had yet to be spoken. "Uh, I don't know. Well, yes, on my part."

"It sure was a nice kiss."

Dewey sighed, thinking of how wonderful everything Michael did in that regard. "Why are you here?"

Emma pulled down the sun visor and checked her lipstick in the mirror. "The cinematographer got the flu so I have a break in filming until Monday and Danny, the executive producer, gave me some of his miles, so here I am. Wasn't that sweet of Danny?"

"When do you have to go back?"

"Sunday. I tried calling you on your cell."

Dewey bit the inside of her cheek. She had turned the damned thing off just before Michael had picked her up. She needed to call her agent, needed to find out the status of her promotion. Her father had left three messages and she needed to face him as well.

"Well," Emma said when Dewey turned silent. "When do I meet the famous Michael?"

"You can meet him tonight."

Knowing that her mother would meet Michael and that it mattered if she approved filled Dewey with an unexpected warmth. For the first time since she could remember, Dewey wanted to confide in her mom.

"We got a marriage license today."

This stopped Emma cold. She pulled off her sunglasses to get a good look at Dewey's face. "What?"

A long, frustrated sigh escaped Dewey's lips. "It's not what you're thinking. We're hoping it'll make Mamaw happy."

Emma's eyes narrowed. "Are you sure that's what you're doing? Making Mamaw happy?"

Deep in the recesses of Dewey's mind she heard a small voice admitting that the license was making *her* happy, but she pushed it away.

"Of course. I mean, I'm not going to marry someone I've just gotten reacquainted with in fourteen years. That would be crazy."

Something about that statement made Dewey wish she could read her mother's mind, for Emma looked away, lost in thought, nibbling on a nail.

Then Dewey remembered Wagner. "Why did you come back,

Mom?"

She looked back, surprised at the question and with a little guilt lingering in her gaze. "I'm here to spend time with you and Mom."

"And no one else?"

At this, Emma didn't bother hiding anything. "Well, if Patrick shows up, that would be *lagniappe*." Emma blushed, using the Louisiana word for "a little something extra."

"Show up where? Are you seeing him again?"

The sunglasses had been returned to their rightful place, but when Emma turned ever so slightly to glance at her daughter, Dewey caught her eye, sly twinkle included.

"He said something about picking me up for dinner at his place tonight," Emma said dreamy, a lovesick smile gracing her lips.

"Boy, he must be good in bed."

"I'd admonish you to not speak of your father that way, but he's not your father."

"I know."

Emma's smile disappeared. "You do?"

After the shock had worn off and Dewey got used to the idea of Wagner's involvement, it really didn't bother her at all, although she doubted seriously she wasn't a Hennessey. In fact, she was excited about the prospect, not that Wagner might be biologically connected, but that someone out there loved her. Better yet, he cared about her — truly cared — and loved her, no matter the genetics.

"I mean, we really don't look alike and it just doesn't, you know, feel like we are," Dewey explained to her mom. "Not to mention there was that blood test and that you don't think so and I trust you. I think a woman knows these things." Dewey twisted a lock of hair around a finger. "It doesn't matter. He's my father one way or another."

"I'm glad," Emma said softly.

Suddenly, they both felt uncomfortable, as if too much bonding too soon was unnatural. They shifted in their seats, Emma rolling down the window for fresh air. "So, where are we going?

"Well, we're in Lafayette, Louisiana, the culinary hub of South Louisiana." Dewey shrugged. "But if you have a better idea."

At this, Emma laughed, and Dewey quickly joined in. "Definitely, let's go eat. I've got a serious *envie* for crawfish."

The rest of the day sped by much too fast. After lunch, where they enjoyed a Cajun plate lunch special that Lafayette was famous for, which Dewey replicated in simple terms for her blog, the two women cleaned Mamaw's house. That night, Dewey and Emma headed off on their "dates" with Michael and Patrick, although Emma returned home more satisfied, Dewey was sure. Michael maintained his distance, always the perfect gentleman, which left Dewey yearning for more.

By Saturday morning her mother hadn't bothered to return home, left a message on Dewey's cell that she was accompanying Patrick to a school function. While Dewey got dressed, she spotted Sandy and Tyler rushing to meet Kevin in the driveway, apparently on their way to a sugarcane festival.

That meant Michael was alone for the day. Dewey started humming an old tune she loved in high school as she pulled on her jeans and the sweater Michael thought was so sexy at Halloween. Just for safe measure, she tucked a condom she always kept in her purse into the back pocket of her jeans, smiling like a teenager all the while.

Her cell phone buzzing took her away from her carnal thoughts. "Hey Janice," she said to her agent.

"When are you getting back out here?" her agent scolded her. "I have food advertisers waiting to speak with you."

Now, Dewey's smile doubled. Her blog was taking off, the last two posts on plate lunch specials immediate hits, and Janice informed her that Harper Collins was discussing a cookbook deal.

"But I think we should wait until other offers come in," her agent added. "I think we can do better."

"Music to my ears," Dewey said.

"Just get your ass back to the West Coast."

Dewey bit the inside of her cheek. Now for the big question. "Janice, I can continue this blog anywhere, right?"

"What do you mean?" Janice asked.

Dewey grimaced and shut her eyes, afraid to say the thought out loud. "I'm thinking of quitting my job."

There was a long pause before Janice answered. "That's a big move."

Dewey exhaled the breath she was holding. "I know."

"Personally, I would wait on jumping off that cliff until the money comes in but yes, I think it's in your future. We need to get the ad count up, of course. I'd have another source of income just in case. But it may be doable. We'll see what the publishers offer."

Having spent years in Hollywood around writers, Dewey knew book contracts didn't pay much and royalties trickled in after the book was published. Monetized blogs could be a steady source of income, but neither paid as well as what most people imagined. Leaving her well-paying job was very much like jumping off a cliff. So was her next thought.

"What I was thinking, Janice, is not only quitting *That's Entertainment*, but moving back to Louisiana."

Dewey couldn't believe she had admitted as much. Was that what she really wanted? To give up her swank Hollywood job and Santa Monica apartment, only four blocks from the sunny California beach?

Surprisingly, Janice laughed. "Well, you do write a blog about Cajun and Creole cuisine."

Dewey smiled. "Yeah, there is that. But it's really scary to think about, you know?"

And oh so very exciting.

"Well, sure honey," Janice answered, and Dewey doubted her agent had a clue as to the craziness happening in her client's life at the moment. "In this day and age of the Internet, you can write about Louisiana cooking in Alaska."

Now that she let herself believe it, the prospect of moving home flooded Dewey's senses and she tingled with excitement. "Thanks Janice."

"Just get back to L.A. so we put the balls in motion. Or at least let me know so we can arrange Skype sessions if you don't."

"I'll be back in L.A. on Sunday."

Dewey glowed thinking about her future, which suddenly seemed so much brighter. She imagined the possibilities of she and Michael moving into Mamaw's house, he teaching high school and she writing in her bedroom, which she would convert into an office. On the weekends and holidays, she'd accompany him on his photography treks, kayaking into the swamps and wetlands of south Louisiana, catching fresh seafood, cooking up unique dishes in Mamaw's kitchen, which she'd renovate as well.

While her mind had her walking down the aisle and accepting a Saveur Award for Best Food Blog and a Beard Award for that amazing cookbook she was to write, her cell phone buzzed again. Before she had time to check the caller ID, she hit the talk button.

"You're still in Louisiana?"

Give it to her father not to mince words. "Hey, Dad."

"I've been trying to get you at work all week because you weren't answering your cell phone and your coworker tells me you're still in Lafayette."

"Wow, you really miss me."

He ignored her, moving right to the point. "I have a business associate who says he knows your boss. Want me to ask him to give this guy a call?"

"Uh, no thanks, Dad."

"Are you sure you want this promotion? They're not going to give it to you sitting in Louisiana for a week."

Dewey cringed, the sore spot in her stomach biting hard for the first time in days. Maybe her mother was right, the ulcer was directly connected to New York. "I fly out this weekend, Dad. I have it under control."

"Bernice is fine, Dewey. Get back to work."

Now, the stress turned to anger. It was one thing to pressure her on her career, quite another to dish her grandmother. "How the hell would you know? I needed to be here, so leave it at that."

And give it to her Dad to be completely oblivious to anything he did wrong. "What? What did I say?"

She glanced through the windows of her bedroom, noticing Michael working in the kitchen below. The scene gave Dewey strength. "Dad, I have to explain something. It's about the promotion."

"What about it?"

"I wasn't the only one up for the job. And I doubt I will get it."

Silence followed, but in the background Dewey could hear her father parlaying instructions to his secretary.

"Dad, did you hear me?"

"What, honey?"

He really was the most infuriating man. "I said I doubt I will get the promotion. They are probably going to give it to a man less qualified but the perfect obedient type, if you know what I mean." Nothing was decided yet but Dewey wanted to end the distasteful conversation, adding, "It's gone. Nada."

Walter cleared his throat. "If you hadn't been in Louisiana all this time…," he said in a brusque manner.

Dewey gritted her teeth and decided to continue the lie. "They told me before I left."

She wasn't sure why she kept misleading her father, except that maybe it would make the move to Louisiana that much easier. She smiled thinking of that scenario.

A pause followed, which unnerved Dewey as much as his words. "Do you think perhaps you might have messed up here, Caroline? Maybe you didn't work hard enough. Being obedient isn't a bad thing, you know?"

Suddenly, with only a few words and just the right tone her father had reduced her, an accomplished journalist and successful food writer, to a wavering neurotic mess. "I worked my ass off, dad," she said defensively, hating the frantic sound of her voice.

"Obviously not quite enough."

Dewey closed her eyes, fighting off the urge to scream. Why did this man have such a hold on her feelings? Why, just once, couldn't he be proud of her?

"I have some good news," she said, hoping this would do the trick. "My last blog posts went viral and I have several big advertisers wanted to come aboard."

"Well, that's nice, sweetheart, but it's not going to pay the rent. And it certainly isn't *That's Entertainment* magazine."

"I might also have a book deal."

Another pause ensued and she could hear her father talking to someone in the background.

"Dad?"

"Are you sure this is a done deal?" he asked when he came back on the line. "Maybe if you go back into their office and talk to your boss like I told you to."

"It's not totally done yet," Dewey said, feeling her self-confidence drain from her like a faucet. "I'll find out for sure on Monday."

"Well, what are you waiting for?"

To move to Louisiana, do what I love and possibly get married to the man of my dreams, Dewey thought. But when her father started fussing about her lack of motivation and assertiveness, lecturing her on what it takes to make it in the business world, all her hopes and dreams faded away. Suddenly, Michael and their trip to the clerk of court's office made Dewey grimace. What on earth were they thinking? They had just gotten back to being on friendly terms and they got a marriage license? As if they would marry with fourteen long, angry years between them. The blog might be successful now but would it remain so? The Internet was a finicky business and hardly anyone she knew made real money that way. Book sales even less so. All her writer friends had day jobs and what kind of day job, at her level of expertise, would she find in Lafayette, Louisiana?

"I think it's time you got back to L.A. and demand what's due you," her father said.

Dewey sighed, resigned to the forces that continually moved her life. "I'll be heading back this weekend."

"Shall I have someone in my office…?"

"No," she said a little too harshly, then added, "thanks. I'll call you first thing on Monday and we can talk after I meet with the powers that be."

They both shared rushed goodbyes, Walter not offering any form of affection or encouragement. Dewey turned off the phone and threw it on her bed, her heart crashing somewhere around her toes.

"Hey Yankee," she heard a voice call from below. "You hungry for breakfast?"

Dewey turned to check herself in the mirror, suddenly hating the coward looking back at her. She pulled off her sweater and replaced it with something more practical, then pulled on a pair of sneakers.

"I'll be down in a minute," she yelled back.

She glanced around the room, taking note of what clothes needed cleaning before she started packing. She'd go see Mamaw first thing in the morning, show her the insane marriage license and hope that would placate things between them, then catch the late afternoon plane back to California with Emma. Mondays were a slow day at the magazine. She'd have a good thirty minutes to talk to Peter before the budget meeting. Time enough to make her demands.

Looking around the room from her youth, her hopes and dreams as damaged as the days her parents talked her into Columbia, her gaze paused on the brilliant daisies Michael had presented her on their first "date."

What was she going to tell Michael?

Chapter Nineteen

MICHAEL STOOD AT THE STOVE, slowly stirring a mixture of flour and oil in an oversized cast iron skillet, what was to become the roux for that night's gumbo, Dewey's farewell meal.

"I don't know how you do it," Dewey said, sitting on the counter, overlooking the tedious process and snapping photos in the process. "It takes forever."

Michael didn't look up, totally absorbed in his spoon moving round and round the bubbling mixture. "Don't tell me you're never made a roux."

"Yes, of course I have, but my blog is about quick and easy Cajun cooking so I always recommend bottled roux."

Michael grimaced as if an arrow pierced his heart. "Lazy-ass Yank."

"Shut up, *couillon*, or I'll call you something worse. And admit it, if there's bottled roux out there that's just as good, why on earth would you make your own?"

Without skipping a beat, his spoon always scraping against the bottom of the skillet to keep the flour from scorching, Michael turned and sent her a sly smile. "It's soothing. It's satisfying. It's about as close as I'm going to get to meditation. Nirvana for that matter. The joy is in trying to make it as perfect as possible."

She watched him concentrate on keeping the flour and oil mixture from burning while achieving the right color. Michael preferred a darker roux with smoked andouille sausage and chicken, sometimes duck caught in the wetlands outside their town. Uncle Pete had brought over some teal earlier that morning so tonight it would be duck.

"Fetch my beer, *s'il tu plait?*" Michael asked, not able to leave the stove.

"This is definitely why you buy bottled roux."

He sent her that trademark sly Arceneaux grin. "No beer, no Arceneaux gumbo."

Dewey jumped off the counter to retrieve his drink on the kitchen table. "Okay, you win."

Outside of Mamaw's, Michael made the best gumbo Dewey had ever tasted. By far. Even her quick and easy gumbo that was pretty damn good didn't match what was developing in front of her. Her mouth watered thinking about what was to come.

"Get over here."

"Huh?"

Michael turned and motioned with his head.

"No way. I don't want to do that."

Michael took a swig of beer, placed the bottle on the counter and grabbed her with his free hand. He pulled her over, then placed the spoon in her other hand and lead her in the constant stirring, one hand over hers, his body enveloping her from behind. Dewey wished they could forget about cooking and she could close her eyes and absorb the feel of him, but his words drew her out of the fantasy. "Pay attention."

"I am."

She really wasn't and he knew it and he started muttering sentences in French.

"I am not lazy," she retorted, grabbing the spoon out of his hand and stirring it around and around the skillet, watching the flour slowly brown and careful not to let the whole thing literally go up in smoke. "This is so boring."

"It makes you introspective." Michael grabbed his drink and

moved to her place on the counter, snapping his own photos and watching her every move as if one wrong turn would ruin his precious meal.

Dewey tried to clear her anxious mind, but one thought kept popping back in. "Are we really going to show Mamaw the license tomorrow?"

"Don't you want to?"

She turned to look at him, but his eyes enlarged and his head motioned back to the stove. "Don't burn my roux!"

Dewey groaned and returned her focus to the skillet. "It's not like I live down the street, you know. Do we really want to get her hopes up?"

Suddenly, the sound of the spoon making its rounds on the cast iron, like a blacksmith sharpening a blade saw, was the only noise in the kitchen. Dewey expected Michael to change the subject or ignore the problem at hand, but he surprised her.

"I can't go to L.A., Dewey."

She stared at the flour turning darker before her, amazed at how disappointing that statement felt, despite the fact that she knew it all along. "I know you can't."

"My family is here. I can't leave them."

Two simple sentences cut straight to her heart and lodged there like a bullet. Wasn't she family?

On the other hand, she knew exactly what he meant and what he had in Lafayette. During the past week she had hung out with them all, watching LSU play Alabama that afternoon, barbecuing delectable things in the back yard, cooking, laughing and "passing a good time," as they say in Cajun country. It felt easy, comfortable, and in a day's time she would give it all up, go back to the cold realities of Hollywood, where family was something she watched on the Silver Screen.

"Sandy needs me," he continued. "She can't handle Tyler alone. Wagner has become like a father and Mamaw, well, I can't leave Mamaw."

"I know," Dewey whispered, but the hurt remained.

"Do you?"

She wanted to look at him, examine his eyes to see what he meant, but tears were too close to the surface. Michael moved along the counter to be closer, to look into Dewey's eyes or keep a watch on his roux, she wasn't sure.

"Mamaw used to always tell us we were loved. I never knew who she was talking about, considering my situation. But that was because I was too busy focusing on my dad. At the same time, I had my Uncle Pete. I had Mamaw. I later had Sandy when Dad remarried."

Dewey nodded. Mamaw had said the same thing to her, always reminding Dewey to be thankful for those in her life, not those who neglected her. She had the Cajun Embassy, the best friends a woman could ask for. She had her mom, and before the year was up, she might have another dad.

Then she thought of her father in New York who waited for her phone call on Monday. She had made up her mind to head back to Hollywood and fight for her promotion but deep down the promise of living here, with Michael, doing what she loved still hung heavy on her heart.

She glanced at Michael and wondered still if he loved her. Could they make a life together, make their own little family?

No, things weren't that simple. Yes, she was grateful for the love in her life, but what about the people she needed most?

"You're burning it."

Dewey quickly looked down and realized she had stopped turning the spoon. She resumed the ritual, wiping away a tear with her free hand without Michael noticing. "Sorry."

After another lengthy pause, Michael brought the subject back up. "Are you having second thoughts?"

"Are you?"

He laughed. "I asked first."

No, they most certainly would not move past high school.

"Again, I live two thousand miles away."

"So, come home."

He said it with such force, like a command, Dewey wanted with all her being to hear it followed with a declaration of love.

"And do what, Michael? I'm an entertainment journalist."

Michael sighed and hung his head, then he shook it while uttering more French expletives. "We're not the third world."

"I know that."

"Journalists from around the globe come here to write about our food, our culture. Zydeco. Cajun music."

"I know that too."

"Isn't that entertainment?"

Dewey let out a large breath. As far as she was concerned, Acadiana had three times as much culture per square inch than all of Los Angeles, but that didn't mean she could make a living here.

"Dewey," Michael continued, "the New York Times and those kinds of people come here regularly. We like the recognition, but we read these articles, spending more time searching to see what they got *right*. And then there's those stupid movies that put Cajuns in New Orleans or make Cajuns look stupid. New Orleanians all sound like they're from Atlanta. And if it's set in Louisiana, you know it involves voodoo, swamps and corruption."

"So, you want me to take on the movie industry as well?"

Michael paused in his diatribe, then smiled. "*Mais*, yeah."

Dewey couldn't help herself; she laughed as well, if anything, to dislodge the lump in her chest. "I'll give it a try."

"You have that blog that everyone's talking about."

"Well, I don't know if everyone's..."

"Can't you live off that?"

She swallowed hard after the lump reached her throat. "Maybe. If I get enough advertisers."

"But you like doing it?"

She loved it. Really loved it. Writing her blog was her greatest achievement in life so far, unless she could finally manage this roux. "Of course, but how will I pay the rent?"

Michael groaned, uttering more phrases in French, making Dewey look up from her work. "Stop calling me that and get real. I mean, really Michael. It takes years to build up a successful blog and make money out of writing."

He stopped his French tirade and shook his head. "I have great health benefits being a teacher, so you wouldn't have to worry about that. You know Mamaw isn't coming home. So you have an empty house next door and it's rent free."

Dewey didn't care about the damn flour for a moment; she paused and gazed into Michael's eyes for confirmation. Because, despite the casualness of what he just said about benefits, which only come with marriage, it was the closest thing to admitting love.

For the first time, she actually believed they might get married.

Michael gazed back, seeming to read her thoughts. Then his brow furrowed and he appeared to want to say something. This could be it, Dewey surmised. Say it, she whispered inside her head. Tell me you care.

Instead, the flour bubbled and Michael jumped to her side. He grabbed the spoon and started stirring again. Neither one said a word as he finished the roux and pushed it off the burner.

Dewey felt it best to change the subject. "How do you know when it's ready?"

"You remember Uncle Pete's boyfriend? Wayne?"

"Yeah."

"When the roux gets as dark as his arm, it's ready."

Dewey laughed. Everyone in her Louisiana family cooked that way. "How much flour do you use?" she had asked Mamaw when they made her famous biscuits.

"Two handfuls," Mamaw had replied. "But handfuls the size of my hands, not yours."

When cooking jambalaya Dewey had asked, "How much cayenne do you put in?"

"Whatever makes it taste right."

"So I need to find a black man in L.A. to determine my roux?" Dewey asked Michael.

"No, you need to find a black man the color of *Wayne*."

Michael began assembling the ingredients to put in the gumbo pot, along with the roux, a concoction that would simmer until the meat became tender. "Remember our first date?" he asked.

Dewey furrowed her brow. "High school or Grand Coteau?"

Now it was Michael's turn to frown. "We never *dated* in high school."

Dewey laughed. "Oh right."

"You said you weren't happy in L.A."

Dewey exhaled deeply and nabbed Michael's beer from the counter, tossing back the ingredients. "It's a long story."

Michael dropped the last of the andouille into the pot and leaned back against the counter. "Unlike a certain someone's *Louisiana Simple* blog, this gumbo is Louisiana Long. So explain."

Dewey discussed the whole story of trying out for the job at work only to be bypassed by a man with less qualifications. She talked about how hard she had worked during the trial period, how many jobs she picks up on a weekly basis when others drop the ball, how management depends on her when the going gets tough but refuses to reward her in the end. By the time she finished, she felt the old anger brewing inside and realized how much she hated going back.

There was a small pause before Michael finally answered. "So quit."

She huffed. "It's not that easy."

He gazed at her, completely serious. "Why not?"

She started to list the many reasons, but for a brief second drew a blank. For a beat, she really had no cause to return to the grind. Thinking back to her phone call that morning, it all came back to her.

"My dad thinks I should go in there and confront my boss, giving the same reasons to promote me as I just listed to you. It's a matter of principle. I deserve this raise."

Michael grimaced when she mentioned her father and then turned back to the stove, shaking his head.

"It's not that easy," Dewey insisted.

He threw the cut sausage and duck rather harshly into the pot, then turned toward her. "It's not easy walking out the door of a place that screwed you? Or it's not easy telling Daddy that you're giving up a plush job to move back to a hick state."

This incensed Dewey. "I've never thought of Louisiana that way."

"Perhaps, but he does, doesn't he?"

Yes, he did, but she wasn't going to tell him that or that her father moved heaven and earth in high school to get her to New York so she wouldn't end up married and pregnant with Michael, living in Louisiana. Even now, she couldn't imagine telling her father that she had given up her plum job in the world's finest entertainment magazine to marry Michael and move back to Lafayette.

Michael seemed to read her thoughts for his eyes narrowed. "You haven't changed a bit," he bit out through clenched teeth. "You're going to give up any chance of happiness by trying to impress that asshole?"

"He's not an ass, he's still my dad."

"Who would have forgotten your birthday if it wasn't for his secretary."

Dewey chewed a nail and looked away, thinking about how he had forgotten last year's completely.

Michael grabbed her shoulders forcing her gaze back. "Dewey, do what you want with your Dad, but don't let him rule your life."

In some deep place inside her soul Dewey knew he was right, but she wasn't ready to admit it and face that painful darkness. "He doesn't rule my life, Michael."

Michael released her, letting forth more French criticism. Dewey couldn't stand it anymore. She spilled her own French expletives and admonishments. He stopped talking and gazed at her, amazed, which ticked her off even more.

"Yes, I speak French, *couillon*," she continued in the Latin language. "I was in French immersion since kindergarten."

Furious, Dewey turned, gripping her hands on the sink and gazing out on the bayou running behind the house. The tranquil scene before her made her wish she wasn't leaving, which only fueled her anger.

"You don't know," she whispered. "You just don't know."

The trouble was, Michael knew exactly how she felt. He would have continued the argument — anything to make her face up to the problems with her father — had she not reverted to French in the middle of it all. Hearing Dewey speak his language fired him up like the heat burning under his gumbo.

He had managed to keep his hands off her since they had obtained the license, wanting to take things slowly, to build up their relationship. Yet, standing there in his kitchen, her chin tilted upwards defiantly as if to fight off the world, Michael didn't care about any of that. She was his Dewey, despite everything, and he needed to let her know, in the only way he knew how.

From her back, Michael pushed her hair from the side of her face, whispering in French for her to take a breath and relax. She responded by shifting away from him, that one muscle leading up to the base of her skull tight as taunt rope.

"I just want you home," he whispered in English as he kissed the small recess of skin where her neck met her shoulders.

The kisses did the trick; she finally began to relax her grip on the sink. But, only slightly.

"I'm not like you, Michael," she whispered back. "I've never been able to stand up to my dad."

That had hardly been his case, considering his father was drunk half the time and avoiding him the other half. He couldn't remember when he had spoken back to his dad, except for the fatal night when he tried to pry the car keys away. For Michael, he had been forced to come to grips with an unbridled anger after his father's death, mainly because he wasn't able to stand up to him anymore. But one thing Michael had learned over the years. After a certain age, a person's life is his own making.

"Dewey, this is your life now. You make of it as you wish."

She started to retort, but he stopped her by gently biting the skin on the back of her neck. "Actually, we're a lot alike." He sucked the skin between his lips, knowing he would brand her with a hickey. "We're both stubborn as hell."

She stiffened, moving her head away a little. "What does that supposed to mean?"

That he wanted her in his bed every day. That these old fears and heartaches of hers holding up a wall, keeping him out, had to come crashing down.

As usual, he wanted to tell her just that, but couldn't find the words. So he spoke with his hands.

Deftly, he reached down and unleashed the top button of her jeans and pulled down the zipper, while his left hand slipped up underneath her sweater and found a perfect breast. He felt her stiffen and mutter his name, but he was going to tear down that wall right now. Instantly, one hand found a nipple and squeezed while the other slipped down her pants to find the origin of all female pleasure.

Dewey gasped and her fingers tightened on the sink and Michael thought he heard her say something, but he wasn't paying attention. He kissed her nape until he reached her ear lobes, then his teeth and tongue teased both while one hand fondled her nipple and the other massaged her below.

Finally, Dewey melted and groaned, leaning her head back against him and stretching her legs apart to give him more room inside. She was hot against his hands, so eager and ready. He could feel her waiting to burst.

"Come to me," Michael whispered in French. "Come home to me."

Dewey called out his name as she shuttered with the climax, falling limp in his arms after the waves of pleasure coursed through her. When Michael shifted his hands, Dewey turned and fell into his waiting arms.

"That's so unfair," she whispered, now nuzzling her face into the side of his neck.

"What? That I can make you happy?" When she didn't answer, Michael wanted to shake her. "You're allowed, you know?"

She straightened, peering up into his eyes, the haze of her passion suddenly gone. "I'm allowed what? To be seduced at a kitchen sink by a French-talking Cajun who's quick with his hands? To get married on a lark to make my grandmother happy?

"Tell me," she continued, her gaze steel, "what happens after we show her the license?"

Michael truly had no clue. It was one future he purposely avoided considering. All he knew was that Mamaw, in some fluke of bizarre reality, was right. They needed to be together. The rest would take care of itself.

Yet, gazing into Dewey's hurt, angry eyes and hearing her questions made him doubt it all. What would they do?

"I don't know, *mon petite chou*," he whispered while the tips of his fingers outlined her face. "I really don't."

She started to retort, but he stopped her with a kiss. "All I know is I want you in my bed."

She turned her head away, brow furrowed, and he knew what she was thinking. That everything led to sex, always had, and what did it all mean? He remembered their lengthy conversation on their big date, when she had confessed about believing he had been with other women. Imagine! His whole life had always been Dewey. Still was.

He gently turned her face back, letting his thumb roll over her lips, then reversing his hand and caressing her cheek with his knuckles.

There was so much he wanted to say, so many unspoken emotions between them. It all rose inside him like a mad rush of adrenaline and halted somewhere near his heart. For a blinding second, Michael swore he could feel his father's sting on his cheek. In that same striking moment, grimacing from the pain of the memory and the fact that he couldn't adequately speak what he felt, he knew Sandy had been right. He was emotionally stifled.

To his surprise, Dewey touched his cheek, as if she knew what memory had flitted across his mind. Then she pulled him close and they embraced, Michael's arms tight about her waist, as if his hold on her could keep her from leaving.

"Stay with me tonight," he whispered, not wanting to lose one minute of touching her.

"What about the gumbo?"

Michael grinned and pulled back. "Sex. Gumbo. Must one have to choose?"

Dewey smiled back, but her hand returned to his face, as if to remind him where they left off. The simple gesture caught his breath.

"Sex first, then gumbo," he whispered, then took her hand, kissed the inside of her palm and led her down the hall, up the stairs and into his room.

Chapter Twenty

THE HOUSE WAS DEADLY SILENT as Sandy led Kevin in through the back door carrying a dead-to-the-world Tyler on his shoulders, his fingers still gripping the Mickey Mouse balloon Kevin had bought him. She passed dirty gumbo bowls on the kitchen table and the stove was a mess – so unlike Michael to leave cleaning for the morning. Unless…

When Sandy opened the door to her bedroom and paused in the hallway to let Kevin bring Tyler inside, she turned her ear to the neighboring door, hoping to hear two voices coming from Michael's room. At the moment, all was quiet, except for the distant thunder announcing a storm heading their way.

She followed Kevin and helped him put her son to bed, then tucked her baby in with a warm blanket. Kevin helped, smiling at the sweet cherub asleep before them.

"He's a sweet kid."

Sandy smiled in the darkness. "Particularly when he's sleeping."

Kevin studied her with the same, appreciative gaze, which made Sandy shift her feet nervously. "Want some coffee?"

Kevin leaned forward and kissed her, as he had all evening long, something chaste and sweet considering Tyler but lurking with the promise of deeper satisfaction later. Sandy was getting used to the constant affection. Almost.

She straightened. "I'll go put the pot on."

She failed to see if Kevin was following down the stairs and hallway, but she felt his presence at the kitchen doorway as she poured the coffee pot full of fresh water. The change in his attitude was as obvious as the air pressure falling outside. "Did I do something wrong?"

Sandy sighed, lost for the adequate words. She wondered if failing to communicate was a genetic trait. Kevin moved to the sink, leaning back against the counter so he could peer into her eyes.

"If you don't want to do this, tell me. I'll go."

Sandy poured the water into the coffeemaker and hit the on button.

"I don't want you to go, that's the problem."

"That doesn't make sense."

Sandy stared at the steam rising from the machine.

"Nothing makes sense in my family, Kevin. Haven't you noticed?"

"Is it Tyler?"

Sandy grimaced as if struck. "Of course, it's Tyler. He's my baby and he always comes first."

Now, it was Kevin who looked assaulted. "When have I not agreed with that?"

That wasn't what she meant. What did she mean? Sandy turned her back to him and began removing cups and saucers from the cabinets.

"Sandy? Damn it, what is going on here?"

Anger pushing her forward, she turned, cups still hanging from her fingertips.

"I was always careful, Kevin. Always. Tyler's dad was a sweet-talking, get-in-your-pants kinda guy and I fell for it, hard, my steadfast logic forgotten along with the condom. And I got pregnant from the first date."

Kevin started to say something, but Sandy continued while she had the impetus. "He took off after that. No money, no word, no nothing. I have no idea where he is. I don't even know who his family is.

"My family was pissed. My friends deserted me. And I ended up with this fabulous child who barely hears me because his brain doesn't have enough chemicals to allow him to focus. If it hadn't been for Michael, I might have thrown myself off a bridge a long time ago. But, here I am."

Kevin gazed at her deeply, his dark eyes appearing larger through his glasses. "Here you are."

She exhaled and blew out years of frustration and anger. "Here I am."

Kevin reached for her, but Sandy stepped back. "I know I've made bad decisions with men, probably because deep inside I knew nothing would come of it. How could anything come of it with Tyler? Who's going to take on a woman with a mentally unstable child? It is a disorder, you know? Doctors didn't make this shit up."

Now, her voice was rising and she worried about waking Michael, and hopefully Dewey who was sleeping alongside him. Her heart thumped loudly in her chest, as if echoing the thunder rattling the windowpanes. Sandy realized that years of people staring at Tyler as if he were a brat, of having to defend the doctors and their diagnoses to family and teachers, plus the hazards of dealing with a hyperactive child had taken a toll on her. She stretched her arms on the counter for support and took a deep breath.

"Sandy."

Kevin was touching her cheek and she felt another hand at her waist, but everything had turned dark before her. She was almost seeing stars from the emotions raging inside her.

"Sandy."

Finally, she took a deep breath and looked up into his eyes, finding Kevin smiling.

"I can understand your defensiveness, but you got the wrong man, babe."

He slipped his arm around her waist and pulled her close, kissing her soundly, not worrying that anyone was watching this time. When he finally pulled back, Sandy did see stars.

"Tomorrow or the next day or whenever you feel the time is right, we'll go visit my mom and she will tell you all kinds of stories about my hyperactive childhood. Then she'll laugh and say she wished for this."

"Wished for what?"

"That I would get to experience what I gave her."

Sandy dropped her head against his forehead. "I can't fall in love with you, Kevin, if you're going to reject us both later."

He placed a finger at her chin and raised her face up to his. "Haven't you heard a thing I've been saying? I love you. I love Tyler. And although I don't know what you've had to deal with — and have to deal with — I do know exactly what Tyler's going through."

When she started to object, he touched a finger to her lips to silence her. "It's time, sweetheart. It's time to let Michael have his own life and for you to have yours. It's time for you to be happy."

Sandy wanted to with all her heart, but old fears and heartaches held her back. Still, looking in eyes that shined love and affection for her was breaking down her defenses.

"You do realize that genetics are against us here."

"You mean, we may have another ADHD kid? Yeah, I've thought of that, but then I'd have that chance with any woman since I carry the gene."

Dear God, Sandy thought. Another ADHD kid?

Kevin appeared as if he read her mind.

"Or maybe one child is enough."

They both smiled, leaning their foreheads together.

"The couch?" Kevin finally asked.

Sandy listened, waiting for some sign of movement from above. Knowing Tyler would not waken and hoping Michael would stay put, she kissed Kevin her yes.

A chorus of birds woke Dewey before dawn. She slipped her feet silently over the side of the bed and glanced out Michael's bedroom window where several species gathered around Mamaw's bird feeder, no doubt part of the Mississippi Flyway migration down south. Like an internal clock, the birds knew when to flee, when to head to safer climates.

The world looked strange from Michael's vantage point, as if her childhood had been flipped like a photo. All those years she had sat at her window talking to Michael as friends, then pinning for him in silence, hoping she'd get a peek at the boy next door and he would feel the same way. Now she was gazing back, spotting her juvenile posters on her wall, the brightly colored comforter on her bed, the silly bowling trophy she won in third grade.

And all the pain of her youth.

Her own alarm clock rang. Time to fly.

Michael was still sleeping, one arm stretched lazily across the bed, his thick black hair tossed across his forehead and a slight smile on his lips. They had made exquisite love the night before, slow and purposeful as if for the very first time.

Holding hands they had entered Michael's room and closed and locked the door behind them.

"In case Sandy and Tyler come home," Michael had said.

Dewey thought to suggest her bedroom but curiosity got the better of her. She gazed around the room she had dreamed about for years, one she knew intimately as a youth when the two had played board games here, listened to CDs and watched old movies on Michael's then ancient television. Somewhere between ninth grade and today, the room became off-limits, especially after the shed incident; Mamaw strictly forbade them anywhere near each other's bedrooms.

It was different than Dewey expected, but then Michael never went gone pecan. The walls were a lovely light gray with an oversized chair by the window where a stack of books was piled. His photographs graced the walls, no doubt his favorites. Dewey recognized the sleepy swamp scene; she had a duplicate hanging over her bed in California.

"I have a confession to make," she whispered as Michael caressed her arms.

"You've never made a roux in your life." He kissed the curve of her neck.

Dewey laughed. "When you come to L.A. I will make you *my* gumbo and you'll be amazed. And no, that's not it."

Michael pulled back to look into her eyes, but his fingers now traveled up from her breastbone to her cheek and she shivered. Then his lips replaced them.

"Mamaw has been buying your photos every Christmas for an anonymous art dealer in California," Dewey said, trying to keep a steady head but leaning sideways to give him more room at her nape. "I'm that person."

Michael paused and gazed back at her questioningly. Then a sparkle began in his eyes and grew until it lit up his face.

"That was you?"

"I'd say that one was my favorite." She nodded toward the swamp scene. "And I do love it. But I'm partial to Geno Delafose. Nothing like a zydeco man in a cowboy hat."

Still sporting a raging grin — Dewey wondered if she admitted her love right then and there if it would have the same impact — Michael headed for his closet and returned wearing a cowboy hat.

"What the...?"

"Door prize at the speech and debate regionals in Dallas." Michael tipped it back, making him look like adorable Curley from *Oklahoma*. The Hugh Jackman version.

Dewey wasted no time encircling her arms about his neck and meeting those smiling lips. Michael didn't hesitate to do the same. He pulled her so close, their hips practically touching, she felt he was as anxious to make love as she was. As they deepened the kisses and his hands roamed over her back, dipping down to the ridge of her bottom, Dewey's fingers headed to his waistband. She managed to release the belt buckle but his hand gripped hers when she attempted the zipper.

"We need to go slow."

Dewey let out a large exhale, her heart still beating wildly. "Why?"

Michael touched his forehead to hers, his breathing ragged as well. "Because we need to do it right this time, *chér.*"

Dewey reached up and caressed his cheek, wanting this man so badly she felt she might combust. "Michael, despite everything that's happened between us, we have always done *this* right."

Michael paused, gazing deep into her eyes. Then he grinned slyly, threw his arms around her waist, picked her up and carried her to the bed. "You're right. Fuck it."

And that was the first of her trips to heaven that night, with Michael's delectable gumbo energizing them at intermission. Clothes were quickly discarded, thrown about the room in abandon but not before Dewey pulled her condom from the back pocket of her jeans.

Michael leaned on an elbow, grinning. "Expecting something?"

"Hell yeah," she answered, and met his lips.

Like so many times before, their rush to fulfillment took on a fevered acceleration, but when they were finally naked on the bed, Michael slowed the process down. He teased with deep, sensual kisses while his hands explored every inch of her body. Dewey, too, slid her hands across his chest, wondering again when he had turned so buff, then trailed a finger down the line of hair reaching to his manhood.

Michael reacted to her touch, smiling slyly and slipping his own fingers between her legs, which made her gasp with pleasure. While he explored her inner femininity, she grabbed his thighs, then reached around to his bottom to pull him closer still.

"Slowly, darling, slowly," he whispered.

Slow would come later, after a bowl of gumbo. Dewey pushed Michael hard so that he released her. She then straddled him while pushing him back on the bed. "Fuck that."

Michael laughed but wasn't about to let her have the last say.

He grabbed her bottom and pushed himself into her, which made Dewey lean back and moan to the heavens. Then with a swift move, the two of them still joined together, he moved Dewey on to her back and began the dance they knew so very well. Gazing into each other's eyes, Michael deftly pulled one of Dewey's leg up around his waist and plunged deeper.

It was lust, pure and simple, Dewey remembered, looking into those dark Cajun eyes. They could have remained that way until bliss washed over them both. But Michael leaned down and kissed her ever so sweetly.

It was the closest he had come to a declaration of love. Even as they had lain in each other's arms afterwards, Michael planting kisses, his arms wrapped tightly around her, words had refused to come. The best of friends, perhaps soul mates, Dewey should have known what was going on inside his mind. But fear and doubts took over by morning's light and now it was time to go home.

Dewey slipped back to her pillow and laid eye to eye with the sleeping man she adored, breathing in his scent, marking the moment to memory. For a moment she imagined jobs, family and responsibilities disappearing with the coming of the dawn. She could slip back under the sheets and hold on to him tightly, wish the world away.

But it was never that easy.

Dewey left the warm bed and gathered her clothes, throwing on her jeans and sweater and quietly exiting the bedroom she had dreamed of for years. She tiptoed around Sandy and Tyler sleeping peacefully on the couch, their arms entwined, gathered her purse and slipped out the back door of the Arceneaux household.

Except for the colorful birds eating breakfast on Mamaw's porch, the house was silent and still, Emma locked in Patrick's arms in a faraway bedroom. Her bags already packed and an Uber waiting on the curb, Dewey commanded herself not to cry as she left by the front door and headed for the Lafayette airport.

Chapter Twenty-one

PATRICK SLOWLY DROVE INTO THE Arceneaux driveway, parking behind Michael's truck as quietly as possible.

"What are you worried about?" Emma said with a laugh. "That the kids will disapprove."

Patrick gently pulled up the emergency brake, then killed the engine. "Hell yeah."

Emma wasted no time erasing the distance between them and Patrick pulled her into his arms, kissing her soundly.

"I so love you," he whispered when they finally came up for air.

"I love you, too," Emma answered, nestling her face into the crook of his shoulder.

He wanted to stay there forever, forget the problems they faced, such as where they would live and how they would juggle careers. And yet, those four words Emma spoke gave him the clarity he needed.

"I'm of retirement age, you know."

Emma met his gaze with a sassy smile. "Are you saying I'm kissing a senior citizen?"

Patrick smiled and weaved a lock of her hair behind an ear. "We're the same age, sweetheart."

Emma grimaced. "Don't remind me. These days all I'm getting are mom and grandmother roles."

"Grandmother? Hardly."

"Well, I wouldn't mind a grandchild."

Neither would he, Patrick thought, which gave him courage.

"I'm a teacher. Retirement comes early — and well it should."

This time, Emma leaned back and cool air settled between them. Patrick didn't know what would come of his next declaration but it was now or never. It was the answer to everything. "I can retire at the end of the school year. Move to Los Angeles in May."

Emma's eyes enlarged and Patrick wondered if she would laugh, then flee, like she did the last time he proposed. Instead, she smiled, first tentatively, then into a large grin. She leaned forward and wrapped her arms about him tightly. "Yes."

They remained locked in each other's arms for what seemed like an eternity until Patrick released her, held her face in his hands and kissed her once more.

"Let's go tell the kids," he whispered.

They giggled, holding hands as they walked up the driveway. As they turned to head into Mamaw's house, Patrick caught movement out of the corner of his eye. Michael sat on his top porch step, staring off toward the bayou.

"Michael?"

Patrick wasn't sure the boy heard for he continued starring, his gaze blank. Shivers rode up Patrick's arms.

"Michael."

This time, his old friend looked his way but those dark Cajun eyes seemed to register nothing. It was then Patrick noticed the note in his hands and Emma voiced what Patrick immediately thought.

"Dewey left?"

Michael came to life then, albeit slightly. He lifted the letter and smiled sadly. "At least I read it this time."

Patrick and Emma joined him on the stoop, sitting on either side.

"She was supposed to leave with me this afternoon," Emma

said. "I don't understand."

Michael handed her the note. "You know your daughter, not one for goodbyes."

Emma shook her head. "No. I've never seen her so happy these last couple of days. Something must have happened."

As Emma stood and began pacing the yard reading the note, Patrick felt betrayed as well. And guilty. Did he do this?

"Is this my fault?" he asked. "Is it because of the paternity test?"

Michael laughed but it was a hollow one. "She had her gumbo. It was time to leave. As she so brilliantly explains in her letter, she has a life back in L.A. that she can't give up."

Emma stopped reading. "She hates her job."

Michael rubbed his hands across his morning stubble. "She told me that too. I guess Louisiana wasn't enough to keep her here."

Emma shook her head and approached them both. She held the note high in her hand. "This has her father written all over it." She looked hard at Michael. "You of all people should know that."

Michael sobered, but his gaze was skeptical.

Emma looked at Patrick. "This has nothing to do with paternity tests either. Dewey has been trying to impress that ass of a father her whole life — forgive me for calling him that but it's true. And now he's pressuring her about a promotion so he can brag to his friends his daughter works at the finest entertainment magazine in the world."

Like the clarity he received in the car, Patrick instantly understood. It had always been that way with Dewey. No matter how many times her father forgot her birthday, cited business as a refusal to come to the phone, pushed her into situations she never agreed with, Dewey still pined for his attention. An anger deep and old rose to the surface, one born of watching another man throw away something beautiful and perfect.

When he looked at Michael, ready to spur the boy into action, Michael was already on his feet, in the yard and gazing down the driveway.

"Your car's behind me," he yelled back to Patrick. "Give me your keys."

A pride so intense rose inside him knowing that Michael wasn't going to suffer in silence this time and that he would fight for the love of his life. That the three people he cared most about in the world would finally be happy. Patrick stood and threw him the keys and Michael headed off.

Emma came to his side and watched as Michael drove off in a fury. She exhaled deeply. "Well, shit."

Patrick turned to the woman he adored — always had — who seemed to glow in the early morning light despite her mused hair and wrinkled clothes. God, he loved this woman.

"What?"

Emma's shoulders dropped and she shook her head. "Damn my mother. She's always right."

Dewey had convinced herself leaving was the right course of action but as the Uber neared the airport, a pain deep inside stabbed at her heart and caused her head to ache. She rubbed her chest and commanded the little voices inside her to cease their racket, that of course she had to return to her job, her apartment, the life she left behind. Then why did she feel as if she were about to come unglued?

She paid the woman and grabbed her bags with the smiley face labels and headed to the Delta counter to officially change her ticket and check her bags. There were three people in front of her and Dewey closed her eyes in frustration, not because she hated waiting in line but because the pause might unravel her for sure. A body in motion and all that. The hiatus worked its magic; a lone tear fell down her cheek.

"Leaving home?"

Dewey opened her eyes to find a middle-aged woman dressed in the scarlet colors of the University of Louisiana at Lafayette.

Afraid to speak and start bawling for sure, Dewey nodded.

The woman rubbed Dewey's arms as if they were family, that friendly comaraderie among strangers so prevalent in South Louisiana. "I know. It's hard leaving those you love."

Again, Dewey could only nod.

"I live in Houston now, got a job there when oil prices fell and my company laid me off. But I sure miss my family in Lafayette." The woman grinned. "Not to mention the food."

More arrows into the heart. Dewey could work here, do what she loved instead of tolling at her miserable job.

"My whole family was at my mom's house last night for gumbo," the woman continued, gazing off as if the family table existed just behind the baggage claim. "With the weather turning cooler…I don't think I had a better meal."

Dewey swallowed hard, wondering if this woman was peeking inside her soul. "Me too," she managed to whisper.

"I don't care what they say about places like New York City, but the food here is to die for." The woman's gaze sparkled. "But maybe it's because of the love we put into it."

For a second Dewey seriously wondered if this woman was sent there by Mamaw. She wouldn't put it past her grandmother to call upon the heavens to deliver an angel her way. Regardless, Dewey got the message. Loud and clear. The pain gripping her heart turned into a burst of sunshine. She knew what to do, and it ignited every cell in her body.

Dewey let go of her suitcase and pulled the woman into a bear hug. "Thank you," she whispered.

The woman hugged her back and laughed. "For what?"

Dewey released her and wiped the tears streaking her face. "For stopping me from doing something really stupid."

"Glad to hear it." And with that the woman hugged her again as if they were, indeed, family. After all, it was Lafayette and no doubt they probably were.

Dewey smiled when the line moved and the woman waved. She pulled her suitcases into the lobby and gazed around. She needed to get home. Fast. Before Michael woke up and realized she was gone pecan.

Dewey sighed and looked heavenward. That was doubtful. Michael was a teacher, rose early. No doubt the damage had been done. What on earth was she thinking? And what was she so afraid of? How could a grown, successful woman making demands of the most powerful man in Hollywood not be able to stand up to her non-committal father and to realize a man's love when she feels it, despite whether he says the words or not? The now familiar pain in her heart returned and her shoulders dropped. She screwed up. Again. Tears found gravity once more.

Dewey had no idea what to do next, stood paralyzed in the middle of Lafayette's airport, when a man ran past in a blur. She caught him out of her peripheral view but didn't think much of it at first. People ran through airports all the time, trying to catch planes.

And yet…

Dewey turned and spotted Michael staring up at the departures board, studying the flights anxiously. He stood intent on figuring out which flight she would have been taking, but he felt her gaze upon him and glanced her way. For a moment he didn't see her, turned back towards the board. Then he realized she was standing next to him and turned again.

More tears emerged and all Dewey could utter was "I'm sorry."

In two strides Michael was at her side, pulling Dewey into his embrace and holding her so tight she could barely breathe. She didn't care. He was here. It was going to be okay.

"I'm sorry," she repeated.

Michael pulled back, took her tear-streaked face into his hands and rested his forehead against hers.

"Don't leave," he commanded. "You can go back to L.A. tonight with your mother but you're not leaving now."

Dewey nodded obediently.

"You understand that? You are not leaving now."

Dewey laughed through her tears. "Yes, sir."

Michael smiled and tears leaked from the corners of his eyes. He sighed deeply, then gazed at her with so much love Dewey thought she would melt on the spot.

"I love you, Dewey Hennessey."

She knew what pain emerged with those words, but she was not his father. And she would not return to an unsatisfied job because *her* father wanted her to. They would find love despite the men who once controlled their lives. Their love would light the way.

"I love you too, Michael Arceneaux."

He kissed her then, long and hard and passionate, not caring who watched. When he finally released her, Michael grabbed her suitcases and took her hand.

"We have some planning to do."

Chapter Twenty-two

NAPS WERE GOD'S GIFT TO the old, Mamaw thought as she snuggled deeper into her armchair. So was the warm sunlight flitting in through her window, warming her face. The autumn glare might have caused discomfort on her eyelids for not the tree branches flowing in the wind outside the home. As she slipped off to slumber, waves of yellow and red danced across her inner vision.

Suddenly, the sunlight disappeared.

Mamaw squinted an eye open and found two smiling faces gazing down from above.

"Wake up old woman," Michael said. "We have a surprise for you."

Mamaw's first reaction was to ignore these two stubborn mules, but the air felt differently. They were up to something, and hopefully something positive. Still, she pulled her shawl about her shoulders and nodded towards Dewey. "Is there a ring on her finger?"

She expected resistance, arguing, but the two passed a knowing smile between them. Then, Dewey leaned over and kissed her sweetly on the cheek.

"Just come with us, please," her granddaughter said.

Mamaw rose from her chair, assisted by the children she loved deeply despite their stubbornness, each one gripping her elbows. She looked from one to another but neither said a word, just smiled as they led her down the hall.

"Where are we going? I already ate breakfast."

"Not the dining hall," Michael said.

She glanced at Dewey for information but Dewey remained silent, that silly smile still playing her lips.

"It's Sunday, y'all," Mamaw added. "We don't have bingo on Sundays."

"Not bingo," Michael said with a laugh.

Now that she got a good look at her two grandchildren, Mamaw noticed they weren't dressed casually, as so many young people loved to do these days. Instead, Michael wore a deep blue dress shirt and tie topped with a navy blue jacket, although he still sported those damn blue jeans. Dewey looked adorable in a lacy white dress, her hair curled and twisted in an elegant knot at the back. Mamaw leaned in close to make sure her eyes weren't deceiving her.

"Are those roses in your hair?"

They paused at the end of the hallway, both still grinning like fools in front of a door.

"What are you two up to anyway?"

Michael leaned down low to kiss Mamaw on the cheek. For not the first time in Mamaw's lengthy lifetime, she wished she had been taller than a mere five feet high.

"See you in a few, old woman," Michael said, then slipped inside the door.

Mamaw turned to Dewey. "What's going on?"

She started to speak but Patrick emerged from behind the door, also dressed in his Sunday best, Sandy following behind.

"Well it's about time you all dressed for Sunday," Mamaw said. "I was beginning to think looking nice for the Lord's day had disappeared with good manners."

Patrick said nothing, held out his arm. Mamaw was still confused but she slipped a hand through the crook of his elbow and allowed him to lead her inside. Patrick glanced over her shoulder and winked at Dewey, so Mamaw looked back too. Dewey stood there, Sandy at her side, beaming for all the world. A relief so intense flooded her senses, but Mamaw wanted to be sure.

"Is someone going to tell me what's going on?"

Patrick pushed the door open wider and a well-dressed man in glasses on the other side opened it further, allowing Mamaw a wide berth. As her eyes adjusted to the dim light, she realized she stood inside the small chapel, its tiny altar adorned with flowers. In an instant, her daughter reached her side, kissing her on the cheek as Patrick had done.

"You win," she whispered. "And we love you for it."

Mamaw wanted to ask if her hopes and prayers had finally been filled, but the words couldn't pass the lump in her throat. Emma slipped a handkerchief inside her palm and Patrick led her down the aisle to the first row. He kissed her hand and gave her a wink as she sat down, then moved to the opposite pew.

The chapel was so small they felt as if sitting side by side so Mamaw asked him, "Is this what I think it is?"

But Patrick had his own lump to contend with. He nodded, tears filling his eyes.

Emma joined her and sat down, her head held high as if she, too, fought off emotions. Mamaw took her hand, knowing that seeing Dewey happy was as vital to her daughter's happiness as it was to her.

"You're a good mother," Mamaw whispered. "You always were."

Tears set free, Emma hugged her tight. "Thank you, Mom. I love you so much."

Mamaw touched her face. "I love you, too, sweetpea." She nodded her head to the other side of the aisle. "What about that good-looking fella?"

Emma laughed and leaned in close. "He's moving to L.A. in May."

Before Mamaw could erupt with delight, soft music began in the back of the room. Tyler was standing proudly by the door, holding one of those newfound technical devices the size of a business card. A woman wearing a ministerial gown walked down the aisle and stood at the altar, then Michael followed, once he knew Tyler understood the use of the technical thing. Michael glanced back at Mamaw and gave her a wink and Mamaw couldn't stand it any longer. She pulled out her handkerchief and patted her eyes to what she knew would become quite a faucet flow.

Sandy came next down the aisle, holding a small bouquet of pink roses and pausing on the other side of the minister.

"I'm best man *and* maid of honor," she announced proudly and everyone laughed.

They all turned to look at Dewey standing by the door, smiling to all the heavens. But Tyler had the last word.

"You're supposed to stand up," he announced a bit too loudly.

While everyone laughed again and stood, Dewey waved to Patrick, motioning for him to join her at the door. Patrick looked confused but did as he was told, reaching her side and leaning close for her instructions. Dewey said something that no one could hear but Mamaw suspected she knew for the man's eyes brimmed with tears. He fought back the emotions, then held out his elbow to her and they walked arm in arm down the aisle. When he placed Dewey at the altar, Michael's face lit up like the coming of the dawn. Mamaw never saw two people more in love.

"We come together today to join Michael Arceneaux and Caroline Hennessey together in marriage," the minister began.

Mamaw never heard much else of the ceremony; she was too busy weeping with joy. When the minister announced Dewey and Michael husband and wife, and the two kissed in wedding bliss, Mamaw couldn't imagine her heart being fuller. With one exception. She peered over at Emma, who had her own handkerchief out.

Emma seemed to read her mind. "We love each other. He's moving to L.A. That's all you're getting for now."

They laughed and hugged each other, then watched as Tyler bounded down the aisle and hugged Dewey and Michael's legs.

Then Patrick rose and hugged the couple, followed by Sandy and some cute boy who seemed to be attached to Sandy in some way. Oh please, lord, Mamaw thought, let this one be smart, attentive and have a good job.

Finally, Dewey and Michael were at her side, hugging and kissing her as she cried into their shoulders.

"Are you talking to us now?" Dewey asked, wiping away her tears.

Mamaw huffed. "That woman is nice and I'm glad we're in a Catholic chapel, but you all need to be married in a real church with a priest."

Michael put his hands on his hips and shook his head. "Or what?"

"Don't tempt me, young man."

Dewey put her arm around Mamaw. "I'm flying to L.A. with mom this afternoon. I'm giving my notice at work and packing up."

"I'm heading there over Thanksgiving break," Michael added, while pulling Dewey close. "Then driving her home."

"Great," Mamaw exclaimed. "A Christmas church wedding."

Dewey sighed and looked heavenward and Michael laughed. Then for some crazy reason, every person in the room, except the minister who was busy listening to Tyler discuss his new music device, surrounded the couple in a group hug. They all laughed and cried until someone mentioned gumbo.

"Dinner at Michael's," Sandy explained. "He has a pot of left-over gumbo and the Hennesseys don't have to be at the airport until six."

"Gumbo!" Tyler yelled when he heard the magic word.

They slowly made their way out of the chapel, Sandy grabbing the flowers, Patrick paying the minister, Tyler talking non-stop. They filed into several cars, Mamaw in the front seat of Patrick's with Emma and Tyler behind. Through the window, Mamaw watched as that cute boy graciously opened the door for Sandy, then kissed her sweetly. Normally, Mamaw didn't approve of public affection but Sandy looked so happy.

"Lagniappe," she whispered through her tears.

"What did you say, Mom?" Emma asked.

"I got everything I wanted, and a little something extra."

They rode as a caravan to the Arceneaux household and the gumbo that awaited them, her babies married, her daughter in love and a hopeful future for Sandy. A bliss so intense captured Mamaw's heart that she closed her eyes and offered up a grateful prayer. It was all she had wanted — and so much more.

Michael's Wild Duck and Sausage Gumbo

*6 teal or woodduck breasts, cleaned and cut into bite-sized
pieces*
Salt and pepper to taste
Cajun seasoning to taste
1 cup vegetable oil
1 cup flour
2 large yellow onions, chopped
1 green bell pepper, chopped
1 yellow bell pepper, chopped
1 cup celery, chopped
1/2 garlic clove, chopped (optional)
*1 pound andouille sausage, or similar pork sausage, cut into
small pieces*
1 32-ounce box chicken broth or stock
Water to bring soup to desired consistency
2 cups cooked Louisiana rice
Green onions, chopped, for garnish

Directions: Cut the cleaned duck into pieces, then season with salt and pepper or Cajun seasoning. In a large pot, brown the seasoned duck pieces in the oil over medium-high heat until brown, about 3 to 5 minutes. Remove the duck and set aside.

Reduce the heat to medium and add the flour for a roux, stirring constantly, being careful not to let the roux burn. Keep stirring until you receive the right darkness of roux. The color and time it takes to finish the roux will depend upon your preference. A light roux may take about 20-30 minutes. A dark, hearty roux up to an hour. Once the right color and consistency has been achieved, add the chopped onions, bell peppers, celery and optional garlic. Cook until the onions are translucent. Add the andouille and cook for about 5 minutes. Add the chicken broth or stock, plus water for preferred consistency, and bring to a gentle boil, then simmer, uncovered for about an hour. Add the duck and simmer for another hour.

Add additional salt, pepper or Cajun seasoning to taste. Remove from heat, serve gumbo over rice and garnish with chopped green onions.

Dewey's Louisiana Simple Chicken Gumbo

1/3 cup vegetable oil
1 pound chicken, cut into small pieces
*1 (16-ounce) Guidry's Creole Seasoning mix**
*1 (32-ounce) jar Cajun Power Chicken Gumbo**
Hot sauce, as needed
2 cups cooked Louisiana rice
Green onions, chopped, for garnish

Directions: In a large soup pot sauté the chicken pieces in vegetable oil over medium-high heat until browned. Add half of the Guidry's Creole Seasoning mix (one cup measured or more to your liking) and cook for an additional 3-5 minutes until onions are translucent and celery and bell peppers are soft. Drain out the oil. Add the entire jar of Cajun Power Chicken Gumbo. Fill the empty jar with water and add to the pot, twice. Stir well over medium-high heat until all is blended and there are no lumps in the roux (what came out of the jar). Add hot sauce if needed. When gumbo starts to bubble, reduce heat to simmer and let cook for about 45 minutes. Serve gumbo over rice and garnish with chopped green onions.

*Walmart carries Guidry's Creole Seasoning mix, which consists of the Cajun Holy Trinity of onions, bell peppers and celery. Cajun Power is Dewey's personal favorite, available in select stores and online at www.cajunpowersauce.com. Other "roux in a jar" products include Savoie's, Richard's and Tony Chachere.

About the Author

Cherie Claire lives in South Louisiana where she works as a travel and food writer and pens several blogs about her unique culture. For Cherie, a bowl of gumbo really does ease most pains. To learn more about her Cajun novels, upcoming events, Louisiana recipes and to sign up for her newsletter, visit her website www.CherieClaire.net.

Write to Cherie at CajunRomances@Yahoo.com.

ALSO BY CHERIE CLAIRE

The Cajun Embassy
Ticket to Paradise
Damn Yankees
Gone Pecan

The Cajun Series historical saga
Emilie
Rose
Gabrielle
Delphine
A Cajun Dream
The Letter